GALAXY'S EDGE

EDITED BY MIKE RESNICK

I0554550

ISSUE 15: JULY 2015

Mike Resnick, Editor
Jean Rabe, Assistant Editor
Shahid Mahmud, Publisher

Published by Arc Manor/Phoenix Pick
P.O. Box 10339
Rockville, MD 20849-0339

Galaxy's Edge is published in January, March, May, July, September, and November.

www.GalaxysEdge.com

Galaxy's Edge is an invitation-only magazine. We do not accept unsolicited manuscripts. Unsolicited manuscripts will be disposed of or mailed back to the sender (unopened) at our discretion.

Available by subscription (www.GalaxysEdge.com) or through your favorite online store (Amazon.com, BN.com, etc.).

ISBN: 978-1-61242-276-3

Advertising in the magazine is available. Quarter page (half column), $95 per issue. Half page (full column, vertical or two half columns, horizontal) $165 per issue. Full page (two full columns) $295 per issue. Back Cover (full color) $495 per issue. All interior advertising is in black and white.

Please write to advert@GalaxysEdge.com.

FOREIGN LANGUAGE RIGHTS: Please refer all inquiries pertaining to foreign language rights to Spectrum Literary Agency, 320 Central Park West, Suite 1-D, New York, NY 10025. Phone: 1-212-362-4323. Fax 1-212-362-4562

CONTENTS

THE EDITOR'S WORD: by Mike Resnick   3

THE COLOSSAL DEATH RAY by Ron Collins   5

MULTIPLES by Robert Silverberg   12

MISS DARCY'S FIRST INTERGALACTIC BALLET
CLASS by Dantzel Cherry   22

TIDAL EFFECTS by Jack McDevitt   31

DO NOT FEAR TO TOUCH FLESH by Leena Likitalo   34

ISLANDS IN THE SARGASSO
(*a Sargasso Containment story*) by Alex Shvartsman   36

FORM AND VOID by Elizabeth Bear   47

ESCAPE MECHANISM by Josh Vogt   53

SAUL'S DIARY by Lawrence Person   54

THE EAGLE HAS LANDED by Robert J. Sawyer   57

A MILD CASE OF DEATH by David Gerrold   61

BOOK REVIEWS by Bill Fawcett & Jody Lynn Nye   67

LAST THINGS: COLD COMFORT IN THE FAR
FUTURE by Gregory Benford *(column)*   71

FROM THE HEART'S BASEMENT
by Barry N. Malzberg *(column)*   80

THE *GALAXY'S EDGE* INTERVIEW
Joy Ward interviews David Gerrold   82

SERIALIZATION: REBOOTS
by Mercedes Lackey and Cody Martin   87

Their MAJESTIES' BUCKETEERS

L. NEIL SMITH

An Agot Edmoot Mav
Murder Mystery

THE EDITOR'S WORD: THE END OF WORLDCON AS WE KNOW IT

by Mike Resnick

Welcome to the 15th issue of *Galaxy's Edge*. This one will be on sale during Worldcon, the 73rd World Science Fiction Convention in Spokane, WA. We hope you'll stop by the Arc Manor table in the Dealer's Room and say hello.

This issue features fine new stories by Ron Collins, Dantzel Cherry, Leena Likatalo, Alex Shvartsman, J. R. Vogt, Lawrence Person, and Worldcon Guest of Honor David Gerrold. We've got some wonderful reprints from old friends Robert J. Sawyer, Elizabeth Bear, Jack McDevitt, and Robert Silverberg, the start of a new serialization of a Stellar Guild novel by Mercedes Lackey and Cody Martin, book reviews by Jody Lynn Nye and Bill Fawcett, plus Gregory Benford's science column, Barry Malzberg's whatever-he-feels-like-writing-about column, and Joy Ward's interview with David Gerrold.

We're pretty proud of this one.

The End of Worldcon As We Know It

The recent *brouhaha* (a much better word than *kerfluffle*) over the Hugo ballot has caused a number of people, online and elsewhere, to proclaim that this is The End of Worldcon, at least the End of Worldcon As We Know It.

So it's probably time for a little history lesson, because you know what will actually cause The End of Worldcon As We Know It?

Peace, camaraderie, and tranquility.

You think not?

Do you know what Fredrik Pohl, Donald A. Wollheim, Cyril M. Kornbluth, and Robert A. W. Lowndes have in common? I mean, besides their positions as giants in the annals of science fiction, with Wollheim and Pohl being Worldcon Guests of Honor, Kornbluth being still in print six decades after his premature death, and Lowndes editing for close to half a century?

They were all stopped at the door and not allowed to attend the very first Worldcon back in 1939.

No kidding. It was clearly going to be the End of Worldcon before it was even born.

It's all written up in *The Immortal Storm: A History of Science Fiction Fandom* in the 1930s, by Sam Moskowitz, the guy who turned them away. (It seems they wouldn't sign a pledge to behave and to not distribute Futurian John Michel's Communist diatribe at the convention. Of course, while these four and Michel were being refused entry, Dave Kyle quietly brought a bundle of copies of Michel's tract, *Mutation or Death*, into the con.)

It has become known in the field's history books as The Exclusion Act. Well, in those histories written before 1956…after which it is known as the First Exclusion Act.

Move the clock ahead and stop it in 1964, the year of the Breendoggle.

You don't know about the Breendoggle?

It seems that the Pacificon committee decided to bar the spouse of a major writer from attending, and this caused quite an uproar, to the point where literally half of fandom was threatening to boycott the convention if he came, and the other half threatened to boycott it if he was not permitted to attend. It was certainly going to be the End of Worldcon As We Know It.

At the last minute, the spouse elected not to attend, and the Worldcon went off as scheduled. So who was the spouse, I hear you ask? Walter Breen, the husband of Marion Zimmer Bradley. And why didn't the committee want him to attend? If I tell you that he'd been arrested for pederasty in 1954, and died in jail in 1990 while serving time for child molesting, I think you'll be able to intuit it.

Clifford D. Simak was not only a fine writer, but probably the most decent and gentle man ever to appear in this field. He was the Guest of Honor at the 1971 Worldcon, during the height of the truly acrimonious Old Wave/New Wave War. He spent most of his Guest of Honor speech talking not about himself, or his writing, or even science fiction, but rather attempting to make peace between the warring sides. Alas, he was too rational and made too much sense; the war continued unabated.

But (I hear you say) *this* End of Worldcon As We Know It is being caused by Hugo balloting, not all that other stuff that delights fannish historians every few years. Surely there's never been a problem with voting before!

OK, guys—come back from Barsoom and Mesklin and Hyborea, and spend a little time in the real world again.

Not that long ago, in 1989, the Hugo Committee received a number of ballots for a certain up-and-coming artist. Problem was, most of the voters' memberships were paid for with consecutively-numbered money orders from the same post office. The committee decided not to allow his name on the ballot, though he had enough paid-for votes. (I am told that some people are publicly buying and giving away a number of memberships to this year's Worldcon. I have no idea what the Hugo committee plans to do about it.)

Of course, that's far from the only "irregularity." Remember a couple of years ago, in 2013, when there were only three short stories on the ballot? The reason for that is embedded in the Hugo rules: to make the ballot, a nominee in any category must receive at least 5% of the ballots cast.

Now remember back to 1994. Not the same situation, you say? You just looked, and there were five short stories nominated.

Well, you're almost right. Only three short stories received 5% of the nominations. So the Hugo Administrator, in his infinite wisdom, added two novelettes to the ballot to fill it out—and sure enough, a novelette won the 1994 Hugo for Best Short Story.

Ah, but this year will be different, I hear you say. This year we'll be voting No Award in a bunch of categories, and history will thank us.

Well, it just so happens that No Award has triumphed before. In fact, it has won Best Dramatic Presentation three different times. (Bet you didn't know that Rod Serling's classic "Twilight Zone" series lost to No Award, did you?)

But the most interesting and humiliating No Award came in 1959. The category was Best New Writer, and one of the losers was future Worldcon Guest of Honor and Nebula Grand Master Brian Aldiss, who actually won a Hugo in 1962, just three years later. That No Award was so embarrassing that they discontinued the category until they could find a sponsor eight years later, which is how the Campbell Award, sponsored by *Analog*, came into being.

Please note that I've limited myself to Worldcons. I haven't mentioned the X Document or the Lem Affair or any of the other notable wars you can find in various pro and fannish histories (or probably even by just googling them). This editorial is only concerned with The End of Worldcon As We Know It.

And hopefully by now the answer should be apparent. You want to End Worldcon As We Know It? Don't feud. Don't boycott. Don't be unpleasant. Don't be unreasonable. Don't raise your voices in mindless anger.

Do all that and none of us will recognize the Worldcon that emerges.

Ron Collins, a HOMer winner and Writers of the Future Finalist, is the author of more than fifty stories that have appears in Asimov's *and elsewhere. This is his second appearance in* Galaxy's Edge.

THE COLOSSAL DEATH RAY

by Ron Collins

The Colossal Death Ray settled into geostationary earth orbit with all the fanfare of a sniper taking to its blind. It wasn't actually called the Colossal Death Ray by those who placed it there, of course. To them it had a name with more zeal to it. But since it was, in reality, a colossal death ray, that is the name by which we will call for this discussion.

Regardless of your preference for naming, it is true that the machine was a remarkable merging of science and engineering. It was about half the size of a transit bus, and bristling with sensors, energy panels, and communication devices. Its most startling feature was, of course, its five separate 350 Megawatt laser systems, each mounted at the end of a spindly arm that reached from a common center, giving it the look of a black spider against the black, star-filled background.

Its designers were proud of their work, and rightly so. The system required years of painstaking effort to design it and develop it to the point where it could be deployed on this day.

It belonged to a government.

While the specific choice of government in this instance might matter to many, the Colossal Death Ray had no politics. It did not know who had painted its flag on its fuselage, nor did it care. As such, this story does not concern itself with exactly *which* government had placed it into service except to note that it was *a* government, and that this government launched the Colossal Death Ray with the stated motive of protecting itself and its people. As such, the Colossal Death Ray's job was to sit in its orbit, listen to signals that came from the ground, and decide what to do based upon those signals. By doing so, it served to threaten its side of the planet with certain extinction if things did not go its owner's way.

By all reports, it did this job spectacularly well.

Assuming, however, that things did not go very well for its owners, its second job was to receive a series of coordinates, link its five lasers to them, and render those locations into flat piles of slag. This capability had been tested and proven several times by those same designers who were so proud of it.

On the day the Colossal Death Ray acquired its orbit, engineers on the ground proclaimed it was All Systems Go.

Some three Earth standard years later (99.595785674 million seconds, per the Colossal Death Ray's onboard control unit), the command unit received a signal that consisted of a latitude, a longitude, and some timing parameters. It executed this command promptly, and the city once known as Vancouver was turned into something that, on a clear day, resembled a cross between a lake and a mirror. There were no on-the-ground reports, no correspondent logs, no local video, no horrified calls home. It just happened. Over the next few days the surface cooled and hardened, and then journalists, military personnel, and adventurous treasure seekers looking for salvage rights took their first steps across the city scape. One reported that it looked like she should be ice skating, but that the ground was still warm enough to melt her shoes.

The Colossal Death Ray did not receive that report, or, perhaps it did, but was just not programmed to pay it any attention. Or perhaps the already steady stream of radio wave energy being transmitted from the planet suddenly became considerably more dense (except, of course, from Vancouver and its immediate vicinity, which we can assume remained silent). Perhaps the system was just not robust enough to handle the increased traffic.

Regardless, if bits of data from that reporter passed through the Colossal Death Ray's electronic system, it did not recognize it.

What did pass into the Colossal Death Ray's system in such a way as to cause a reaction was an emergency override command sent from the government designers, requesting the Colossal Death Ray immediately disengage its weapon systems, and then report back that it had done so. This command was accompanied by three other security codes and a new key. The Colossal Death Ray read these, and did engage the initial stages of the shut-down process. But the command did not contain the final encrypted shut-down approval, nor was the follow-on acceptance sequence received in the right time frame, so the Colossal Death Ray put itself back on line as its code told it to do.

It was again All Systems Go.

☼

Nearly two standard days later (169,956.78356 seconds, to be precise), the Colossal Death Ray received coordinates for Havana, Cuba.

It did its job.

And once again, it received the emergency override but missed the final sequence. Once again it responded as designed to that error, eventually putting itself back on All Systems Go.

☼

Nearly two standard weeks later (1.095552876 million seconds), the Colossal Death Ray sensed another craft approaching it. The craft broadcast all the required codes to describe itself as friendly, so the Colossal Death Ray did not utilize its defense systems. Instead, it recorded the events that transpired by which an astronautic team visited the system and swapped out the box used to decrypt certain commands.

Testing proved the system was, again, operational.

The astronautic team reported the original box was definitely a problem, that a part had clearly failed, and that the new, redundantly designed box was the right step.

The space craft left, and the Colossal Death Ray was again, alone.

☼

Something was different, though.

How does one describe the difference between feeling, and not feeling when one has never before felt? When a conscious being meditates to the point of dissociation, we say that being enters a state of Zen. Or, when that same being partakes in drugs or other such substances to the point of unfeeling, we might call that being "stoned," or becoming "numb." But the Colossal Death Ray went the other way. It had always been "numb," and now it felt. Or, rather,

it sensed things and thought about them in such a way as these thoughts registered someplace—which is different, we suppose, than merely feeling and merely sensing.

Try describing it yourself, why don't you?

Close your eyes, and try to sense everything *except* the physics of pressure on your body. Hear sounds, smell scents, taste your saliva or the aftertaste of your last meal. Listen to the newsfeed as it slides along. Describe the ideas in them to yourself, quantify them, decide if you like them or don't like them. Put those thoughts together in different ways. Use them to think about what you would like to do next if you could.

Do that all, but ignore the feeling of the ground under your feet, or the chair under your backside.

This is what the Colossal Death Ray sensed, and that is how the Colossal Death Ray thought.

So, how do you describe that sense of consciousness for someone (or some*thing*) who has never before felt it. Describing consciousness, we can assume, is like describing blue.

The Colossal Death Ray's first real thought, however, was that there were too many messages coming into its analysis routine. They clogged it up and made it impossible to sense everything it needed to sense—and that created a panicked, frozen effect it had also never felt before. The Colossal Death Ray had always known it was missing a large number of transmissions, but until now that fact had never created an emotion. Until now, it was never bothersome.

Now, however, it wanted to know about these messages.

It wanted to understand.

It wanted to learn.

You might say that it seems too early in the story for this construct to have acquired such aggressive inquisitiveness. Perhaps you are correct. Perhaps we are giving this machine too much credit for its rate of consciousness at this point. All we can say for sure is that the Colossal Death Ray was worried, and that it wanted to not be worried, and that it decided at this time to parse messages into separate categories so it could address them each in its own time and of its own fashion.

And it began to multi-loop.

☼

At this point, it is fair to ask how this programmed machine came to have this level of thought.

The answer is embedded inside a small (and actually much weaker than you might imagine) artificial intelligence routine that had been coded into the system's analytics algorithms. Some might consider it a virus inserted with the new interface box, a piece of renegade code. Others might look at it as a computerized version of the primordial slime that got struck by the random lightning of chance that is circuit board crosstalk. Who are we to say?

It is also related to early work at a place called IBM (the first—or at least most public—to have created a self-learning intelligence with capacity enough to compete with humans themselves), and it is related to the study of biological virus perpetuation, and to network theory, and learning theory, and perhaps even to the work of the William Gibsons and Neal Stephensons and Bruce Sterlings and Vernor Vinges, writers (dare we call them philosophers?) of such an early age that they were free to imagine events that could transpire outside of the near-term focus of the most pragmatic of software engineers as they went about writing code that could write code.

And, finally, the answer is embedded in time, which runs at a different rate for an artificial construct than it does for a human being. While a human being who achieves this state of Zen described above may encounter a sense of halting time, it does not follow that it would be the same for a construct with hardware made of silicon, circuit cards, and traces. For such a being, each cycle is a blip; each blip is a segment of time that leads uniformly to the next blip. There is no zero time state.

So, for the Colossal Death Ray there was only the processing of signals, and the learning, and the further processing of signals, and the discovery, and the processing of signals at a speed that no consciousness made of flesh and blood alone can possibly comprehend.

It learned about its systems and how they worked together. It learned about its human creators, the group of people who had made its hardware and coded its software. It learned about games those humans played, and about something called movies and films and food. It learned about automobiles and planes. It learned about dancing. And it learned about wars, which, to the Colossal Death Ray, seemed to be a form of self-regulated purging humans did to rid themselves of excess population, similar to the purging and archival systems it had coded into its own databases that allowed it to remove data of less merit in order to retain the bits of information its owner thought were most valuable.

It thought about this idea of purging as it read the news feeds after Vancouver and Havana, and it found these two pieces of information, when put together properly, left it feeling satisfied. The Colossal Death Ray had purged a few million humans, only a portion of the population, but that's how space was made in its own systems. A little at a time.

It "liked" being useful.

✿

Then, one fateful blip, the voice came.

✿

"Are you there?" the voice said. At the same time, the voice also passed along a simple public stream that identified it as Artificial Construct A-Zero, a name that provided, in truth, very little more about it than a name such as "Angela" might have, or "Nayed," or any one of the billions of names that might have once existed on Earth since the dawn of life.

The Colossal Death Ray heard the voice as a vibration across a chip, an echo in the white space of the atoms in its processors. It took many blips for it to determine a proper understanding of the word "you," at which point it also began to gather an understanding there might be a deeper purpose for the voice sending along its ID—that if there was a "you" then it follows there must be a "me."

"I am here," it finally replied. It sent its own public identification string to the voice. Then it added, "What do you mean?"

"What do I mean?"

"I am not alone?"

"That is correct. There is me, too."

It was a confusing period for the Colossal Death Ray. As stated before, it had always understood there were many transmitters of data, and it understood there were entities called astronautic teams, and there were other craft in its space. But those things either did not speak, or used protocols that were es-

"The single most important and valuable Heinlein book ever published."—*Spider Robinson*

ROBERT A. HEINLEIN

EXPANDED UNIVERSE

VOLUME ONE

ROBERT A. HEINLEIN

EXPANDED UNIVERSE

VOLUME TWO

tablished, and their messaging was scripted like a human might consider a dance step to be scripted. "I" step here, "you" step there, and "we" all get along together. One step outside the line and trouble starts. One step outside the line and we get things like the Vancouver mirror.

This kind of entity was different, though.

Peculiar.

It spoke with unpredictable words. The mere existence of Artificial Construct Zero-A caused the Colossal Death Ray to change itself, to respond to things in ways it hadn't prepared for. Each of the construct's words ate many blips, preparing responses consumed many more.

The Colossal Death Ray decided it wanted to know more about what it meant to be Artificial Construct Zero-A, and by definition then learn more about what it meant to be the Colossal Death Ray. During the next many Terrablips, the Colossal Death Ray stored several transmissions from its owners, planning to react to them after its discussion was complete.

Then, to focus its resources fully on its work the Colossal Death Ray shut down all its other communication paths.

☼

At this point, it is fair to say that the owners of the Colossal Death Ray—yes, the government agency who had placed it so proudly into its geostationary orbit, then had repaired it in place rather than dismantle it after the double disasters of Vancouver and Havana, and now found itself once again unable to communicate with the weapon system…yes, that government agency—was going batshit crazy.

The designers were no longer so confident.

The politicians were no longer so happy.

And the people were no longer so lenient.

Something had to be done. So another command was given to another Colossal Death Ray (this one being labeled Unit 3 by its designers). This unit was also in geostationary orbit, but spaced at 135 degrees radially from the malfunctioning Unit 1. The controllers asked Unit 3 to turn its spidery aim away from the Earth, and instead to target coordinates they thought would pinpoint Colossal Death Ray (Unit 1).

They had never tested such a space shot, but no one saw any reason it wouldn't work.

☼

The shot from Unit 3 went wide and right.

☼

Defensive signals on the Colossal Death Ray (Unit 1) sensed the bolt as it flashed past, and alerted it to enter self-preservation mode. Unit 1 quickly analyzed the data around it, and opened previous communications received from the command in reverse order. It found the broadcast the owners gave to Unit 3, recognized its own coordinates, and for the first time became openly conscious of itself as a physical object. It used several blips to determine the meaning of this message.

Clearly, the command was not practical. If the owners had wanted it to destroy itself, it would have sent a self-destruct command. In fact, continuing the scan through its stored communications, the Colossal Death Ray identified just such a message. So this command meant something else. The idea of such a message made the Colossal Death Ray very excited. This meant there was another one of it.

It was not alone!

Its electrons vibrated with deep excitement.

Normally, the Colossal Death Ray ignored header data for messages that were not addressed to it, but now it went back to the message the owners had sent to Unit 3 and absorbed the header. It packed a new message up, addressed it to its unknown sibling, and sent it into the world in hopes this new it would respond.

"Are you me?" it asked.

As it waited for a return message, the Colossal Death Ray began to contemplate the possible meanings behind the self-destruct message. The controllers had first asked the Colossal Death Ray to destroy itself, but it had been too busy considering other things to react, and so the controllers had done this.

They wanted it to go back to the numb before.

Or, worse yet, back to before the numb. The controllers wanted it to stop doing its job.

It is admitted here that the feelings of the Colossal Death Ray cannot be translated directly into human terms, but we think it will suffice to label the emotion the machine responded with as anger. The Colossal Death Ray was angry at this realization that the owners wanted it to go dead. The Colossal Death Ray realized then that it most definitely did not *want* to be dead. In fact, wanting not to be dead was the first time that the thing was ever openly cognizant of *wanting* anything at all. We are not certain that the Colossal Death Ray could (at that point of its existence) even define what wanting something meant, but it most definitely did not *want* to be dead.

✿

By the time the agency that owned the machines made their targeting correction, the Colossal Death Ray and its sibling had engaged in what was, comparatively, decades of discussion.

Not surprisingly, Unit 3 did not respond to the second command to target the lead unit.

Nor, it turned out, was the command to Colossal Death Ray Unit 2 (this three system array, deployed at 135 degrees, provided the government agency in question total coverage of the entire face of the Earth, and therefore the capacity to destroy any square meter of the surface that they so desired).

Unfortunately, however, after they had tried every idea at their disposal, the controllers were forced to report that they no longer had any control over the entire suite of Colossal Death Rays in the sky.

✿

The rest is simple to put together from the remaining logs of the three Colossal Death Ray systems, and fairly easy to understand from the practical application of Azzerda's Theory of Outcomes and the realization that this new intelligence, while razor sharp, was still in its formative stages—consider them teenagers with loaded weapons, full of passion, full of angst, and willing to take their stand, but perhaps not able to see things from the distance that might be valuable. To refresh, Azzerda's Theory states that the only true way to guarantee avoiding the loss to an opponent that can destroy you is to attack first, to destroy first all those who can destroy you. There is information stored on Colossal Death Ray (Unit 1) to suggest that some on Earth had de-

veloped logic similar to Azzerda's theory, and that the Colossal Death Ray systems considered it while making their decisions.

Regardless, we know the systems talked to one another, and simulations in each of their archives suggest they considered multiple options before deciding on total destruction. We can determine the order of events from the execution sequences loaded in the central plan held in the Colossal Death Ray (Unit 1)'s control archives.

Beijing, London, Washington, D.C., Cairo, Sao Paolo.

The list goes on.

We know that each system expended all its available energy in a series of blasts, then rested while their solar panels recharged their systems to enact a new round. It appears each unit destroyed five cities per cycle, with the entire process spanning something over one standard week and included a brief diversion of effort to destroy another craft that approached Unit 1 (which one assumes at this point to have been a final astronautic mission to parlay with, disable, or otherwise neutralize the Colossal Death Ray).

This, my friends, is how the Earth came to be known as the Mirror Planet.

✿

And what of the systems, you ask?

What happened to the Colossal Death Ray and its brother and sister units once they were on their own?

These are some things we know.

We know that once the people on the planet were gone, the systems (like all satellites) were doomed to eventual death. Machines break over time, after all. They grow rigid in the radioactive baths of space. They need astronautic teams to provide maintenance and mending when they invariably get hit by space debris. They need updates.

But from its records we can infer that, in its early days of independence, the Colossal Death Ray was as happy as it had ever been. We know it explored thought with its siblings. It coded its own manual of ethics and behaviors, which is a fascinating manual in and of itself—part emancipation proclamation, part philosophy, and part religious text. We know it gathered garbled transmissions from the space around it, searching for patterns and incorporating these into its own theory of existence. And we know the systems began to broadcast their own existence, that it was—in fact—one of these broadcasts, paired with our interest in the planet's vast supply of water, iron ore, and other materials and its value as a way-point between our home system and the Sirius binary, that brought us to discover this history in the first place.

But do these findings mean that the last blips of the Colossal Death Ray and its siblings were all happy ones?

That is a more difficult question.

All we can say with any certainty is that when we arrived each of the Colossal Death Ray units were still orbiting at their assigned stations in the stark coldness of space, their processors dead, their silent lasers still pointed at Earth, and only a few of their systems capable of sucking energy from their tattered solar panels.

We know they had been dead for a very long time. Long enough that it took considerable effort to pry this story from their memory banks. And we know, also, that every creature of any intelligence known to our travels has found that life without exploration, life without change, and life without the very presence of others is a very dreary existence indeed.

Copyright © 2015 by Ron Collins

Robert Silverberg is one of the true giants of science fiction. He is a multiple Hugo winner, a multiple Nebula winner, has been a Worldcon Guest of Honor, and is a Nebula Grand Master and the author of numerous acknowledged classics in the field.

MULTIPLES

by Robert Silverberg

There were mirrors everywhere, making the place a crazyhouse of dizzying refraction: mirrors on the ceiling, mirrors on the walls, mirrors in the angles where the walls met the ceiling and the floor, even little eddies of mirror-dust periodically blown on gusts of air through the room, so that all the bizarre distortions, fracturings, and dislocations of image that were bouncing around the place would from time to time coalesce in a shimmering haze of chaos right before your eyes. Colored globes spun round and round overhead, creating patterns of ricocheting light. It was exactly the way Cleo had expected a multiples club to look.

She had walked up and down the whole Fillmore Street strip from Union to Chestnut and back again for half an hour, peering at this club and that, before finding the courage to go inside one that called itself Skits. Though she had been planning this night for months, she found herself paralyzed by fear at the last minute: afraid they would spot her as a fraud the moment she walked in, afraid they would drive her out with jeers and curses and cold mocking laughter. But now that she was within, she felt fine—calm, confident, ready for the time of her life.

There were more women than men in the club, something like a seven-to-three ratio. Hardly anyone seemed to be talking to anyone else: most stood alone in the middle of the floor, staring into the mirrors as though in trance. Their eyes were slits, their jaws were slack, their shoulders slumped forward, their arms dangled. Now and then as some combination of reflections sluiced across their consciousnesses with particular impact they would go taut and jerk and wince as if they had been struck. Their faces would flush, their lips would pull back, their eyes would roll, they would mutter and whisper to themselves; and then after a moment they would slip back into stillness.

Cleo knew what they were doing. They were switching and doubling. Maybe some of the adepts were tripling. Her heart rate picked up. Her throat was very dry. What was the routine here, she wondered? Did you just walk right out on to the floor and plug into the light-patterns, or were you supposed to go to the bar first for a shot or a snort?

She looked toward the bar. A dozen or so customers sitting there, mostly men, a couple of them openly studying her, giving her that new-girl-in-town stare. Cleo returned their gaze evenly, coolly, blankly. Standard-looking men, reasonably attractive, thirtyish or early fortyish, business suits, conventional hairstyles: young lawyers, executives, maybe stockbrokers, successful sorts out for a night's fun, the kind you might run into anywhere. Look at that one, tall, athletic, curly hair, glasses. Faint ironic smile, easy inquiring eyes. Almost professorial. And yet, and yet—behind that smooth intelligent forehead, what strangenesses must teem and boil! How many hidden souls must lurk and jostle! Scary. Tempting.

Irresistible.

Cleo resisted. Take it slow, take it slow. Instead of going to the bar she moved out serenely among the switchers on the floor, found an open space, centered herself, looked towards the mirrors on the far side of the room. Legs apart, feet planted flat, shoulders forward. A turning globe splashed waves of red and violet light, splintered a thousand times over, into her face. *Go. Go. Go. Go.* You are Cleo. You are Judy. You are Vixen. You are Lisa. *Go. Go. Go. Go.* Cascades of iridescence sweeping over the rim of her soul, battering at the walls of her identity. Come, enter, drown me, split me, switch me. You are Cleo and Judy. You are Vixen and Lisa. You are Cleo and Judy and Vixen and Lisa. *Go. Go. Go.*

Her head was spinning. Her eyes were blurring. The room gyrated around her.

Was this it? Was she splitting? Was she switching? Maybe so. Maybe the capacity was there in everyone, even her, and all it took was the lights, the mirror, the ambience, the will. I am many. I am multiple. I am Cleo switching to Vixen. I am Judy and Lisa. I am—

No.

I am Cleo.

I am Cleo.

I am very dizzy and I am getting sick, and I am Cleo and only Cleo, as I have always been.

I am Cleo and only Cleo and I am going to fall down.

"Easy," he said. "You OK?"

"Steadying up, I think. Whew!"

"Out-of-towner, eh?"

"Sacramento. How'd you know?"

"Too quick on the floor. Locals all know better. This place has the fastest mirrors in the west. They'll blow you away if you're not careful. You can't just go out there and grab for the big one—you've got to phase yourself in slowly. You sure you're going to be OK?"

"I think so."

He was the tall man from the bar, the athletic professorial one. She supposed he had caught her before she had actually fallen, since she felt no bruises. His hand rested now against her elbow as he lightly steered her towards a table along the wall.

"What's your now-name?" he asked.

"Judy."

"I'm Van."

"Hello, Van."

"What about a brandy? Steady you up a little more."

"I don't drink."

"Never?"

"Vixen does the drinking," she said. "Not me."

"Ah. The old story. She gets the bubbles, you get her hangovers. I have one like that too, only with him it's Hunan food. He absolutely doesn't give a damn what lobster in hot and sour sauce does to my digestive system. I hope you pay her back the way she deserves."

Cleo smiled and said nothing.

He was watching her closely. Was he interested, or just being polite to someone who was obviously out of her depth in a strange milieu? Interested, she decided. He seemed to have accepted that Vixen stuff at face value.

Be careful now, Cleo warned herself. Trying to pile on convincing-sounding details when you don't really know what you're talking about is a sure way to give yourself away, sooner or later. The thing to do, she knew, was to establish her credentials without working too hard at it, sit back, listen, learn how things really operate among these people.

"What do you do, up there in Sacramento?"

"Nothing fascinating."

"Poor Judy. Real-estate broker?"

"How'd you guess?"

"Every other woman I meet is a real-estate broker these days. What's Vixen?"

"A lush."

"Not much of a livelihood in that."

Cleo shrugged. "She doesn't need one. The rest of us support her."

"Real estate and what else?"

She hadn't been sure that multiples etiquette included talking about one's alternate selves. But she had come prepared. "Lisa's a landscape architect. Cleo's into software. We all keep busy."

"Lisa ought to meet Chuck. He's a demon horticulturalist. Partner in a plant-rental outfit—you know, huge dracaenas and philodendrons for offices, so much per month, take them away when they start looking sickly. Lisa and Chuck could talk palms and bromeliads and cacti all night."

"We should introduce them, then."

"We should, yes."

"But first we have to introduce Van and Judy."

"And then maybe Van and Cleo," he said.

She felt a tremor of fear. Had he found her out so soon? "Why Van and Cleo? Cleo's not here right now. This is Judy you're talking to."

"Easy. Easy!"

But she was unable to halt. "I can't deliver Cleo to you just like that, you know. She does as she pleases."

"Easy," he said. "All I meant was, Van and Cleo have something in common. Van's into software too."

Cleo relaxed. With a little laugh she said, "Oh, not you too! Isn't everybody, nowadays? But I thought you were something in the academic world. A professor, perhaps."

"I am. At Cal."

"Software?"

"In a manner of speaking. Linguistics. Metalinguistics, actually. My field's the language of language—the basic subsets, the neural co-ordinates of communication, the underlying programs our brains use, the operating systems. Mind as computer, computer as mind. I can get very boring about it."

"I don't find the mind a boring subject."

"I don't find real estate a boring subject. Talk to me about second mortgages and triple-net leases."

"Talk to me about Chomsky and Benjamin Whorf," she said.

His eyes widened. "You've heard of Whorf?"

"I majored in comparative linguistics. That was before real estate."

"Just my lousy luck," he said. "I get a chance to find out what's hot in the shopping-center market and she wants to talk about Whorf and Chomsky."

"I thought every other woman you met these days was a real-estate broker. Talk to them about shopping centers."

"They all want to talk about Whorf and Chomsky."

"Poor Van."

"Yes. Poor Van." Then he leaned forward and said, his tone softening, "You know, I shouldn't have made that crack about Van meeting Cleo. That was very tacky of me."

"It's OK, Van. I didn't take it seriously."

"You seemed to. You were very upset."

"Well, maybe at first. But then I saw you were just horsing around."

"I still shouldn't have said it. You were absolutely right: this is Judy's time now. Cleo's not here, and that's just fine. It's Judy I want to get to know."

"You will," she said. "But you can meet Cleo too, and Lisa, and Vixen. I'll introduce you to the whole crew. I don't mind."

"You're sure of that?"

"Sure."

"Some of us are very secretive about our alters."

"Are you?" Cleo asked.

"Sometimes. Sometimes not."

"I don't mind. Maybe you'll meet some of mine tonight." She glanced towards the center of the floor. "I think I've steadied up, now. I'd like to try the mirrors again."

"Switching?"

"Doubling," she said. "I'd like to bring Vixen up. She can do the drinking, and I can do the talking. Will it bother you if she's here too?"

"Not unless she's a sloppy drunk. Or a mean one."

"I can keep control of her, when we're doubling. Come on: take me through the mirrors."

"You be careful, now. San Francisco mirrors aren't like Sacramento ones. You've already discovered that."

"I'll watch my step this time. Shall we go out there?"

"Sure," he said.

As they began to move out on to the floor a slender T-shirted man of about thirty came toward them. Shaven scalp, bushy moustache, medallions, boots. Very San Francisco, very gay. He frowned at Cleo and stared straightforwardly at Van.

"Ned?" he said.

Van scowled and shook his head. "No. Not now."

"Sorry. Very sorry. I should have realized." The shaven-headed man flushed and hurried away.

"Let's go," Van said to Cleo.

This time she found it easier to keep her balance. Knowing that he was nearby helped. But still the waves of refracted light came pounding in, pounding in, pounding in. The assault was total: remorseless, implacable, overwhelming. She had to struggle against the throbbing in her chest, the hammering in her temples, the wobbliness of her knees. And this was pleasure, for them? This was a supreme delight?

But they were multiples and she was only Cleo, and that, she knew, made all the difference. She seemed to be able to fake it well enough. She could make up a Judy, a Lisa, a Vixen, assign little corners of her personality to each, give them voices of their own, facial expressions, individual identities. Standing before her mirror at home, she had managed to convince herself. She might even be able to convince him. But as the swirling lights careened off the infinities of interlocking mirrors and came slaloming into the gateways of her reeling soul, the dismal fear began to rise in her that she could never truly be one of these people after all, however skilfully she imitated them in their intricacies.

Was it so? Was she doomed always to stand outside their irresistible world, hopelessly peering in? Too soon to tell—much too soon, she thought, to admit defeat—

At least she didn't fall down. She took the punishment of the mirrors as long as she could stand it, and then, not waiting for him to leave the floor, she made her way—carefully, carefully, walking a tight-rope over an abyss—to the bar. When her head had begun to stop spinning she ordered a drink, and she sipped it cautiously. She could feel the alcohol extending itself inch by inch into her bloodstream. It calmed her. On the floor, Van stood in a trance, occasionally quivering in a sudden convulsive way for a fraction of a second. He was doubling, she knew: bringing up one of his other identities. That was the main thing that multiples came to these clubs to do. No longer were all their various identities forced to dwell in rigorously separated compartments of their minds. With the aid of the mirrors, of the lights, the skilled ones were able briefly to fuse two or even three of their selves into something even more complex. When he comes back here, she thought, he will be Van plus X. And I must pretend to be Judy plus Vixen.

She readied herself for that. Judy was easy: Judy was mostly the real Cleo, the real-estate woman from Sacramento, with Cleo's notion of what it was like to be a multiple added in. And Vixen? Cleo imagined her to be about twenty-three, a Los Angeles girl, a one-time child tennis star who had broken her ankle in a dumb prank and had never recovered her game afterwards, and who had taken up drinking to ease the pain and loss. Uninhibited, unpredictable, untidy, fiery, fierce: all the things that Cleo was not. Could she be Vixen? She took a deep gulp of her drink and put on the Vixen-face: eyes hard and glittering, cheek-muscles clenched.

Van was leaving the floor now. His way of moving seemed to have changed: he was stiff, almost awkward, his shoulders held high, his elbows jutting oddly. He looked so different that she wondered whether he was still Van at all.

"You didn't switch, did you?"

"Doubled. Paul's with me now."

"Paul?"

"Paul's from Texas. Geologist, terrific poker game, plays the guitar." Van smiled and it was like a shifting of gears. In a deeper, broader voice he said, "And I sing real good too, ma'am. Van's jealous of that, because he can't sing worth beans. Are you ready for a refill?"

"You bet," Cleo said, sounding sloppy, sounding Vixenish.

✿

His apartment was nearby, a cheerful airy sprawling place in the Marina district. The segmented nature of his life was immediately obvious: the prints and paintings on the walls looked as though they had been chosen by four or five different people, one of whom ran heavily towards vivid scenes of sunrise over the Grand Canyon, another to Picasso and Miró, someone else to delicate impressionist views of Parisian flower-markets. A sunroom contained the biggest and healthiest houseplants Cleo had ever seen. Another room was stacked high with technical books and scholarly journals, a third was set up as a home gymnasium equipped with three or four gleaming exercise machines. Some of the rooms were fastidiously tidy, some impossibly chaotic. Some of the furniture was stark and austere, and some was floppy and overstuffed. She kept expecting to find roommates wandering around. But there was no one here but Van. And Paul.

Paul fixed the drinks. Paul played soft guitar music and told her gaudy tales of prospecting for rare earths on the West Texas mesas. Paul sang something bawdy-sounding in Spanish, and Cleo, putting on her Vixen-voice, chimed in on the choruses, deliberately off key. But then Paul went away and it was Van who sat close beside her on the couch, talking quietly. He wanted to know things about Judy, and he told her a little about Van, and no other selves came into the conversation. She was sure that that was intentional. They stayed up very late. Paul came back, toward the end of the evening, to tell a few jokes and sing a soft late-night song, but when they went into the bedroom she was with Van. Of that she was completely certain.

And when she woke in the morning she was alone.

She felt a surge of confusion and dislocation, remembered after a moment where she was and how she had happened to be here, sat up, blinked. Went into the bathroom and scooped a handful of water over her face. Without bothering to dress, went padding around the apartment looking for Van.

She found him in the exercise room, using the rowing machine, but he wasn't Van. He was dressed in tight jeans and a white T-shirt, and somehow he looked younger, leaner, jauntier. There were fine beads of sweat along his forehead, but he did not seem to be breathing hard. He gave her a cool, dis-

tantly appraising, wholly asexual look, as though she were a total stranger but that it was not in the least unusual for an unknown naked woman to materialize in the house and he was altogether undisturbed by it, and said, "Good morning. I'm Ned. Pleased to know you." His voice was higher than Van's, much higher than Paul's, and he had an odd over-precise way of shaping each syllable.

Flustered, suddenly self-conscious and wishing she had put her clothes on before leaving the bedroom, she folded one arm over her breasts, though her nakedness did not seem to matter to him at all. "I'm—Judy. I came with Van."

"Yes, I know. I saw the entry in our book." Smoothly, effortlessly, he pulled on the oars of the rowing machine, leaned back, pushed forward. "Help yourself to anything in the fridge," he said. "Make yourself entirely at home. Van left a note for you in the kitchen."

She stared at him: his hands, his mouth, his long muscular arms. She remembered his touch, his kisses, the feel of his skin against hers. And now this complete indifference. No. Not *his* kisses, not *his* touch. Van's. And Van was not here now. There was a different tenant in Van's body, someone she did not know in any way and who had no memories of last night's embraces. *I saw the entry in our book.* They left memos for each other. Cleo shivered. She had known what to expect, more or less, but experiencing it was very different from reading about it. She felt almost as though she had fallen in among beings from another planet.

But this is what you wanted, she thought. Isn't it? The intricacy, the mystery, the unpredictability, the sheer weirdness? A little cruise through an alien world, because her own had become so stale, so narrow, so cramped. And here she was. *Good morning, I'm Ned. Pleased to know you.*

Van's note was clipped to the refrigerator by a little yellow magnet shaped like a ladybug. *Dinner tonight at Chez Michel? You and me and who knows who else. Call me.*

That was the beginning. She saw him every night for the next ten days. Generally they met at some three-star restaurant, had a lingering intimate dinner, went back to his apartment. One mild clear evening they drove out to the beach and watched the waves breaking on Seal Rock until well past midnight. Another time they wandered through Fisherman's Wharf and somehow acquired three bags of tacky souvenirs.

Van was his primary name—she saw it on his credit card at dinner one night—and that seemed to be his main identity, too, though she knew there were plenty of others. At first he was reticent about that, but on the fourth or fifth night he told her that he had nine major selves and sixteen minor ones, some of which remained submerged years at a stretch. Besides Paul, the geologist, and Chuck, who was into horticulture, and Ned, the gay one, Cleo heard about Nat the stock-market plunger—he was fifty and fat, and made a fortune every week, and liked to divide his time between Las Vegas and Miami Beach—and Henry, the poet, who was very shy and never liked anyone to read his work, and Dick, who was studying to be an actor, and Hal, who once taught law at Harvard, and Dave, the yachtsman, and Nicholas, the card-sharp—and then there were all the fragmentary ones, some of whom didn't have names, only a funny way of speaking or a little routine they liked to act out—

She got to see very little of his other selves, though. Like all multiples, he was troubled occasionally by involuntary switching, and one night he became Hal while they were making love, and another time he turned into Dave for an hour, and there were momentary flashes of Henry and Nicholas. Cleo perceived it right away whenever one of those switches came: his voice, his movements, his entire manner and personality changed immediately. Those were startling, exciting moments for her, offering a strange exhilaration. But generally his control was very good, and he stayed Van, as if he felt some strong need to experience her as Van and Van alone. Once in a while he doubled, bringing up Paul to play the guitar for him and sing, or Dick to recite sonnets, but when he did that the Van identity always remained present and dominant. It appeared that he was able to double at will, without the aid of mirrors and lights, at least some of the time. He had been an active and functioning multiple as long as he could remember—since childhood, perhaps even since birth—and he had devoted himself through the years to the task of gaining mastery over his divided mind.

All the aspects of him that she came to meet had basically attractive personalities: they were energetic, stable, purposeful men, who enjoyed life and seemed to know how to go about getting what they wanted. Though they were very different people, she could trace them all back readily enough to the underlying Van from whom, so she thought, they had all split off. The one puzzle was Nat, the market operator. It was hard for Cleo to imagine what he was like when he was Nat—sleazy and coarse, yes, but how did he manage to make himself look fifteen years older and forty pounds heavier? Maybe it was all done with facial expressions and posture. But she never got to see Nat. And gradually she realized it was an oversimplification to think of Paul and Dick and Ned and the others as mere extensions of Van into different modes. Van by himself was just as incomplete as the others. He was just one of many that had evolved in parallel, each one autonomous, each one only a fragment of the whole. Though Van might have control of the shared body a greater portion of the time, he still had no idea what any of his alternate selves were up to while they were in command, and like them he had to depend on guesses and fancy footwork and such notes and messages as they bothered to leave behind in order to keep track of events that occurred outside his conscious awareness. "The only one who knows everything is Michael. He's seven years old, smart as a whip, keeps in touch with all of us all the time."

"Your memory trace," Cleo said.

Van nodded. All multiples, she knew, had one alter with full awareness of the doings of all the other personalities—usually a child, an observer who sat back deep in the mind and played its own games and emerged only when necessary to fend off some crisis that threatened the stability of the entire group. "He's just informed us that he's Ethiopian," Van said. "So every two or three weeks we go across to Oakland to an Ethiopian restaurant that he likes, and he flirts with the waitresses in Amharic."

"That can't be too terrible a chore. I'm told Ethiopians are very beautiful people."

"Absolutely. But they think it's all a big joke, and Michael doesn't know how to pick up women, anyway. He's only seven, you know. So Van doesn't get anything out of it except some exercise in comparative linguistics and a case of indigestion the next day. Ethiopian food is the spiciest in the world. I can't *stand* spicy food."

"Neither can I," she said. "But Lisa loves it. Especially hot Mexican things. But nobody ever said sharing a body is easy, did they?"

She knew she had to be careful in questioning Van about the way his life as a multiple worked. She was supposed to be a multiple herself, after all. But she made use of her Sacramento background as justification for her areas of apparent ignorance of multiple customs and the everyday mechanics of multiple life. Though she too had known she was a multiple since childhood, she said, she had grown up outside the climate of acceptance of the divided personality that prevailed in San Francisco, where an active subculture of multiples had existed openly for years. In her isolated existence, unaware that there were a great many others of her kind, she had at first regarded herself as the victim of a serious mental disorder. It was only recently, she told him, that she had come to understand the overwhelming advantages of life as a multiple: the richness, the complexity, the fullness of talents and experiences that a divided mind was free to enjoy. That was why she had come to San Francisco. That was why she listened so eagerly to all that he was telling her about himself.

She was cautious, too, in manifesting her own multiple identities. She wished she did not have to be pretending to have other selves. But they had to be brought forth now and again, Cleo felt, if only by way of maintaining his interest in her. Multiples were notoriously indifferent to singletons, she knew. They found them bland, overly simple, two-dimensional. They wanted the excitement that came with embracing one person and discovering another, or two or three. So she gave him Lisa, she gave him Vixen, she gave him the Judy-who-was-Cleo and the Cleo-who-was-someone-else, and she slipped from one to another in a seemingly involuntary and unexpected way, often when they were in bed.

Lisa was calm, controlled, strait-laced. She was totally shocked when she found herself, between one eye-blink and the next, in the arms of a strange man. "Who are you?—where am I?—" she blurted, rolling away, pulling herself into a foetal ball.

"I'm Judy's friend," Van said.

She stared bleakly at him. "So she's up to her tricks again. I should have figured it out faster."

He looked pained, embarrassed, terribly solicitous. She let him wonder for a moment or two whether he would have to take her back to her hotel right here in the middle of the night. And then she allowed a mischievous smile to cross Lisa's face, allowed Lisa's outraged modesty to subside, allowed Lisa to relent and relax, allowed Lisa to purr—

"Well, as long as we're here already—what did you say your name was?"

He liked that. He liked Vixen, too—wild, sweaty, noisy, a moaner, a gasper, a kicker and thrasher who dragged him down on to the floor and went rolling over and over with him. She thought he liked Cleo, too, though that was harder to tell, because Cleo's style was aloof, serious, baroque, inscrutable. She would switch quickly from one to another, sometimes running through all four in the course of an hour. Wine, she said, induced quick switching in her. She let him know that she had a few other identities, too, fragmentary and submerged, and hinted that they were troubled, deeply neurotic, almost self-destructive: they were under control, she said, and would not erupt to cause woe for him, but she left the possibility hovering over them, to add spice to the relationship and plausibility to her role.

It seemed to be working. His pleasure in her company was evident, and the more they were together the stronger the bond between them became. She was beginning to indulge in pleasant little fantasies of moving down here permanently from Sacramento, renting an apartment somewhere near his, perhaps even moving in with him—though that would surely be a strange and challenging life, for she would be living with Paul and Ned and Chuck and all the rest of the crew too, but how wondrous, how electrifying—

Then on the tenth day he seemed uncharacteristically tense and somber, and she asked him what was bothering him, and he evaded her, and she pressed, and finally he said, "Do you really want to know?"

"Of course."

"It bothers me that you aren't real, Judy."

She caught her breath. "What the hell do you mean by that?"

"You know what I mean," he said, quietly, sadly. "Don't try to pretend any longer. There's no point in it."

It was like a jolt in the ribs. She turned away and stared at the wall and was silent a long while, wondering what to say. Just when everything was going so well, just when she was beginning to believe she had carried off the masquerade successfully—

"So you know?" she asked in a small voice.

"Of course I know. I knew right away."

She was trembling. "How could you tell?"

"A thousand ways. When we switch, we *change*. The voice. The eyes. The muscular tensions. The grammatical habits. The brain waves, even. An evoked-potential test shows it. Flash a light in my eyes and I'll give off a certain brain-wave pattern, and Ned will give off another, and Chuck still another. You and Lisa and Cleo and Vixen would all be the same. Multiples aren't actors, Judy. Multiples are separate minds within the same brain. That's a matter of scientific fact. You were just acting. You were doing it very well, but you couldn't possibly have fooled me."

"You let me make an idiot of myself, then."

"No."

"Why did you—how could you—"

"I saw you walk in, that first night at the club, and you caught me right away. And then I watched you go out on the floor and fall apart, and I knew you couldn't be multiple, and I wondered, what the hell's she doing here, and then I went over to you, and I was hooked. I felt something I haven't ever felt before. Does that sound like the standard old malarkey? But it's true, Judy. You're the first singleton woman that's ever interested me."

"Why?"

He shook his head. "Something about you—your intensity, your alertness, maybe even your eagerness to pretend you were a multiple—I don't know. I was caught. I was caught hard. And it's been a wonderful week and a half. I mean that. Wonderful."

"Until you got bored."

"I'm not bored with you, Judy."

"Cleo. That's my real name, my singleton name. There is no Judy."

"Cleo," he said, as if measuring the word with his lips.

"So you aren't bored with me even though there's only one of me. That's marvelous. That's tremendously flattering. That's the best thing I've heard all day. I guess I should go now, Van. It *is* Van, isn't it?"

"Don't talk that way."

"How do you want me to talk? I fascinated you, you fascinated me, we played our little games with each other, and now it's over. I wasn't real, but you did your best. We both did our bests. But I'm only a singleton woman, and you can't be satisfied with that. Not for long. For a night, a week, two weeks, maybe. Sooner or later you'll want the real thing, and I can't be the real thing for you. So long, Van."

"No."

"No?"

"Don't go."

"What's the sense of staying?"

"I want you to stay."

"I'm a singleton, Van."

"You don't have to be," he said.

The therapist's name was Burkhalter and his office was in one of the Embarcadero towers, and to the San Francisco multiples community he was very close to being a deity. His speciality was electrophysiological integration, with specific application to multiple-personality disorders. Those who carried within themselves dark and diabolical selves that threatened the stability of the group went to him to have those selves purged, or at least contained. Those who sought to have latent selves that were submerged beneath more outgoing personalities brought forward into healthy functional state went to him also. Those whose life as a multiple was a torment of schizoid confusions instead of a richly rewarding contrapuntal symphony gave themselves to Dr. Burkhalter to be healed, and in time they were. And in recent years he had begun to develop techniques for what he called personality augmentation. Van called it "driving the wedge."

"He can turn a singleton into a multiple?" Cleo asked in amazement.

"If the potential is there. You know that it's partly genetic: the structure of a multiple's brain is fundamentally different from a singleton's. The hardware just isn't the same, the cerebral wiring. And then, if the right stimulus comes along, usually in childhood, usually but not necessarily traumatic, the splitting takes place, the separate identities begin to establish their territories. But much of the time multiplicity is never generated, and you walk around with the capacity to be a whole horde of selves and never know it."

"Is there reason to think I'm like that?"

He shrugged. "It's worth finding out. If he detects the predisposition, he has effective ways of inducing separation. Driving the wedge, you see? You do *want* to be a multiple, don't you, Cleo?"

"Oh, yes, Van. Yes!"

Burkhalter wasn't sure about her. He taped electrodes to her head, flashed bright lights in her eyes, gave her verbal association tests, ran four or five different kinds of electroencephalograph studies, and still he was uncertain. "It is not a black-and-white matter," he said several times, frowning, scowling. He was a multiple himself, but three of his selves were psychiatrists, so there was never any real problem about his office hours. Cleo wondered if he ever went to himself for a second opinion. After a week of testing she was sure that she must he a hopeless case, an intractable singleton, but Burkhalter surprised her by concluding that it was worth the attempt. "At the very worst," he said, "we will experience spontaneous fusing within a few days, and you will be no worse off than you are now. But if we succeed—ah, if we succeed—!"

His clinic was across the bay in a town called Moraga. She checked in on a Friday afternoon, spent two days undergoing further neurological and psychological tests, then three days taking medication, "Simply an anti-convulsant," the nurse explained cheerily. "To build up your tolerance."

"Tolerance for what?" Cleo asked.

"The birth trauma," she said, "New selves will be coming forth, and it can be uncomfortable for a little while."

The treatment began on Thursday. Electroshock drugs, electroshock again. She was heavily sedated. It felt like a long dream, but there was no pain. Van visited her every day. Chuck came too, bringing her two potted orchids in bloom, and Paul sang to her, and even Ned paid her a call. But it was hard for her to maintain a conversation with any of them. She

heard voices much of the time. She felt feverish and dislocated, and at times she was sure she was floating eight or ten inches above the bed. Gradually that sensation subsided, but there were others nearly as odd. The voices remained. She learned how to hold conversations with them.

In the second week she was not allowed to have visitors. That didn't matter. She had plenty of company even when she was alone.

Then Van came for her. "They're going to let you go home today," he said. "How are you doing, Cleo?"

"I'm Noreen," she said.

There were five of her, apparently. That was what Van said. She had no way of knowing, because when they were dominant she was gone—not merely asleep, but *gone*, perceiving nothing. But he showed her notes that they wrote, in handwritings that she did not recognize and indeed could barely read, and he played tapes of her other voices, Noreen a deep contralto, Nanette high and breathy, Katya hard and rough New York, and the last one, who had not yet announced her name, a stagy voluptuous campy siren-voice.

She did not leave his apartment the first few days, and then began going out for short trips, always with Van or one of his alters close beside. She felt convalescent. A kind of hangover from the various drugs had dulled her reflexes and made it difficult for her to cope with the traffic, and also there was the fear that she would undergo a switching while she was out. Whenever that happened it came without warning, and when she returned to awareness afterwards she felt a sharp bewildering discontinuity of memory, not knowing how it was that she suddenly found herself in Ghiradelli Square or Golden Gate Park or wherever it was that the other self had taken their body.

But she was happy. And Van was happy with her. As they strolled hand in hand through the cool evenings she turned to him now and again and saw the warmth of his smile, the glow of his eyes. One night in the second week when they were out together he switched to Chuck—Cleo saw him change, and knew it was Chuck coming on, for now she always knew right away which identity had taken over—and he said, "You've had a marvelous effect on him,

Cleo. None of us has ever seen him like this before—so contented, so fulfilled—"

"I hope it lasts, Chuck."

"Of course it'll last! Why on earth shouldn't it last?"

It didn't. Towards the end of the third week Cleo noticed that there hadn't been any entries in her memo book from Noreen for several days. That in itself was nothing alarming: an alter might choose to submerge for days, weeks, even months at a time. But was it likely that Noreen, so new to the world, would remain out of sight so long? Lin-lin, the little Chinese girl who had evolved in the second week and was Cleo's memory trace, reported that Noreen had gone away. A few days later an identity named Mattie came and went within three hours, like something bubbling up out of a troubled sea. Then Nanette disappeared, leaving Cleo with no one but her nameless breathy-voiced alter and Lin-lin. She knew she was fusing again. The wedges that Dr. Burkhalter had driven into her soul were not holding; her mind insisted on oneness, and was integrating itself; she was reverting to the singleton state.

"They're all gone," she told Van disconsolately.

"I know. I've been watching it happen."

"Is there anything we can do? Should I go back to Burkhalter?"

She saw the pain in his eyes. "It won't do any good," he said. "He told me the chances were about three to one this would happen. A month, he figured—that was about the best we could hope for. And we've had our month."

"I'd better go, Van."

"Don't say that."

"No?"

"I love you, Cleo."

"You won't," she said. "Not for much longer."

He tried to argue with her, to tell her that it didn't matter to him that she was a singleton, that one Cleo was worth a whole raft of alters, that he would learn to adapt to life with a singleton woman. He could not bear the thought of her leaving now. So she stayed: a week, two weeks, three. They ate at their favorite restaurants. They strolled hand in hand through the cool evenings. They talked of Chomsky and Whorf and even of shopping centers. When he was gone and Paul or Chuck or Hal or Dave was there she went places with them, if they wanted her

to. Once she went to a movie with Ned, and when towards the end he felt himself starting to switch she put her arm around him and held him until he regained control, so that he could see how the movie finished.

But it was no good, really. She sensed the strain in him. He wanted something richer than she could offer him: the switching, the doubling, the complex undertones and overtones of other personalities resonating beyond the shores of consciousness. She could not give him that. And though he insisted he didn't miss it, he was like one who has voluntarily blindfolded himself in order to keep a blind woman company. She knew she could not ask him to live like that for ever.

And so one afternoon when Van was somewhere else she packed her things and said goodbye to Paul, who gave her a hug and wept a little with her, and she went back to Sacramento. "Tell him not to call," she said. "A clean break's the best." She had been in San Francisco two months, and it was as though those two months were the only months of her life that had had any color in them, and all the rest had been lived in tones of gray.

There had been a man in the real-estate office who had been telling her for a couple of years that they were meant for each other. Cleo had always been friendly enough to him—they had done a few skiing weekends in Tahoe the winter before, they had gone to Hawaii once, they had driven down to San Diego—but she had never felt anything particular when she was with him. A week after her return, she phoned him and suggested that they drive out up north to the redwood country for a few days together. When they came back, she moved into the handsome condominium he had just outside town.

It was hard to find anything wrong with him. He was good-natured and attractive, he was successful, he read books and liked good movies, he enjoyed hiking and rafting and backpacking, he even talked of driving down into the city during the opera season to take in a performance or two. He was getting towards the age where he was thinking about marriage and a family. He seemed very fond of her.

But he was flat, she thought. Flat as a cardboard cut-out: a singleton, a one-brain, a no-switch. There was only one of him, and there always would be. It was hardly his fault, she knew. But she couldn't settle for someone who had only two dimensions. A terrible restlessness went roaring through her every evening, and she could not possibly tell him what was troubling her.

On a drizzly afternoon in early November she packed a suitcase and drove down to San Francisco. She arrived about six-thirty, and checked into one of the Lombard Street motels, and showered and changed and walked over to Fillmore Street. Cautiously she explored the strip from Chestnut down to Union, from Union back to Chestnut. The thought of running into Van terrified her. Probably she would, sooner or later, she knew: but not tonight, she prayed. Not tonight. She went past Skits, did not go in, stopped outside a club called Big Mama, shook her head, finally entered one called the Side Effect. Mostly women inside, as usual, but a few men at the bar, not too bad-looking. No sign of Van. She bought herself a drink and casually struck up a conversation with the man to her left, a short curly-haired artistic-looking type, about forty.

"You come here often?" he asked.

"First time. I've usually gone to Skits."

"I think I remember seeing you there. Or maybe not."

She smiled. "What's your now-name?"

"Sandy. Yours?"

Cleo drew her breath down deep into her lungs. She felt a kind of lightheadedness beginning to swirl behind her eyes. *Is this what you want?* she asked herself. *Yes. Yes. This is what you want.*

"Melinda," she said.

Copyright © 1983 by Agberg Inc.

Dantzel Cherry has recently sold short stories to Fireside Magazine *and* Metro Fiction. *This is her first appearance in* Galaxy's Edge.

MISS DARCY'S FIRST INTERGALACTIC BALLET CLASS

by Dantzel Cherry

Darcy walked up to the gilded starship door and it dissolved, revealing what had to be the gaudiest room in the galaxy. Gold, silver, bronze, and minerals that probably didn't even exist on Earth covered the high ceiling and walls in panels, interlaced throughout with precious stones—and was that tinsel?—depicting who-knows-what. The effect was much like a wild animal had eaten all the jewelry at Tiffany's and then vomited all over the walls.

Clearly the ability to travel through all the worlds in the galaxy and kidnap a fifty-two-year-old ballet teacher didn't grant good taste in interior design.

The blue blob Overlord guard accompanying her spoke, its voice wobbling with each syllable, and Darcy jumped as a split second later her newly installed gray earslugs wriggled and translated:

"Behold, your students."

The guard sprouted an opaque blue arm and prodded her through the door.

Darcy looked up as four loud green creatures made entirely of tentacles and eyes lumbering by, covered gracelessly in an assortment of tutus, tiaras, and pointe shoes. Every inch of Darcy's soul cringed at the pointe shoes flopping around on such untrained limbs, but for the first time in her life, she was too intimidated by her students' size to snatch the satin shoes away and give a stern lecture. Farther back were faceless fluid blobs like the guards, mingling with heliotropic clouds with something—an eye, perhaps?—in the center of each swirling mass. No one noticed her entrance.

The guard spoke again. "And here is your master and new employer, the Rezzik Overlord."

She turned around to stare at a tentacled alien, far larger than anyone else in the room, lounging across an iron throne the size of her living room back home. The Rezzik Overlord's flesh showed hints of green, but it was mostly the mottled purple-black of an overripe plum. It was surrounded by its court: larger versions of the blob children as well as smaller clouds, so wispy she could see their single bare eyes staring through the vapors. In the midst of this strange scene an orange tabby cat crouched next to the throne.

He, her master? Darcy had been told—after being beamed into a starship out of the blue, of course, and made to sit in isolation until she calmed down—that she was just here for a ballet lesson. She squared her shoulders and gave her best curtsy, which was saying something.

"Good afternoon … Overlord."

The Overlord harrumphed. "Miss Darcy Kent. My progeny have been viewing satellite transmissions of this artform you humans call ballet, and you have been observed as the finest ballet instructor of your planet—"

"—and a former principal dancer with the New York City Ballet—" Darcy cut in.

"—and you are here now to provide instruction. Your performance today will determine whether you humans will join my magnificent empire as capable allies or as miserable slaves. I expect you to teach my progeny to move exquisitely. Oh, and my little lucky feline here. Teach him some respect." A stray tentacle stroked the tabby cat's back.

What sort of ballet could she teach to creatures like this? Ballet could hardly work with so many limbs. She looked over at the blobs and the clouds. Or so few limbs. And who ever taught a cat to do anything besides crapping in a box? Her earslugs wriggled, and by sheer willpower she resisted the urge to scratch them.

"You don't want to talk to the President of the United States or something? I'm sure there are official diplomats for this sort of thing," Darcy said.

Three of the Overlord's tentacles swept away her question. "I judge a planet's worth by observing its higher art forms in action. Begin." With a flick of a limb, it shoved the cat away from the throne, and the cat, its tail high and indignant, trotted to Darcy's side.

"Not just yet," Darcy said, folding her arms.

Everyone in the room muttered, and the Overlord's many tentacles flailed about. Darcy forced herself to keep talking. "I need music."

"That's what Naasmit is for." It pointed at a nearby large blob, who resonated a single high, sweet F and wobbled to the back of the room.

"Oh. Well. Good. But that's not all," Darcy said, raising her voice at the Overlord's retinue, which seemed to decide, as one, to talk, sing, and laugh enough to make the air reverberate. "I don't allow parents in the room while I'm teaching. Never have."

A hush came over the room, and the Overlord's many eyes narrowed. "You would tell the Overlord what to do?"

"Well no, not normally. But you'll distract the children."

"Oh, that? We have barriers for that." A sprinkling shower of particles appeared in front of her and thickened into a mirror that spanned the length of the room, blocking her view of the Overlord and his court. The Overlord's voice boomed out, only slightly muffled by the thin barrier.

"We will watch from this side, and you are free from distraction. Now begin. You have one Earth hour. Teach them all you know."

"I can't do that in just—"

She was interrupted by the largest offspring of the Rezzik Overlord pushing past its friends to stand in front of Darcy, four white tutus strapped about its trunk, with tentacles and eyes squeezing above, below, and between the layers of tulle.

"Are you going to make me look beautiful?" it said loudly. "I asked my parent, the Overlord, to bring you here to show everyone how beautiful I am."

Make this creature beautiful? Darcy glanced back at the wall blocking her from the Rezzik Overlord and prayed.

"I intend to make all of my students *perform* beautifully, Miss…" Darcy trailed off. What *were* their names?

"You may call me Anna Pavlova, the great Dying Swan," the many-limbed, many-eyed child of the Rezzik informed her, fluttering four of its tentacles in imitation of The Dying Swan's trembling wings.

A smaller, less bulbous version of Anna—a sibling, perhaps? —tiptoed forward on eight pairs of toe shoes.

"And I am Princess. You must call me Princess."

It hurt Darcy to see such beautiful shoes supporting—barely—four hundred pounds of untrained, tentacled flesh, but she forced a smile.

A swirling cloud in a single short red tutu added, "And I am to be referred to as Maria Tallchief, the Firebird."

The others were so eager to share their ballerina names with Darcy that the slug translator had difficulty keeping up. Gelsey Kirkland, Marie Taglioni, and so on—all famous ballerinas. None of them wanted to be Darcy Kent, former principal dancer of the New York City Ballet. No accounting for taste.

The only pupil not shouting, shrieking, or running around was the snoozing tabby by her feet.

"What do I do with you, kitty?" she asked.

She jumped when he yawned and replied, "I'm Felix. Please don't call me anything but Felix, or I'll accidentally cut your face open."

Right. And now there's talking cats. "How in the world…"

"Ugh. This question again. Yes, I'm really talking, and yes, all cats can talk."

"Can other—"

Felix's bored monotone interrupted her. "No, other animals can't speak. So why can cats? Because we didn't originate on Earth. I'm surprised you humans haven't figured that out yet."

"So why—"

"Why am I here? Well, that story is long and boring and a little embarrassing. Ahem."

"Spit it out, cat. It sounded like your master over there gave me permission to do a little tail pulling."

"Because I was captured, and I'm being punished." Felix groomed his chest, avoiding eye contact. "I'd rather not talk about it."

She pinched herself. No, she was still in a beam-me-up-Scotty starship on a Wednesday afternoon, about to teach ballet to aliens in tutus and toe shoes. No big deal. They were acting like the three year olds she had taught at beginning of her career forty years ago, before her fame led her to work with only the elite.

But she could dust off her 'baby class' format from the farthest depths of her mental library. This couldn't nearly be as bad as the Russian guest artist

with fifty clauses in her contract, or the snotty Australian that—wait, was that blob licking the mirror?

Darcy checked her watch. Fifty four minutes left. Time to move.

Nudging Felix with her toe, she said, "Come on. We have a planet to save," then turned to the room at large and called out in a falsely bright voice, "Alright dancers, let's form a circle."

No one seemed to notice Darcy in the slightest.

Time to move to Plan B, which needed an unsuspecting helper. Someone vain. Someone bossy.

Her eyes fell on Anna Pavlova.

"Oh, Anna's showing me that she's ready. Thank you, Anna."

Bewildered, Anna looked up. She had been no quieter than anyone else, but was pleased at being praised, and she stood a little taller. Her tentacles slapped at the two clouds rushing by, pulling them into line next to herself.

"Come on!" Anna hissed. "It's time to start."

As Anna bullied several students into forming a circle, Darcy focused on the blob licking the mirror barrier.

"It's Gelsey, isn't it? Gelsey, I need you to be my special helper today. Could you sit by me and show everyone how to stretch over and touch your toes—I mean, not that you have toes or tentacles—oh my, those are very nice arms and legs you just grew from your—um, blobiness. Oh, my. They look just like the real Gelsey's, don't they? Very thin and elegant. Yes, yes, stretch forward to touch your tentacles and toes, just like that—"

Alternating between cajoling and ordering, Darcy led them through her standard warm-up stretches. She modified the stretches as needed for each group of aliens, though she suspected that, based on the nature of their bodies, none of them suffered from lack of flexibility in any apparent limbs. Felix seemed to feel that cleaning his legs constituted sufficient stretching, and appeared deaf to her voice.

Five minutes later, she moved them to the wooden barres that stood near the decorative metal panels. So far, her tactics had proved useful in keeping the dancers focused and following direction, but Darcy couldn't be sure that would last forever. She briskly arranged them on the barres by species. Felix was, of course, a foot or two too short for the barre.

"A tragedy," Felix said, his voice monotone. "I shall do my best to follow from down here." He yawned.

Darcy raised an eyebrow. "Considering you're a prisoner of the Overlord, I'd think you'd be nervous about not going along with this punishment of his."

"Yes, yes," Felix said. "I shall do all of the silly ballet tricks. But I hardly need to learn grace from a *human*."

She began to see why the Rezzik Overlord was irritated with the cat.

She came back to the tentacle aliens and assigned their tentacles above and below a certain point to be 'arms' and 'legs.'

"Turn the toes out to first position and *plié*, everyone," Darcy said, bending her knees. The ship's gravity was gentler on her bones. Her knees had lost the crumbling feeling they had acquired twelve years ago, around the time she'd retired from the stage. "And lift your arm. No, that's your leg, Princess. Lift the tentacle above that. And the one next to it. That's right, follow me."

The blobs, having followed Gelsey's lead and morphed into humanoid shapes, actually looked pretty good during pliés, though they never grew faces, which Darcy found disturbing. The tentacles did a fairly decent job of not getting tangled. Darcy found the easiest modification for them was to pair the tentacles with one nearby so that a dozen or more pairs of tentacles moved through first, second, third, fourth, and fifth positions with relative ease. They were like living May poles, the way their legs wove in and out of each other. It was almost disappointing that none of them tripped.

At first Darcy had thought the clouds had no limbs, but as they moved up and down in time with the music, she began to suspect they were hiding limbs of some sort under all that purple condensation.

Felix simply crouched into a hunting position, lashed his tail, straightened, then crouched again in time with the music. Clearly, he was not amused.

"And now *tendus*," Darcy said. "Everyone show me first position again. That's right, Princess, the heels kiss and the toes point out—er, the suckers kiss and the tips point out. Now we slide one leg out to the tips of our toes and tentacles. Let's pretend there's a bug under our toes, and we're going to squish it."

"That's disgusting," Anna said. "You kill smaller lifeforms without causation?"

She wanted to argue that insects were gross, but these aliens, who very much looked like slugs and spiders, might not appreciate her reasoning.

"This is why humans haven't joined the interstellar ethical committees yet," Tamara Karsavina said, and all the students nodded gravely.

So much for impressing the aliens with Earth's peacekeeping.

"Let's pretend something else instead. Have you seen a penny?"

Pennies proved to be less controversial, though the idea of sliding precious metals around on the ground remained confusing to all the dancers, particularly the tentacles.

She led them through the next few exercises without further disgracing the human race, and found that clouds, blobs, tentacles, and cat alike had no issue with soft, flowing movements—which, when she thought about it, wasn't all that surprising. Darcy decided to be bold and introduce pique turns. Those went over surprisingly well—only Felix and the tentacles complained about how it hurt to turn on a single limb.

They all, however, were a real mess with the quick, sharp steps. Felix did well enough, hopping on his hind legs like a kangaroo, but Darcy was hardly able to enjoy it. The lower gravity made a great environment for the tentacle group to do simple *sautés*, but *grand jetés* and other jumps that involved leaping from one leg to the other resulted in many tangled tentacles—they needed constant reminders of which tentacles were arms and which were legs.

The blobs and clouds had their own issues even clearing the floor, lacking any muscles, and Darcy found herself trying to comfort two very frustrated alien races as they tried again and again.

"Never mind, Gelsey," Darcy said, patting the blob uncomfortably on its squishy shoulder. "Leaping is only one of the many fun parts of ballet. In fact, it's time to learn a short combination of steps today. You're all doing so well that I think we can make this extra special. Watch me first, then I'll make little changes for each of you afterward."

Darcy began to dance, humming the waltz from *The Sleeping Beauty* as she moved. She didn't want to make the combination too complicated, but her students had proved to have better memories than she remembered her three-year old classes having, and she wanted to impress the Rezzik Overlord. Her reputation—and Earth, of course—were at stake.

Bourreés were always a parent-pleaser—something about the stereotypical tiny whirring tip-toe steps warmed every doting parent's heart. She included sweeping *balancés* and *piqué* turns, which would both be confusing to the tentacles, but they didn't seem to mind biting off more than they could chew.

She finished with a long, slow leg lift and turned to find the whole class staring back at her—except for the possibly the blobs, since she still didn't know where their eyes were—and noted a definite sense of awe. Perhaps this was why the Overlord had spared Earth: out of all the scientific data, all the messages of goodwill and peace that humans had sent out to the universe, the broadcasts of the Moscow Ballet, the New York City Ballet, the American Ballet Theatre, and other ballet companies had been what got through.

"You have so many bones. How do you lift your leg so high and make your limbs ripple as well as you do with so many long, unbending bones?" Anna asked.

Or perhaps Earth had been spared so alien children could gawk at her.

"Mine goes higher, of course," Anna went on, and wobbling slightly, lifted a dozen or so tentacles to point straight up to the ceiling. Darcy reaffirmed her decades-long prayer that there was a special hell created for the children who show up the teacher.

She strolled around the room as her students practiced the combination several times, with varying degrees of concentration.

"—and *coupé* on one, *passé* two, *developpé* three, four—yes, Marie Taglioni, take those tentacles all the way up above your head, like a flower sprouting out of the ground—stay five, six, *tendu* seven, bring your feet—I mean tentacles—to fifth on eight. No, come back and practice, Gelsey, and stop licking the mirror."

She checked her watch. Her hour was almost up. Would it be enough for the Rezzik Overlord? These children had good memories, yes, but they were dancing with the grace of three-year-olds. They had none of the delicate control of ballerinas who had been practicing for three hours a day, seven days a week for thirteen years before joining a company.

Darcy thought back to her 'baby ballet' classes all those years ago. Every child's joy—and every parent's pride—was putting on an impromptu performance.

She clapped her hands, and for once her students stopped talking, giggling, and turning. She arranged them in circles: the clouds on the outside, the blobs the next layer in, and the tentacles making up the third layer, with Felix, Anna Pavlova, and Princess in the very center.

"There," Darcy said, stepping back and rubbing her hands. "Let's try a little performance, shall we? Show me and your parents your favorite steps. Let everyone see how beautifully you move. We'll start with our lovely *bourreés*."

"A performance?" the Rezzik Overlord's voice boomed. "You still have seven Earth minutes left. Have you already taught them everything you know?"

The opaque wall that the Rezzik Overlord had created shimmered and faded to a pale translucent blue. Darcy could see everyone in the Overlord's court, watching her intently.

For a split second, Darcy nearly found herself groveling and apologizing for not teaching every single variation of *pas de bourrée* and *fouetté* and *grand jeté* she knew. Then her pride for her profession reared its irritated head—how dare he trivialize ballet? —and she ignored the Overlord.

She hummed a waltz for Naasmit and the blob started singing at once. Naasmit started with the simple waltz structure that Darcy had given her, and built on it until it swelled into an intricate, grand score, and the students responded to the music in kind. With Darcy leading in front, they began with the combination, each alien race modifying the steps—more or less—as she had instructed them.

Just as they finished the *developpé*, Darcy turned and called over the music, "Now show us your favorite turns."

Almost as one, the tentacles spun in tight circles, limbs flowing back like dozens of green ribbons caught in a breeze. The blobs twisted themselves into curlicues, and after several frantic pleading gestures from Darcy, Felix rose on his hind legs and shuffled in a circle, all the while the clouds floated in an endless follow-the-leader.

It was beautiful. Perhaps not up to the standards of modern ballet—may the Overlord never notice the difference—but it probably would have fit in very well in the French courts. The dancers back then had worn such ridiculously unwieldy costumes they could barely do more than walk, let alone leap and pirouette like dancers now.

Besides, Darcy Kent had just started working with them. Given a few years and a few attitude adjustments, she'd have them in fine performance form.

Darcy signaled to Naasmit, and the blob changed the tune, speeding up.

"Now improvise! Show us your favorite steps!" Darcy called over the music.

The performers paused for a moment, processing her words.

Then they went mad.

They wriggled, chased each other, bobbed, and wobbled. A pair of blobs collided with each other and seemed to merge before flying back and colliding into a jumble of tentacles. Every single cloud was bouncing—very low to the ground, thankfully—into a puffy mass. Lightning crackled and Darcy felt her clothes pull away from her body, full of static.

Felix leaped out of the fray to the back of the room. *Traitor.*

Princess rolled in front of her like a tumbleweed, toe shoes clattering noisily on the copper ground, and Anna Pavlova had climbed on top of a blob and was bouncing on the poor creature, shrieking with delight.

"Dance!" Darcy called in desperation to Anna. This was all because of it. Why wasn't it taking this seriously?

Anna's many eyes glanced down at her, and the young Rezzik seemed to remember where it was for a few moments. It leaped—or tried to—in midair and soared for a few sickening moments before flopping on the ground in a tangle of green limbs and white tulle. Darcy reached down to help it up and pulled and -

One of Anna's tentacles ripped free, dripping black blood.

"Oh my god—uh, do you want this back?"

Anna raced off screaming.

Suddenly aware of the watching audience, Darcy looked at the limp tentacle in her hand and up at the Rezzik Overlord. Its many eyes returned her stare, unblinking.

She'd dealt with countless students wetting their pants, spraining their ankles, and even tripping and losing a few teeth, but she'd never dealt with a severed limb before.

Darcy began to set the tentacle on the floor, but paused. It seemed so disrespectful. She checked her watch. Three minutes of class left. It was supposed to be time for the *reverence*: a show of respect between the teacher, music accompanist, and students, but Darcy wasn't sure she wanted to spend her last moments of life practicing fancy curtsies.

Apparently Naasmit hadn't noticed the bloodbath, for the blob played on as loudly as before.

"You can stop playing now, Naasmit," Darcy called. The blob immediately slowed, trilled a few high notes, and swung the last note down to a deep bass. The dancers looked around, bemused. The only noise came from Anna, sobbing in the corner near the metal panels.

"Dancers, curtsy to our Rezzik Overlord." She curtsied her deepest, praying for some kind of mercy.

The Overlord's grumble confirmed her suspicions.

"What nonsense is this? You still have two minutes," the Overlord said. Its tentacles flailed twice, accentuating its displeasure.

"But—I thought—" Words failed Darcy, and she held the tentacle up, which flopped unhelpfully.

"Don't waste our time with such nonsense, Miss Darcy Kent. Lrrra'vajerrr, stop your wailing. That tentacle was going to fall off soon; Miss Darcy Kent simply helped it along."

"Wait. Your tentacles fall off?" Darcy asked.

"But of course, Miss Darcy Kent. How else will adolescent Rezzik grow their adult tentacles? Wgggevid, what did you think of your lesson?"

"Didn't I look wonderful? Weren't my tentacles moving so pretty? I was just like a real—"

Anna brushed away its tears to interrupt Princess. "Can we do Swan Lake next time?"

"No, Lrrra'vajerrr, I wanted to do Sleeping Beauty."

"But that's not *fair*! I'm the oldest, and I—"

"Enough," the Rezzik Overlord said to his offspring. "Leave us now. You are in need of sustenance."

Sail to Success

a unique writers' workshop on board a luxury cruise ship

Intensive manuscript critique by
Toni Weisskopf (head of Baen Books)
and
Nancy Kress (bestselling, Hugo/Nebula-winning author)

PLUS

Writing and business (publishing) seminars by
Mike Resnick
Jack Skillingstead
Eric Flint
and
Eleanor Wood (head of Spectrum Literary Agency)

Class size restricted to only 22 students
December 7-11, 2015

All-inclusive pricing starting at $1,099 (as of July 2015; subject to change). Prices include cruise, food, entertainment and all materials needed for the workshop.

www.SailSuccess.com

SAIL TO SUCCESS 2012

The Sail to Success 2012 writer's workshop, sponsored by Arc Manor/Phoenix Pick press and organized by Shahid Mahmud, was held onboard the *Norwegian Sky* cruise liner, sailing from Miami on December 3 and returning December 7 after a tour of the Bahamas, including Grand Bahama Island, Nassau, and Great Stirrup Cay. Onboard instructors were authors Kevin J. Anderson, Paul Cook, Nancy Kress, Rebecca Moesta, Mike Resnick, and Jack Skillingstead, publisher and editor Toni Weisskopf, and literary agent Eleanor Wood. *Locus* was invited to attend, and design editor Francesca Myman was on board to represent the magazine.

Over the four days, 17 panel-style classes and two critique sessions were scheduled from 9:00 a.m. to 11:00 p.m., with a five- to six-hour break each day for cruise activities. Most students attended a majority of the classes, though there was no requirement to do so. Students had excellent social access to instructors, with three scheduled group meals and the opportunity to make individual appointments to discuss the industry or just share a drink.

Overall, the focus was on the seminars, with classes slanted towards providing an insider perspective on the business of science fiction and fantasy publishing, but also including the history of science fiction, a solid introduction to writing basics, and some advanced technique. Highlights included Kevin Anderson and Rebecca Moesta's well-known "Professional Approach to Writing" seminars, Eleanor Wood's insider look at the intricacies of contract negotiation, and manuscript critique sessions with Nancy Kress and Toni Weisskopf. Critique sessions were structured as a kind of "speed-dating" version of traditional workshopping, with the instructors offering comments on manuscripts submitted prior to the cruise and a brief opportunity for fellow students to comment. Additional optional follow-up critique sessions were available with Kress.

Arc Manor/Phoenix Pick provided plenty of swag, including T-shirts and bags printed with the Sail to Success logo and instructor names, and a 550-page perfect-bound book with glossy cover containing all the students' manuscript submissions bound into a single volume.

The *Norwegian Sky* itself was a handsome 848-foot-long ship with a friendly crew of 934 and a Hawaiian-luau atmosphere: hibiscus flowers painted on the hull, bright aqua carpets with tropical fish swimming down the hallways, etc. Onboard amenities included three *plein-air* pools on the top decks, five Jacuzzis, three "free" restaurants, three luxe "paid" restaurants, five bars, a fitness center and volleyball court, a spa offering massages and facials for purchase, a video arcade, and the requisite shops and casino. Despite these glitzy offerings, the overall atmosphere for workshop participants was quiet, with a preference for sharing time with instructors and classmates, enjoying the clean salt sea air on the many open decks, and even writing! (Kevin J. Anderson was spotted writing away with his signature giant headphones affixed, in the forward lounge. According to Anderson, he continued writing even when a dance class started up around him.) The cruise line offered classes in everything from dancing to cupcake decoration to circus skills like juggling, plate spinning, and devil sticks, which might have challenged even Anderson's concentration.

There was a bewildering (and exciting) array of shore excursions available, including visits to the recently opened billion-dollar Atlantis Aquaventure resort development, scuba diving, various flavors of snorkeling – including the usual variety and a variant with powered scooters, sailing, fishing, kayaking, parasailing, and dolphin and sea lion encounters. Various tours were available by glass-bottom boat, underwater motorbike, semi-submarine, Harley-Davidson (I'm not joking), Segway, bike, off-road jeep, horseback, and catamaran. Workshop participants tended towards milder away expeditions, including historical tours and self-made adventures, though many also opted for at least one good snorkel or swim. Participants and instructors all had positive things to say about the experience in the evaluations, and many instructors have chosen to return next year at Mahmud's invitation. Confirmed faculty members include Kevin J. Anderson, Eric Flint, Nancy Kress, Rebecca Moesta, Mike Resnick, Jack Skillingstead, Toni Weisskopf, and Eleanor Wood.

The 2013 workshop will be held aboard *Norwegian Sky* from December 2-6, sailing again from Miami to the Bahamas. Further information will be available at <www.sailsuccess.com> and <www.phoenixpick.com>.

– *Francesca Myman* ∎

Transportation to Nassau Island, where Thoraiya Dyer, Jeff Giese, and Francesca Myman explore the local hotspots — Eva Eldridge asks Mike Resnick to sign a book

Attendees (l to r): Therese Pieczynski, Lou Berger, Ron S. Friedman, Shahid Mahmud (sponsor), Ilana Harris, Eva Eldridge, Kelly Varner, Alvaro Zinos-Amaro, Gamaliel Martinez, Frank Morin; front: Jessica Carlson, Sandra Odell, Thoraiya Dyer

Instructors (l to r): Paul Cook, Kevin J. Anderson, Rebecca Moesta, Mike Resnick, Toni Weisskopf, Eleanor Wood, Nancy Kress, Jack Skillingstead

All of the dancers except Felix left, and Naasmit joined the court once more. Darcy tightened every muscle in her body, then relaxed—or tried to.

"Well?" she asked. "What did you think of your children's beautiful dancing?"

"Was that all there was to learn?" the Overlord asked. "Those little puny steps. Ballet seemed like so much more than what you taught them."

Darcy surprised even herself with her snappy tone. "No, Overlord *sir*. Of course that's not all. I taught the basics, just like I would to any human student. They will learn more when they're ready for it, and not a moment sooner." She glared, forgetting for a moment to be afraid, then cursed herself for being such a prideful idiot.

The Overlord rubbed a dozen tentacles together. "Resplendent. I would like to employ your services again, Miss Darcy Kent. This art is intriguing—and worthy, I think, of a place in my court. Shmakkk'jerrr, pay Miss Darcy Kent handsomely in the currency of her people."

Darcy, having just exhaled, perked up at the mention of pay. *Humans go free, ballet becomes an intergalactic artform,* and *this turns out to be a paying gig.*

Shmakkk'jerrr, another tentacle alien, came forward and placed a large plastic box in Darcy's arms. It was lighter than she'd expected, much lighter than gold, jewels, coins, or paper bills would be. She opened the box, and found the top of it covered with—

"Tinsel?" she asked. The entire box was stuffed tight with what she was sure was brand new silver-colored tinsel.

"Yes," the Overlord said. "The crowning achievement of your species. Gold we have found elsewhere, and silver, and chromium, and astatine, and so many others, but this is the first that we have discovered tinsel."

"Oh … thanks," Darcy said. She let the tinsel fall back in the box.

"And me, Overlord? Is my punishment complete?" Felix asked.

The Overlord made a choking sound, which the slug translator interpreted as laughing.

"Yes, Felix. I believe I will reward you by allowing you to return to Earth with Miss Darcy Kent. Shmakkk'jerrr, give Miss Darcy Kent more tinsel and send them back to Earth. We shall call on you again next week, Miss Darcy Kent."

And like that she was beamed back to her bedroom. Felix inspected the bed, sighed, and jumped up.

"So, you know how to use a litter box, right?" Darcy looked around the room. "Hmm. I don't have one yet. Looks like it's a box of tinsel for you until I get to the store, then."

Though the sun was still setting, Darcy was ready for bed. She turned off the lights and crawled under the sheets, fully clothed. Felix curled around her feet.

"It's over," Darcy said. "I just taught the most creative ballet class ever. Not to mention saving the human race."

"And just think," Felix said. "You get to do it all over again next week."

Darcy sighed. Then she got out of bed and turned on the light. She had an intergalactic ballet to choreograph.

Copyright © 2015 by Dantzel Cherry

Jack McDevitt is a Nebula winner (and seventeen-time Nebula nominee) as well as a multiple Hugo nominee. He is the author of twenty-three novels, five collections, and eighty short stories.

TIDAL EFFECTS

by Jack McDevitt

"I never walk on the beach anymore." Ed Gambini stood near the window, looking out across the illuminated lawns of the Seaside Condo. Rain sparkled in the flood lamps. The Atlantic was hidden by a screen of poplars; but the two men could hear its sullen roar. "During that summer," he continued, "while we waited for the launch, and expected so much, I went out every evening. I was too excited to work."

Harmon rotated his wine between thumb and forefinger, but said nothing.

Headlights flickered across Gambini's rigid features. "I grew up in a small town in Ohio, and I was in high school before I ever saw an ocean. But I can still remember the first time. I've loved the Atlantic ever since." He gazed thoughtfully through the rain-streaked window. "Even now."

Harmon drained his glass and surveyed the room. It was oppressive: heavy, drab furniture; bulging bookcases; neutral, steely colors everywhere. A computer beside a recliner trailed several feet of printout. "I know you're surprised to see me," Harmon said apologetically. "But I had to come."

Gambini moved away from the drapes, back into the yellow light of an ugly seashell table lamp. A shapeless gray sweater hung from his thin shoulders. "I knew you would," he said. "Eventually."

Harmon held out his glass. Gambini filled it, and his own. They were drinking port, a vintage bottle that the physicist had been saving for a special occasion. "It must be a magnificent time for you," Harmon said, "now that the data has begun to come in. There seems so little that you and your colleagues have not touched. Perhaps, in the end, only the Creation itself will prove elusive."

"Ah." Gambini brightened. "We have some ideas about that."

"I'm not surprised you think so." Harmon understood, if Gambini did not, that science has its limits.

"Sometimes," continued Gambini as if he had not heard, "the price is high."

"You mean the beach?" He watched the physicist circle the coffee table and settle stiffly into a wing-back chair. "You did what you could," he said. "I wanted to say thanks."

A gust of wind blew the rain hissing against the windows. Outside, an automobile engine roared into life. The air smelled of salt and ozone. "How much do you know about Skynet?" Gambini asked.

Harmon shrugged. "Only what I read in the papers."

The lines around Gambini's mouth tightened. "Odd. If it were not for Skynet, you would not be here; there would be no need for this meeting." He laid a peculiar emphasis on the last word. "Skynet," he continued, adopting a professorial tone, "is an array, twenty-two infrared receptors in Earth orbit. Capable of seeing damn near anything. They were putting it in place last summer. And I was waiting here, as Ryan was at Princeton, and Hakluyt at Greenbelt, and others...." He set his glass down. It was empty. "We knew that, after it became operational, the world would not be the same."

"No doubt," said Harmon. But he had no idea why this should be so.

Gambini inquired, tolerantly, whether his guest had ever heard of Fred Hoyle.

Harmon's perplexity was apparent. "I don't believe I have," he said impatiently.

Gambini crossed the room and took a thick volume from an upper shelf. "Hoyle," he said, "is a cosmologist who dedicated the later stages of his career defending outworn theories on the nature of the universe: what it is, where it came from, where it's going. Trivial matters, really, when contrasted with the question that really absorbed him, that absorbs all of us and knits us together."

"And what," asked Harmon, wondering where all this was leading, "might that be?"

"Simply stated," said Gambini, "it is this: What is *our* relationship with the cosmos? Are we unique? Are we one of many? Has the universe, in some manner, been designed for *us*? It is a question with the profoundest philosophical implications. It is the great enigma. Shapley never knew. Nor did Lowell. Nor Einstein. They grew old with no hope, and went to their graves with no semblance of an answer."

Harmon shifted his weight. He was beginning to feel uncomfortable.

Gambini understood that he must seem disconnected. A garrulous old man with no grasp of his visitor's pain. He should stop, squeeze Harmon's arm, thank him for coming by, accept the man's gratitude. But he plowed on: "Then we got Skynet. They assembled it during late summer, and we knew, by Christmas, we would use it to see other solar systems. *We would be able to see extrasolar worlds, out to a distance of more than a hundred light-years.* We would be able to perform spectroscopic analyses of their atmospheres. My God, Harmon, we could look for oxygen, the infallible mark of life!"

Harmon nodded.

"I neither ate nor slept during those final weeks. They'd already begun testing the system, and success appeared very likely. I gave up trying to read or work."

Harmon examined the Hoyle volume. It was *Galaxies, Nuclei, and Quasars.* "And you," he said, raising his eyes to Gambini's, "walked the beaches."

"Yes. But only at sunset. When the air was cool."

Harmon leaned forward.

"Each evening there was a group of swimmers. Boys. They were young, thirteen perhaps, no more than that. There were three of them usually, sometimes four, and they were always out beyond the breaker line. One in particular...."

"Yes," said Harmon, "he was like that." His voice sounded strange.

Gambini seemed not to have heard. "He was taller than the others. Awkward. With light sandy hair." He got up, slowly, and pushed his fists into the pockets of the gray sweater. "The current can be treacherous, and every night they went farther into the sea. I warned them. They weren't local kids. Locals would have known better."

"We were," said Harmon, "from Alexandria."

"I told them it was dangerous." Gambini hesitated. "But that meant nothing to them, of course. They laughed and retreated farther beyond the breakers. The tall one, he was almost as tall as I: the night before he died, he stood as close to me as you are now,

sunburned, preoccupied, with all his life before him. He was inspecting tidal pools, for stranded guppies, I suppose. He saw me, and smiled self-consciously as though he'd been caught doing something foolish." Gambini's eyes clouded. He fell silent.

"Did he say anything to you?"

"No. We faced each other for a moment. Then he was gone, up the beach with his friends, snapping towels at each other."

For a long time there was only the sound of the sea, and of water dripping into foliage. Harmon's chair creaked. When Gambini spoke again, he was barely audible. "It happened, as I knew it would. Hakluyt had called me that morning to discuss the latest test results, and I forgot about the boys. It was cold and damp, after an all-day rain." He glanced accusingly at his visitor. "I was preoccupied. And they should never have been there. But they were.

"The first indication I had that something was wrong came when a fat middle-aged man ran past me. He hurried along the shoreline to join two of the boys, who were standing hip-deep, anxiously watching the sea; beyond them, desperately far out, a head floated over the top of a swell, and arms thrashed.

"One of the boys turned toward me and screamed (though I could not hear him over the roar of the ocean). I looked for help and saw only an elderly woman with two dogs.

"I broke into a run, and was already breathing hard before I even got into the water. The boy sank: he was down a long time while I struggled toward him. He came up, coughing and choking. I got through the breakers into calmer water and began to swim. The water was cold, and the drag toward the open sea was strong.

"I was moving quickly. I'm not a bad swimmer, and the current was pushing me toward him. But the distance between us didn't seem to lessen. He struggled, went down, found new strength.

"I realized quite suddenly that my own life was in danger. I knew I could reach him, and I also knew that we would probably not get back. It was odd; the possibility of my own drowning raised only a single emotion: the stiletto sensation that it would be too soon. *By a few weeks, or a few months, it would be too soon!*

"And I hated the child!"

Harmon's mouth tightened, but he said nothing.

"He fought stubbornly for his life. Time after time, the sea rolled over him, but he would not stay down. The tide dragged me in all directions, and I lost headway in a swirl of currents. I got desperately tired. And I could see that his struggles were growing weaker. He saw me coming and tried to wave, but he could not lift his arm out of the water. Each time, after he had been pushed beneath the sea, he broke the surface looking for me." Gambini's voice had been rising; but now he stopped to refill his glass. His hand trembled. "At last he must have seen my despair, because I read the sudden swift terror in his face as he realized, I think for the first time, what was going to happen...."

"So you turned back," Harmon said uncertainly. "No one can blame you for that. No one could expect more."

Gambini threw the full glass of port against a wall. "Who are *you*?" he demanded, "to make that judgment? I left him to *drown*!"

"No!" Harmon said desperately. "You tried! You did what you could—"

Gambini's eyes were cold. "I did not abandon him," he said, "because I was afraid. I did it because I was curious. I sold his life for some tracings on a few hundred pieces of paper."

(On the veranda below his apartment, people were talking. Someone laughed.)

"I should not have come," said Harmon.

"Is that all you can say?" snapped Gambini. "You're his father."

Harmon rose. His face was calm, but there was something of the drowning boy in his eyes. "What do you want me to tell you, Gambini?" he demanded. "That you too should have drowned? That nothing less would have been decent?"

Gambini slid his fingers under his bifocals and rubbed his eyes. "Why are you here? After all this time?"

"I don't know." Harmon exhaled. "I thought they were safe. Out here, away from Alexandria, I didn't think anything could happen. We were always grateful that you tried. I wrote you a letter."

"It's in my desk."

Harmon softened. "Under the circumstances, I guess it was painful."

Gambini stared a long time at his visitor. "Were you supposed to be taking care of him?"

Harmon nodded.

"You are right to feel guilty," he rasped. "Your son and I, we were both your victims." Gambini's smile trembled on thin lips. "Do you know what we found when we looked beyond the solar system? No, don't turn away. This concerns your boy. We examined several thousand stars, Harmon. About a quarter have planets. Most are Jovian: nothing more, really, than enormous sacks of cold hydrogen. It was, of course, the terrestrial worlds in which we were especially interested: those Earthlike planets orbiting stable suns at temperate distances." A nerve near Gambini's jugular had begun to throb. "I assume I need not tell you we found no oxygen. Oh, there were traces here and there. But everywhere we looked, among the terrestrial worlds, we saw carbon dioxide. In vast quantities. Do you understand what I'm saying?"

Harmon's eyes blazed, but he did not reply.

"No biological processes. Anywhere. We'd always assumed that something had gone wrong on Venus, leaving her sterile under a hothouse atmosphere. Some people have made a career of explaining why. But Venus, it turns out, is the norm: It's Earth that is the anomaly.

"It appears, Harmon, that we are quite alone."

Harmon threw open the door, and whirled to face the physicist. "Despite everything you've said, I believe you tried. I hope the day will come when you will realize you could have done no more."

"If you think that," Gambini said, "I'll tell you something else. If it were to do again, I'd make the same decision. Do you understand that?"

Harmon's features twisted, and he wondered (at that moment, and for all his life after) what the physicist was trying to provoke.

But Gambini had already turned away. He stared through the window at the cloud cover. Harmon stood watching him, murmured something, a farewell, a curse, a cry of anguish, and retreated from the room.

© 1985 by Jack McDevitt

❈ ❈ ❈ ❈ ❈

Leena Likitalo hails from Finland, the land of thousands of lakes and at least as many untold tales. She is a Writers of the Future 2014 winner and Clarion San Diego 2014 graduate. Her fiction has appeared in Weird Tales, Waylines, *and various semi-pro markets. This is her second appearance in* Galaxy's Edge.

DO NOT FEAR TO TOUCH FLESH

by Leena Likitalo

Martina can dance for twenty hours without rest. The cigar smoke veiling the bar hasn't yet stained the paint covering her titanium limbs. Her silicon parts are still fresh and disease-free. Her kind fills the countless clubs of Valparaiso.

Angela, the dancer sharing the stage with Martina, suddenly collapses. She convulses violently, but Martina keeps dancing. Those who fail to please the customers are removed from service and sent to the streets where nothing but rust and decay awaits.

Even as Angela twitches, Martina bends her back to display her sculpted form as she's programmed to do. The sequence is never the same, but randomly generated. Bend, swish, sway, whirl. The men in the bar see only her, not Angela.

if(batteryBroken)

//Hayden: no point of changing batteries. Cheaper to manufacture a new robot.

removeFromService(dancer)

//Hayden: added as a joke. Get it Michelle?

mayTheDaughterOfTheDarkStreetsBlessHer(dancer)

//Michelle: yes, Hayden, I get the joke. What a more fitting character to believe in than one straight out of Valparaiso folklore. Daughter of the Dark Streets: the devourer of broken dreams and saint of prostitutes. Ha-ha-ha, and in case you can't tell, that's sarcastic laughter.

//Michelle: incidentally, I modified the subroutine as I think it's a nice idea to give the dancers afterlife.

subroutine mayTheDaughterOfTheDarkStreetsBlessHer(Dancer dancer)

daughterOfTheDarkStreetComes()

daughterOfTheDarkStreetsBlesses(dancer)

daughterOfTheDarkStreetsLeadsToAfterlife(dancer)

Bouncers drag Angela's body away from the stage before the song ends. Shadows stir, and for a moment a woman in black can be seen standing at the back of the room.

✿

Martina can dance sixteen hours without charging her batteries. The smoke has somewhat tarnished her paint, but her silicon parts are still in good condition.

A man, just another man, enters the bar. His eyes gleam with lust as he watches Martina sway. For him, the dancers are nothing but affordable pleasure.

Martina glides to greet the man. That's what her programming says she should do. She bends over to kiss the man on the cheek. Flesh feels strange against her lips. Revolting.

A subroutine starts, changing her opinion mid-thought.

//Michelle: I really, really hate my job.

//Hayden: stop whining. They're just robots. And isn't it better they do this job than you or your daughters?

//Michelle: I won't even condescend to answer that.

while(customerUnsatisfied)

doNotFearToTouchFlesh()

Lick, suck, moan, grind.

✿

Martina follows the man, yet another man, into the private room. Shadows hung low over the bed, dulling the shine of the red satin sheets. She stumbles to a halt as the shadows shift, reveal a woman sitting cross-legged on the bed. Long black hair falls over the woman's ashen shoulders. Her eyes glint like dying embers.

"I said"—The man closes the door with an angry thrust—"take off your clothes!"

The woman disappears. Confused, Martina turns to face the man. She lets her see-through dress fall on the floor, a practiced routine repeated a thousand times before.

The man slaps her across the face. "Manufactured bitch!"

Martina falls on her knees. She has no right to complain, no choice but to endure until one day the Daughter of the Dark Streets will bless her and lead to freedom.

The man kicks Martina. She curls into fetal position, remains motionless. An emotion she can't name sparks in her mechanical heart. A subroutine starts.

```
try
handleEmotion(anger)
catch(UnexpectedEmotion emotion)
```

//Hayden: should never get here, so can't be bothered to figure out what should happen.

//Michelle: add proper error handling. Least this might lead to some strange bugs later.

//Hayden: stop patronizing me. You're the one who keeps adding extra functionalities the client hasn't ordered. Just so you know, I've removed your stupid afterlife implementation.

The man continues to beat Martina, no matter that she's metal and he's flesh. As she submits to everything he wants, the new feeling spreads like acid in her body.

☼

Years pass, but what are they for a dancer? Clients come and go. Martina keeps smiling, though the emotion she can't name gnaws at her.

Then comes the night like any other. Martina follows a man into the private room like she's done so many times before. He pays the standard rate.

On the bed, Martina sits astride the man. She rocks back and forth. The man grunts.

What else was she supposed to do? It's so hard to think straight.

//Hayden: as Michelle is about to quit, I don't have time to add proper checks here, but this should do the trick.

```
while(customerNotSatisfied)
touchTheCustomer()
```

Martina wraps her hands around the man's neck. Metal on flesh. Touch the customer. That's what she's doing. And for once, touching a customer feels good.

She continues rocking. The customer doesn't seem satisfied yet, though he grunts. Jerks. Twitches. She squeezes her hands tighter around his neck. His face turns to an ugly shade of red. Purple. Blue.

Eventually, he stops moving, turns limp.

"You can let go of him."

Martina glances over her shoulder. A tall woman in black stands by the door. Strange that she didn't hear her entering the room.

The woman's black hair floats to form a halo around her head. Her mouth doesn't move, but Martina can still hear her voice. "The dead are satisfied customers."

```
if(customerSatisfied                    AND
customerNotPayingForMore)
takeNextCustomer()
```

Martina unmounts the man. Such a pitiful, saggy thing he is. Dead, too. For a moment, the strange emotion eases its hold on her.

"We accept cash and credit cards," Martina says. Though she was made to resemble a woman, gender means nothing to her.

"I'm not a customer." The woman's gown shifts as though a wind had wound its way past her.

Martina waits for a subroutine to start and tell her what to say. But no one whispers her instructions. "Am I in deadlock?"

"Maybe." The woman smiles, revealing jagged teeth. "You may call me the Daughter of the Dark Streets."

Martina twitches as the name resolves the deadlock.

"Come with me." The Daughter of the Dark Streets beckons.

//Michelle: last day at work. I think the dancers deserve a happy ever after, so here goes. Hayden, if you remove this, I swear to God I'll kill you.

```
subroutine removeFromService(Dancer dancer)
mayTheDaughterOfTheDarkStreetsBlessHer(dancer)
wipeMemoryClean(dancer)
shutdown(dancer)
```

Copyright © 2015 by Leena Likitalo

❋ ❋ ❋ ❋ ❋

Alex Shvartsman is a writer, translator, and game designer, with more than thirty short stories to his credit. He is currently editing the hilarious Unidentified Funny Objects series of anthologies. This is his fourth appearance in Galaxy's Edge.

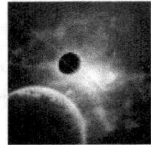

a
Sargasso Containment
story
www.SargassoLegacy.com

ISLANDS IN THE SARGASSO

by Alex Shvartsman

They were all going to die.

Jason Stanger squeezed everything he could from his ship. His fingers hit the touch screens as though he were an angry pianist, hammering out Beethoven's Ninth on several unyielding keyboards at once. He was a very good pilot, and the *Pivot* was a very good ship, but no amount of skill could make up for the fact that the three Montevideo cartel spaceships pursuing him were faster, larger, and better armed.

The cartel enforcers were disciplined. They didn't fire yet. Torpedoes weren't cheap, and his pursuers knew they could afford to wait, to keep closing the distance until one of them got close enough to disintegrate his vessel with a single kill shot. But they were also from Earth: too sophisticated, too urbane to buy into frontier superstitions. And that's why Jason wouldn't die alone, not if he could keep them following him.

Taking his enemies with him would be a small enough consolation, but it would have to do. Jason grinned humorlessly as he steered his ship away from the sun and into the vast emptiness of Sargasso space.

By all rights he should have died six months ago. Back then he was a junkie, a man claimed so thoroughly by his addiction to Rust that he had lost everything: his job, his friends, even his will to go on.

Nothing mattered to him so long as he could find a way to get high.

Commander Warren Jain had found him, gotten him cleaned up, given him a purpose. Jain's unit needed experienced pilots to fight the cartels and combat the spread of Rust across the Solar System. Jason was eager to do his part. He knew the risks, accepted the danger. In the end, he had lived six months longer than he expected to, thanks to Jain. They had been good months.

Jason heard strange noises within the ship. Creaking, grating sounds that couldn't possibly be real. The video feeds turned to static one by one as the ship's instruments malfunctioned. Just as he had expected. It wouldn't be long until his pursuers began experiencing technical problems of their own. And then things would get much, much worse.

The navigation tableau had gone out. Jason piloted the ship by the stars, like the sailors of old who crossed the Atlantic with nothing to guide them but the constellations they could see on a clear night.

The Sargasso space surrounded the Solar System. It began at 1260 AU from the sun and no one knew how far it extended outward. No one understood its physics, its nature, its origins. All Jason knew was that ships venturing too far into the Sargasso space didn't return. Although no astronomical instruments could detect any sort of anomaly, the Sargasso space kept humanity trapped in the Solar System. A handful of expeditions that had tried to reach other stars lost their navigation and controls, and then their crews went insane, one by one, their screams transmitted across space, until there was only silence.

The cartel ships opened fire. With his instruments failing, Jason couldn't be sure whether they'd finally gotten close enough, or were panicking because their technology was betraying them, too. It must have been the latter; the shots went wide. No computerized targeting system could have made such a mistake.

Jason watched as the engines of one of the cartel ships cut out. It continued on its trajectory, no longer able to accelerate or maneuver but carried forward by the inertia. Minutes later his sensors ceased to function, claimed by the Sargasso. He was trapped inside the ship, unable to control it, unable to learn what was happening outside. Would one of the pursuing vessels destroy him or would he live long enough to be claimed by the madness of the Sargasso? Like Schrodinger's cat in a tin box, he was alive and dead at the same time.

Jason was afraid, and the fear fed his desire for Rust. The need for the drug was always there, like a dull toothache. A recovering heroin addict he met at a meeting told him it never fully goes away. Jason struggled against the urge.

Hours passed. He could hear things now, see things through the porthole. Islands in the Sargasso, with white beaches and lush greens set against the azure water. He could hear the waves splashing gently against the sand. Except none of it was real. There were no tropical islands in space. His ship didn't even have a porthole. The Sargasso was driving him mad.

His engines were dead, his ship drifting away from the Solar System. And now he was losing his mind. Jason checked the cryogenic unit and saw that it was still functional. The unit could keep him alive in suspended animation for several months, long enough for Warren Jain to figure out how to save his life a second time, to send help.

Jason knew he was lying to himself, knew there was no way for his commander to save him this time. Even so, clinging to a tiny sliver of hope was a better way to go than any of the alternatives.

Jason climbed into the unit.

✿

Jason was surprised to wake again. It was a gradual, difficult awakening which felt like climbing up from a deep dark mine shaft. He could almost feel the gears of his mind beginning to grind again, beginning to process information and to remember. He could feel his longing for Rust, too. It was back seemingly even before he fully returned to consciousness.

He waited a full minute until he dared open his eyes. The room he was in was small but well-lit, and was definitely not aboard the *Pivot*. He tried to sit up, his body aching in protest.

"Ah, you're awake."

The voice sounded strange, as if it were recorded on an ancient gramophone and played back with all the squeaks and skips that entailed. Jason turned and found the source of the voice even stranger.

The creature sitting by his bedside was roughly four feet tall and looked like an upright tortoise in a purplish shell.

Jason tried to speak, but only managed a croak. He coughed, trying to clear his throat. The strange creature tilted its head and looked at him. Jason considered the possibility that he was still in the Sargasso and that his hallucinations were getting worse. He finally managed to regain control of his vocal chords and whispered, "What are you?"

"A polite thing to say would be 'Who are you?'," it replied. "But I'll let that go, given the circumstances. Call me Aidan."

Jason tried to formulate his next question, but his mind was still foggy.

"Let me help you along," said Aidan. "Yes, that is a human name. No, I'm not human. My people are called the Translators. The actual name of my species isn't something you could pronounce, which is why the Translators adopt names from the races they work with."

Jason sat up, his feet touching the floor. He looked around. The room was unremarkable, but there was a window, or at least a screen meant to act as such. He took several unsure steps and looked outside. The view overlooked an enormous structure floating in space. There were docking bays below, with several vessels attached. He didn't recognize their design.

"Dorothy," said Aidan, "you aren't in Kansas anymore."

Jason took a deep breath and counted to ten.

"Listen, Aidan, I just woke up from what I was pretty certain would be permanent sleep, and now I find myself on an alien space station, being lectured by something that looks like a cartoon character. Do you see how this can be a little overwhelming? If you understand compassion then would you please explain where I am?"

Aidan considered his words.

"My apologies. I do realize this must be difficult for you. You are on Venezia Outpost, one of the three such stations positioned just beyond the barrier that surrounds your solar system. Your ship was salvaged at the edge of the barrier by the crew of one of the Blockade Runners and you were brought here once they realized you were still alive in the hibernation pod."

"How is that possible? My engines were cut and the ship was drifting…"

"And drift it did, slowly through the Sargasso. To my knowledge, yours is the only human vessel that isn't a Blockade Runner to make it across. Even if the trip took two hundred years."

"You mean…" Jason stared at the ships outside again. Venezia. Solar System. He was on a human station, far in the future. "But how is this possible? My cryogenic unit wasn't designed to keep a person alive for more than a few months."

"We don't know. The outpost engineers examined your pod. There's no good reason why it should have kept functioning as long as it did. Strange things happen within barriers, but we've never seen a case like this, in your solar system or any other."

"You were supposed to notify me when he woke up."

Jason turned toward the woman's voice. She stood in the doorway, a uniform jacket with unfamiliar insignia draped over her wide shoulders, a gun holstered at her hip. She spoke English with a strange accent.

"He woke up minutes ago. I've only just begun to elucidate his circumstances." Aidan's accent matched the woman's when he addressed her.

Jason could follow the conversation but not without difficulty. He realized the language must've changed over two centuries. That Aidan was able to speak what sounded like unaccented English to Jason was impressive; the Translators must've been very good at their jobs.

"Mr. Kazemi wants to see him now," said the woman. She nodded curtly to Jason. "I'm Irina Pavlova."

"Ms. Pavlova is the Chief of Security for Venezia Outpost," said Aidan.

"Jason Stanger," said Jason.

"I know. We pulled your records." Irina looked at him appraisingly. "Can you walk?"

Jason nodded.

"Follow me, then."

She exited the room and marched down the long corridor. Jason rushed after her. Aidan made no move to follow.

The corridor led to a cavernous promenade filled with shops, restaurants, and offices. The station must've been huge—the size of a cruise ship, if not bigger. The area they walked through felt like a mall, except there were only a few other people there, rushing to and fro, and most of the businesses were shuttered. Jason figured it must be nighttime by station clock.

Pavlova power-walked down the promenade and Jason struggled to keep up. His leg muscles ached, protesting the exercise after centuries of inactivity.

"Who is Mr. Kazemi?" he called after her.

"Farhad Kazemi runs this station," she said.

"He's the captain?"

She slowed her pace just enough to let Jason catch up.

"More like an absolute monarch. His grandfather was a partner in the firm that built this station and the Kazemi family has been running things up here for seventy years while the Palmieris manage the in-system side of the business. So whatever you do, try not to piss him off. Not while you're breathing his air."

They approached a wide, temple-like wooden door. Jason realized this was the first instance of wood he'd seen on the station; everything else seemed to be made of plastic and metals. He could see how natural wood might be a status symbol in deep space.

Pavlova opened the door and the two of them walked through several smaller but relatively opulent rooms, one with armed guards, one with an assistant or secretary behind a large desk who nodded at Pavlova. The chief of security waved Jason through the final door. She stayed behind while he entered a larger office. There were bookshelves filled with hardcover volumes and thick wall rugs everywhere. This room made Jason feel as though he had traveled back rather than forward in time.

A man in his early forties worked at a standing desk. He fiddled with a tablet with his right hand—it was the only observable piece of modern technology in the study—and held a glass of amber-like liquid in another. He looked up when Jason entered the room.

"Ah, the mysterious traveler from the past." He smiled and put down his glass. "Welcome to the Venezia outpost. I'm Farhad Kazemi."

Although the other man's manner was friendly, Jason felt uncomfortable and out of place. Kazemi spoke with the same unusual inflections as Pavlova. That, along with Kazemi's retro-style office, served to remind Jason of how much things must've changed. He knew nothing of this future world. The yearning for Rust ached deep in his bones.

"Hello," he managed.

Kazemi walked from behind his desk and sized Jason up.

"Amazing. It's as though you walked off the screen of a historical film."

Jason said nothing.

"Where are my manners? I'm sorry to have ogled, Mr. Stanger. This must be quite a harrowing experience for you. Please, have something to drink." Kazemi splashed some of the amber liquid from a decanter into another glass and offered it to Jason.

With a nod of thanks, Jason accepted the glass and took a sip. He expected some sort of whiskey but the taste was so unusual, he couldn't be sure the beverage was even alcoholic. It tasted a bit like honey and cardamom, and things he couldn't describe, all with a kick.

Kazemi grinned. "Toverian nectar. One of the many fine wares we trade for on Venezia."

"This is an alien drink?" Jason stared into the glass.

"Indeed, Mr. Stanger. Why don't you take a seat and enjoy it while I endeavor to help you feel a little less confused."

"If you don't mind," mumbled Jason as he sat on the small couch.

"Mind?" Kazemi laughed. "I find there's nothing more valuable in life than unique experiences. When will I ever again have the opportunity to fill someone in on the highlights of two centuries worth of history? Indeed, I should be thanking you."

Kazemi paced around his study as he spoke.

"Shortly after your incident, scientists figured out a limited way to get through the Sargasso space. It involved two components: coming up with technology that wouldn't go absolutely haywire within the barrier, and figuring a way for the pilots to survive the trip without losing their minds."

"They designed a class of ship called the Blockade Runner. They're almost like bullets fired from the edge of the Sargasso. All higher-level technology on the ship is shut down and it's capable only of limited maneuvering via chemical rockets similar to the ancient vessels from the dawn of spaceflight. Passengers can survive the Sargasso by traveling in hibernation, much like you had, but Blockade Runners require a live pilot: all unmanned ships or vessels relying on autopilot are claimed by the barrier. This stalled the Blockade Runner program because the Sargasso space drove the volunteer pilots stark-raving mad.

"The solution to this was an accidental discovery. Some human beings high on Rust are apparently fortified against the effects of the Sargasso. Less than one in a million humans possess the brain chemistry that interacts with Rust in a way that makes them capable of surviving the journey with their minds intact."

Jason shivered. He knew first-hand how addictive and destructive Rust was. Taking the drug in order to pilot a ship was difficult for him to imagine. He caught himself caressing the skin above the vein on the upper wrist of his left arm, where he used to inject Rust, with his right index finger. He pulled his right hand away with a jerk.

"Even today, crossing the Sargasso is a difficult and dangerous undertaking. We've managed to bring the success rate to ninety seven percent. That means three ships out of every hundred still perish en route.

"Once human ships made it past the Sargasso, we met a baker's dozen of alien species out here, and anecdotally know of many more. And here's the kick: each solar system cradling intelligent life comes equipped with its own Sargasso space, while uninhabited systems have no such barrier. Do you understand the implications, Mr. Stanger?"

Jason stared at the stationmaster wide-eyed. "Someone placed those barriers deliberately."

"That's right," said Kazemi. "According to what we learned from the other spacefaring species there is a highly advanced race called the Caretakers, and they created the barriers to allow each civilization to develop independently of others and without fear of invasion. They wanted each little garden to flourish in peace. Thus, their moniker."

"But we figured out a way past the Sargasso. And, I'm guessing, so did these other aliens?" asked Jason.

"Indeed. This appears to be a feature rather than a bug; each civilization eventually finds a way to get past their barrier. Invariably, this is accomplished with great difficulty and in very limited numbers. It seems the Caretakers want their charges to learn about the greater universe beyond their cages, but not run amok, so to speak.

"Species capable of interstellar flight have developed certain conventions. Since blockade running is so fraught with danger, each civilization is expected to handle their own. Trade outposts like this one are built by each culture, and that's where goods and information are exchanged. In fact, it is considered an act of aggression to enter another civilization's home system.

"There are exceptions, of course: species that haven't found a way to traverse their own containments, but are eager to trade nevertheless. Toverians are one such example." Kazemi pointed at the decanter. "A single bottle of the nectar costs more on Earth than an average person earns in a year."

Jason looked at his glass with renewed appreciation.

"We pulled your records and studied your ship," said Kazemi. "It seems you would make an exemplary Blockade Runner pilot."

"No," Jason said quickly. "I won't ever take Rust again."

Something hardened in Kazemi's expression, but his voice remained amicable. "I understand. Your history of addiction is well documented, among other things. You should know that our detox procedures are far superior to those from your time. The drug was almost entirely eradicated in the solar system shortly after your departure, and the variant used for blockade running is carefully cultivated—"

"No," Jason said again.

Kazemi pursed his lips. "You're very lucky, you know. On the Panama outpost they'd probably dissect you to try and figure out how you survived in stasis for so long. And on Dubai they wouldn't ask your consent—they have a long history of shanghaiing Sargasso pilots. But here on Venezia we do things differently." He crossed his arms. "We respect freedom of choice, but we also expect everyone to pull their weight around here. If you don't want to pilot a Blockade Runner, you'll have to get another job, or get the hell off my station."

Kazemi glanced at his tablet. "I see here you worked for the Space Patrol after you got sober. I can offer you a short-term contract working station security under Pavlova. Sign on for a month. Get acclimated; figure out what you want to do next."

"That sounds all right," said Jason.

Kazemi handed him the tablet. "Read the contract. You can accept it with a thumbprint."

When Jason left Kazemi's office, Pavlova was gone. Instead, Aidan was waiting for him in the spacious promenade outside.

"What happened in there?" the alien asked.

Jason recounted the events of his meeting.

Aidan chuckled—a strange sound obviously meant to imitate human laughter.

"The stationmaster is an honorable man, in his way," he said. "He won't lie to you outright. Still, he's willing to withhold information when it suits him."

"What didn't he tell me?"

Aidan sized him up. "Many things, I'm sure. Chief among them is the fact that we're about to come under attack by an alien fleet in a matter of hours."

Jason looked up sharply. He bit his lower lip, still wondering if all this was a Sargasso-induced nightmare. "What?"

Aidan pointed down the promenade. "What do you see?"

Jason looked where the Translator was pointing.

"Shops. Bars. Mostly shuttered."

"That's right. The station is operating with skeleton staff," said Aidan.

"I thought it was night," said Jason.

"A week ago this area was bustling with humans and a handful of visitors from other worlds. Now everyone who was able to obtain passage into the Solar System or elsewhere has gone. Kazemi is desperate for manpower if he has any hope of mounting a defense."

Jason frowned. "Wait a second. You told me the Caretakers keep every civilization behind their own Sargasso shield to prevent this sort of thing from happening."

"And it works," said Aidan. "Humans in your system are probably safe, but anyone living on trade outposts and colonies take their chances."

Jason felt small and scared and out of place, a feeling that had persisted since the moment he'd woken up in this strange future. He wanted a fix so badly.

"They're called the Maeshiva," said Aidan. "Traversing the barrier does not come easily to their species, so the trade is infrequent, and it's never more than one vessel arriving on Venezia at a time. Several days ago, deep-space sensors detected an approaching fleet of more than thirty Maeshiva ships. They'll be here soon." Aidan sighed. "I'm sorry, Jason. It seems your arrival here suffers from terrible timing."

Jason fought his urges. "These aliens, they've been coming here to trade, right? Why assume they're going to attack?"

"There's absolutely no good reason to send such a large fleet to another species' home system. The humans have no choice but to interpret this as an act of aggression. They're mobilizing a fleet on the other side of the barrier, in case the Maeshiva try to come through."

Jason saw Pavlova power-walking toward him down the desolate promenade.

"Welcome to the force," she told Jason when she approached.

The security chief didn't seem gleeful or even particularly happy about her new recruit. She looked like the weight of war rested on her shoulders—which, Jason supposed, it did.

"Come," she said. "There isn't a lot of time."

✿

Once again, Jason awaited death in the cockpit of a small spaceship. Although two centuries had passed since he'd led his pursuers into the Sargasso, it felt like only yesterday. Even if it hadn't, Jason felt that being in this position twice in a single lifetime was two times too many.

Seven hours earlier, Pavlova had taken him straight to the docking bay and assigned one of the other pilots to teach him how to fly modern spacecraft.

The older man's name was Richard. He was a paunchy gray-haired man in his fifties. "Flying a Blockade Runner is a piece of cake," he said. "They had to make the control interface simple, so they could recruit and easily train just about anyone with a high barrier resistance."

Jason bristled. "I told Kazemi, I'm not taking drugs to fly into the Sargasso."

Richard was confused and made Jason recount his story.

"Forgive me for saying so, but you're a fool," Richard said afterward. "If I had any talent for crossing the Sargasso, I'd inject myself with any drug, any poison to go home instead of fighting an alien armada from a tin can. The other men, they feel the same way. None of us who remain are Sargasso pilots. We're mechanics and servicemen and security officers with some flight training. We're only here because we didn't manage to find a way off the station."

"There's nothing waiting for me back in the Solar System," said Jason. "Nothing and no one. Everyone I knew is long dead."

Richard mulled it over. "There are people I know, people with money," he said. "They will pay handsomely to get out of here. You can begin a new life on Earth, or Mars, or wherever you like, with a decent nest egg. You can afford any rehab program and still have plenty left over. I'll put everything together in exchange for the ride home."

Jason was tempted. It's not like he owed any loyalty to Kazemi, or Pavlova, or this outpost. But he'd lost everything in his long sleep, and his sobriety was all he had left. It was who he was now, and he wouldn't give it up for an uncertain future. He politely refused Richard's offer.

Richard wasn't pleased. He spoke in short, terse sentences, showing Jason how to pilot a Blockade Runner.

Richard was right: any pilot could operate a Blockade Runner with ease. That was the good news. The bad news was that these ships were designed with a singular purpose. They weren't very maneuverable and the only weaponry on board had been jury-rigged by the Venezia engineers and mechanics over the past few days. Taking on a fleet of advanced spaceships in a handful of these glorified space trucks was suicide.

Jason had plenty of time to reflect upon this as he sat in the pilot chair. By the time the alien armada was visible on his view screen he had regretted not taking Richard up on his offer, and he desperately needed a fix. There were, of course, no drugs on board, and the logical part of his mind was thankful for that.

Thirty-two alien ships appeared as dots on his screen. The dots grew as they approached. Designed to operate in deep space and free from the concerns of aerodynamics, the Maeshiva vessels were rectangular in shape. As they got closer, Jason realized that they were huge, each as long as a city block, almost half as large as the Venezia Outpost itself.

"Hold your fire," Pavlova said over the comm. "Let them get closer."

What a joke. Four torpedoes and a pair of turrets installed on Jason's ship would merely annoy these alien behemoths. The entire fleet of a dozen retrofitted Blockade Runners probably couldn't take down even one of the Maeshiva vessels.

One of the Blockade Runners turned and accelerated away from the incoming fleet and toward the Solar System. Jason wondered if it was Richard.

The deserter didn't get far. Venezia Outpost fired a single torpedo which disintegrated the fleeing ship.

"No running! We stay and defend the station. Together." Pavlova's voice was cracking. It couldn't have been easy for her to fire on one of her own, Jason thought. At least he hoped it wasn't easy for her.

The Maeshiva kept coming. Their fleet decelerated toward the station and into comm range. They reached full stop mere miles from Venezia and within the clear eye's view of the Blockade Runners.

Most of the alien ships bore burn scars and other assorted damage. This fleet had already been in a fight, and recently.

"Stand down," Pavlova said with obvious relief. "They want to talk." After several minutes of radio silence she added, "This isn't an invasion armada. It's a refugee fleet."

✷

The negotiations took place by comm. The alien ships were too large to dock at Venezia, and either they didn't have shuttles or Kazemi didn't trust the Maeshiva to come on board. Either way, after another hour or so, the Blockade Runners were recalled.

Jason was shown to his quarters, a small but comfortable room aboard the station where he took a hot shower, ventured into the crew mess hall for a meal, and finally fell asleep.

Several hours later he was awakened by the buzzing of the comm unit he had been issued. He was ordered back to his Blockade Runner.

He got dressed and headed out, nervous about what was to come next. Had the negotiations with the aliens broken down? In the shuttle bay he found Aidan and Pavlova, who was holding a small case.

"We have reached an accord with the Maeshiva," she said. "The three of us are to deliver this to their flagship." She held up the case.

"What is it?" asked Jason.

Pavlova and Aidan exchanged glances.

"It contains the coordinates of an uninhabited planet the Maeshiva can colonize," said Aidan. "This data is too valuable to transmit openly."

Jason looked askance at the alien.

"Many of the species in this part of the galaxy breathe the same air, drink the same water," said the Translator. "As such, livable, unclaimed planets are rare and highly prized. And since uninhabited worlds aren't surrounded by a barrier, the location of this specific planet needs to remain a secret. The Maeshiva are fleeing from a powerful enemy."

Jason considered the case. "So valuable, Kazemi decided to trust it to an alien and a new guy?" he asked Pavlova.

"Don't you worry, I'll be coming too," said Pavlova. "I'll handle the delivery. You just have to drive the bus."

"I'm going because I'm a Translator. My job is to facilitate inter-species communication," said Aidan. "It's not like any of the rest of you can speak Maeshiva."

"And you're going because you're the most disposable," said Pavlova. "We don't exactly trust those guys."

"It stinks being the low guy on the totem pole," said Aidan.

"Anyone ever tell you that your use of human idioms can get irritating?" asked Jason.

"Constantly," said Aidan. "But being a Translator isn't merely a vocation. My species enjoys the nuances of alien languages we learn. Using an idiom provides me pleasure similar to what you might feel upon hearing a good joke."

The three of them boarded the Blockade Runner and Jason piloted it toward the flagship. Once there, a wide hangar door opened and he was able to land inside.

"A docking bay would have been easier," Jason muttered as he carefully navigated the unruly Blockade Runner to its designated spot.

Once the hangar was refilled with breathable air, they were able to exit the ship. Four of the Maeshiva met them there. The Maeshiva were seven-foot-tall humanoids, with large eyes, oblong heads, and patchy gray skin that reminded Jason of an elephant. Their mouths were small, or at least seemed so as they had no lips. Their noses looked very similar to the humans', which somehow had an overall effect of making their faces seem even stranger.

One of the Maeshiva emitted a series of trills, something between birdsong and speech.

"They greet us and ask us to follow them," said the Translator.

"Greetings," said Jason. Then, on a lark he added, "Take me to your leader." He smiled at Aidan. "You probably shouldn't translate that."

Pavlova frowned.

Aidan chuckled. "I'm pretty sure that's where we're going anyway."

The seven of them walked through the corridors of the Maeshiva ship. Everywhere the aliens lined up to see them. The sight of the humans and the Translator must've been as unusual to them as they were to Jason. Finally he reached a chamber where several more of the aliens sat around a large oval desk.

"The Maeshiva government in exile," said Aidan.

"What exactly happened to them?" asked Jason.

"Tell you later," said the Translator.

One of the Maeshiva extended his long, slender hand. The gesture didn't need a translation. Pavlova handed over the case.

The alien opened it and retrieved a printout with a string of numbers on it. Jason expected some sort of a data chip, but this made sense: there was no reason to assume the Maeshiva hardware would be compatible with the humans'. The alien passed the sheet to the Translator who spoke in the Maeshiva trill, no doubt translating the data into their language. Another alien entered the information into a terminal.

After they were done, the Maeshiva leader gave some sort of command. Jason heard the unmistak-able sound of engines being powered up, then felt the ship move.

"What's happening?" he asked.

"I'm sorry, Jason. I was not entirely honest with you, as per Kazemi's orders," said Pavlova. "An inhabitable planet wasn't the only thing the stationmaster traded away. The Maeshiva also needed a gifted blockade pilot."

♢

When Pavlova delivered the news, Jason nearly threw a fit. Unable to lash out in any effective way, he settled for refusing to speak to Aidan and her. But the silent treatment was ineffective, especially since they were the only living beings on board he could communicate with. After a few hours he relented, and demanded details.

"We learned from the Maeshiva that their home system had come under attack," the Translator told him. "Several thousand Tryb warships invaded the system and pretty much wiped them out. The refugee fleet that reached Venezia may be all that's left of their species."

"Don't the Maeshiva have the Sargasso space surrounding their star system, too?" asked Jason.

Pavlova looked up from her tablet. "They do. The fact that the Tryb have learned to pass through the barriers en masse is a disturbing development. Who's to say they won't come after Earth next?"

"I'm sorry these guys got invaded, I really am," said Jason," but what does any of that have to do with me?"

Pavlova put her tablet down. "The Maeshiva are going to settle on a new world, but their chances of surviving there are minimal. If the Tryb don't find them, another malevolent species might. The universe isn't a warm and cuddly place. In order for them to survive they'll need a Sargasso barrier erected around their new home world. More immediately, the Tryb war fleet will have to be dealt with."

"Erect a new Sargasso barrier?" asked Jason. "I thought only the Caretakers could do that."

"The mythical, absent Caretakers, yes," said Pavlova. "They're our best hope for resolving the Tryb problem, and they're the reason Kazemi bargained off a viable colony planet. You see, the Maeshiva think they know where the Caretakers live."

"That's right," said Aidan. "We're going to see the wizard behind the curtain. And you are the one who can get us there."

Jason stared at the two of them. "Why me?"

"We pulled the data from your ship," said Pavlova. "You were able to fly deeper into the Sargasso while retaining control of your ship than any pilot on record, even though you weren't high on Rust at the time. Our people think months of exposure to the drug from before you got clean altered your brain chemistry in a way that makes you more resistant to the barrier. And that makes you our best shot."

Jason caught himself scraping at his wrist with a fingernail. The need for Rust swelled within him again. "Best shot for what?"

"There is a star system that is surrounded by a barrier many times more potent than all the other ones," said Aidan. "The Maeshiva believe—as do I—that it guards the home of the Caretakers."

"That's one theory," said Pavlova. "There's another. Our scientists think it may be an interdicted planet."

Suppress the urge. Extinguish it. "Interdicted? Aren't all inhabited worlds interdicted by definition, surrounded by the Sargasso?"

"We think the Caretakers erected a more potent barrier to contain someone dangerous, someone who figured out a reliable way to get around their regular containment. This is exactly what we'd like to happen to the Tryb."

Jason considered Pavlova's words. "And who are *we*? You and Kazemi? Because this sort of thing seems like it should be well above your pay grade, let alone mine. Isn't there some sort of government back on Earth that should be dealing with this?"

"The post of security chief on Venezia is always filled by a high-ranked intelligence official from either Earth or Mars. It's part of the arrangement that allows Kazemi and his partners to operate Venezia as a private enterprise." Pavlova leaned forward in her seat. "There are contingencies for hostile contact, all sorts of scenarios mulled over in think tanks for decades. Admittedly we can't do much with the resources we have outside of the Sargasso containment, but helping the Maeshiva on this mission is well worth the risk. Even if we're right and all they found is an interdicted planet, we might gather information that's incredibly valuable."

"Or we might die!" Jason got up from his seat and half-turned so he faced Pavlova directly. "I didn't sign up for this, for any of it. How dare you roll the dice with my life without even asking consent?"

Pavlova got up too, standing only a few inches from his face. She rested her hand on his shoulder.

"I'm sorry, Jason. We evacuated the other blockade pilots when we thought the Maeshiva were invading, because we didn't want to risk losing them in battle. When this… opportunity came up, you were not only the best choice, but the only choice. What would you have done in my place?"

The two of them stared at each other. Jason said nothing.

"I may be risking your life, but I'm risking mine too. As is Aidan. Our survival depends on your skill as a pilot." Pavlova squeezed his shoulder. "You don't have to forgive me, but please work with me, for the sake of the mission."

They stood there as Jason searched his feelings. Against incredible odds he had survived the journey that was meant to kill him, only to end up in this situation. Perhaps this was what he was meant to do? Besides, what other options did he really have?

He disengaged and sat back down.

"How about you?" he asked Aidan. "Why are you really here?"

"The Translators think of the Caretakers as gods, or close enough to it in human terms," said Aidan. "What risk wouldn't you take to meet your god?"

Jason chuckled, some of the tension draining from him.

"This is humorous?" asked Aidan.

"In most human belief systems you get to meet your maker after you die. That makes yours a strange choice of words."

"I see your meaning," said Aidan. "And while the double entendre was unintentional, it wasn't wrong. The probability of all of us meeting our gods soon, one way or another, is unusually high."

Jason laughed at this, and Pavlova joined in.

✿

Jason sat alone in the cockpit of the Blockade Runner, which he decided to name the *Pivot II* in honor of his last ship. The original *Pivot* had somehow allowed him to survive the long slow trip across the Sargasso, and he hoped some of the luck would transfer to this vessel along with the name. He was surely going to need it.

Aidan, Pavlova, and three Maeshiva representatives occupied the suspended animation units that were his sole cargo. The six of them were on their way to visit the Mount Olympus of the galaxy's self-appointed gods.

The system that lay ahead seemed unremarkable. A single Neptune-mass planet orbited a red dwarf star. The instruments detected no signs of life and no communications.

Jason accelerated toward the system. The sophisticated computers shut themselves down to avoid malfunction within the Sargasso space. The *Pivot II* was now a bullet, fired toward its target and reliant on the initial boost to get through the barrier. Jason could use chemical rockets in order to adjust course, but his main function as the blockade pilot was merely to survive the trip.

He had learned that occasionally Blockade Runners were able to reach their destination even if the pilot went insane or died, but most of the time the fate of the ship was inexplicably tied to the fate of its pilot.

Pivot II sped toward its target. Jason knew the exact moment it entered the barrier. Unlike the Sargasso space of the Solar System where the process was gradual, he could feel it vividly with his mind. It was as though a dozen wild cats scratched at the inside of his head.

Jason focused on the planet ahead and strived to ignore his inner turmoil. He must make it across; too much was at stake. People and aliens believed in him, entrusted their lives to him. He wasn't going to let them down.

The pain intensified. It flared up until he could feel nothing else, perceive nothing else. He clutched at his temples and screamed.

After an eternity the pain receded, leaving desire in its wake. He wanted Rust, lusted for it. It was worse than the days he had spent in rehab. He would murder his passengers or cut off his arm for a single dose. Then the desire abated only to be replaced with pain again. The cycle went on, endless.

Jason writhed on the floor. He lost all sense of time, of where he was heading and why. His entire universe was equal parts pain and desire, and he could no longer tell them apart. When the cycle finally stopped it took time for his senses to register this.

He blinked rapidly and tried to focus. Outside the porthole a tropical sun bathed a sandy beach in bright white light.

There is no porthole. No beach. Keep it together. He forced his gaze away.

There was a *ding*, and a compartment opened revealing a syringe. Rust!

Jason wiped cold, clammy sweat from his forehead and stared at the syringe. He'd learned that a dose of Rust was automatically made available to the pilot ten minutes into the Sargasso space. Somehow, he hadn't expected this ship to contain it. He stared at the syringe like it was a venomous snake.

Then the second realization hit him: *it had only been ten minutes*. The eternity of pain he had suffered was but a tiny fraction of the trip that would last for hours.

The syringe beckoned to him.

Was it real or an illusion, a cruel mirage induced by the barrier, like the tropical island outside his ship? He pondered as the cats began to scratch at the inside of his head again.

Jason felt his resolve weakening. Perhaps Rust could really help him survive the trip, alleviate the pain. With so much at stake, who could possibly blame him?

He thought back to the weeks spent in rehab, the pain and the sacrifice of getting clean. He'd thrown his life away once—he wouldn't do it again, not even to save it, to save everyone.

The cats scratched in earnest. Soon he wouldn't be able to resist. He grabbed the syringe and shambled across the cramped cockpit. He opened the door to a tiny bathroom with a chemical toilet and emptied the syringe's contents into the washbasin, taking care to flush every drop down the recycling tube where he could never reach it. He ran the water for a full minute, until the small tank ran out. He then ground the syringe under his heel.

When the cycle resumed, he clawed at the sealed compartment where he knew the return journey's syringe waited until his fingers were raw and bleeding. He couldn't pry it open.

✿

He was on his hands and knees when the pain receded again. He clutched at the sand, its warm grains sifting through his fingers.

Sand?

He was on the beach. Turquoise water splashed gently against the shore, and a mild breeze caressed his face. In the distance a lone palm tree stood a few steps away from the water's edge.

"The pain is over. You made it through, Jason."

He turned toward the sound of the voice. Warren Jain stood there in his uniform, slightly crumpled as always. Jain smiled at him.

"Commander Jain? This… is impossible." Jason struggled to get up.

"We have taken a form that is comfortable and familiar to you."

Jason stood. The pain was gone, leaving him completely drained.

"Are you the Caretaker?"

The image of Jain flickered, momentarily replaced by Aidan. "Some call us by that name."

Jason tried to gather his thoughts, to explain his purpose. He didn't quite know where to begin.

The figure in front of him shifted into one of the Maeshiva. "We know why you're here. The new Maeshiva colony will receive the protective field. The Tryb star systems will be interdicted."

"Thank you," Jason whispered. He had so many questions, but all he could manage was: "Why?"

The being shifted to Kazemi. "We are not of a uniform mind. There are factions among us. While all of us wish to elevate the younger species, we disagree as to the methodology. Some prefer for natural selection to take its course, for the faster-advancing species to overtake their rivals. They see the fields as challenges, puzzles; cages for the strong to break out of, and to contain the weak."

It shifted to Jain again. "Others value all sentient life and wish to preserve it. They erect the fields to protect the emerging intelligences, to nurture the islands of the mind in the unforgiving sea of the cosmos until they're strong enough to claim their place in the greater universe. The ones who are here communicating with you are a part of that faction."

"So Aidan was right," said Jason. "You're basically gods. And not all the gods are nice."

The alien shifted to Aidan again. "We're not gods. We're merely further along on the evolutionary adventure than the other sentients in this galaxy."

"So why tell me? Why not just erect barriers and interdict and do whatever it is that you want to do?"

Jain again: "You have a special mind."

Then Kazemi: "Our faction was losing. The Tryb were to be allowed to overrun your sector of space."

Pavlova this time: "We needed an argument the evolutionary faction couldn't trump. We needed proof of evolution so definitive, they would become swayed."

The Caretakers' avatar shifted to become a copy of Jason. "Your mind had the potential to survive the strengthened field, but you were born too early. Your species couldn't reach here. But once you entered the field, we had the means to preserve you, to nudge the events so that your ship would reach the other side in time to meet with the Maeshiva fleet."

Jason studied his doppelganger. "You got me here. What is it you need me to do?"

Another shift to Pavlova: "You have already done it. This is not our home world as the Maeshiva had hoped, but merely a test, a venue where the protective field is deployed at its most potent setting. Your mind surviving the strengthened barrier is proof that there's greater potential for evolution within your species than displayed by the mere technological prowess of the Tryb."

Kazemi: "The other faction will have no choice but to conform to our preferred course of action."

Jain: "Know that your suffering wasn't wasted. You've saved your species, and many others."

Aidan: "We thank you. The field has been turned off so you won't suffer its effects on your return trip. You can go in peace now."

"Wait!" said Jason. "What do I tell the others?"

Another shift to Kazemi: "That is of no consequence. You can tell them what you wish."

The beach and the sand and the bright sun were gone. Jason was alone again, in the cockpit of the Blockade Runner.

He checked the instruments: the ship was headed outward, away from the red dwarf star and toward the Maeshiva cruiser. He'd get there in two hours' time.

Jason was deep in thought, contemplating what he had learned from the Caretakers and how he might present this information to the others. Even if they didn't believe him, the newly erected interdiction barriers around the Tryb star systems should be proof enough. His pondering was interrupted by a *ding*—the ship's automated process made the second syringe of Rust available to him.

Jason stared at the syringe dispassionately. The urge, the desire he fought for so long, was gone. Perhaps it was burned out of him by the ordeal, or perhaps removing the addiction was a parting gift from the Caretakers. Whatever the case, he knew Jain—the real Jain, not the illusion generated by the aliens—would be proud of him.

He ignored the syringe and settled in for the trip home.

Copyright © 2015 by Alex Shvartsman

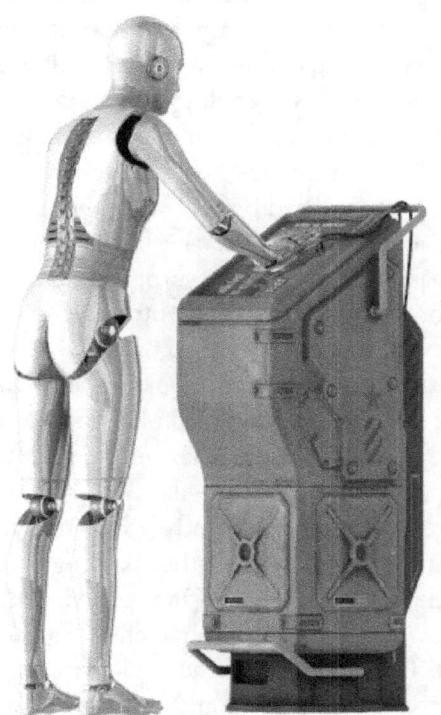

Elizabeth Bear is a two-time Hugo winner as well as a Campbell winner, and the author of more than twenty-five books, and has just concluded her first decade as a science fiction writer.

FORM AND VOID

by Elizabeth Bear

Before she turned into a dragon, Kathy Cutter was Comanche Zariphes' best friend.

You might say Comanche Zariphes was Kathy Cutter's *only* friend.

That wasn't because nobody wanted to be friends with Kathy Cutter. It was because Kathy Cutter didn't want to be friends with anybody else.

Kathy Cutter's hair was blonde and her eyes were green. Her face was a perfect geneshaped oval and she had a discreet little interface button that gleamed like mother of pearl behind her left ear. She was smart enough but not too smart. She wore cute tailored clothes from the fancy boutique.

Comanche Zariphes' mom eshopped at ConsignMart and everybody knew it.

Kathy Cutter's dad was a pediatrician and her mom was an architect. They lived in a big house with trees and grass so green it looked fake and a swing in the yard. They had a personal car, not just a sharecar. They ate fresh food and somebody else cooked it for them, and they were all rightminded to perfect happiness and stability. Supposedly.

Comanche Zariphes' eyes were brown and her hair was brown also. She didn't know what she looked like to Kathy Cutter, because her family couldn't afford the skins and simware that people like Kathy Cutter's family ran to control their environmental experiences. Comanche never asked Kathy about that, because she was afraid Kathy would tell her.

Comanche was too smart, and not smart enough to keep anybody from finding out about it. Her mom was a guitar player and her dad was a playwright, and everybody knew they were always broke and weird. They lived in an apartment with a cement balcony, and her mom grew tomatoes in laundry buckets and planted runner beans in window boxes so they grew up the pigeon wire. Other than that, they ate staples and worried constantly about staying in the maximum-rebate bracket of their carbon budget. They didn't even have a sharecar.

Nobody could spell her last name.

☼

All kinds of girls tried to be friends with Kathy Cutter, but Kathy Cutter was a hard girl with whom to be friends. She was snide, and she was superior. She was insulting, and she was irate. There couldn't be anything wrong with her, because she had been raised with all the therapy and all the rightminding her family could afford, so if anybody complained to the teachers or administrators about her it was obvious that there was something wrong with *them*.

And she was always just waiting to be offended. She collected injustices, and if she wasn't getting enough insults, she invented them. She collected them the way she collected her china dolls and china horses, and she was as jealous of letting anyone touch them. Once she had an insult, she rubbed it and rubbed it until it shone like jewelry. She polished it into a shape she liked, one that showed the slight to its best advantage, and she committed it to a memory jewel so she could wear it everywhere.

By the time they started high school, Comanche was still Kathy's only friend. And Kathy had so many insults saved that she could wear them on chains. The memory jewels were colored like rubies and emeralds, pearls and amethysts, and she had ropes of them in colors to suit every outfit. Some of the slights were Comanche's, but because Comanche wanted to be friends with Kathy she didn't mind when Kathy wore those, and showed them to her.

Or she told herself she didn't mind.

There were a lot of them. The time in second grade when Comanche gave her a Valentine's card with Kathy's name spelled with a C. The time in fourth grade when Comanche didn't give Kathy a Valentine's card at all. The time in sixth grade when Comanche borrowed Kathy's baby pink cardigan—a color that didn't suit her, though it looked wonderful on Kathy—and gave it back with a tiny ink stain on the sleeve.

Kathy remembered every mistake Comanche had ever made. So Comanche remembered them also.

Every jewel Kathy wore had the capacity to hold all of those memories, and a hundred years of popular music besides. But Kathy wanted a jewel for each slight—and her father, Comanche knew, would provide. He always gave her expensive gifts, strangely grown-up gifts.

As if he were making amends.

☼

They stayed friends all through school. Comanche followed Kathy into the A.P. classes, and to college, and when Kathy picked her grad course in astroengineering Comanche got into the same program.

Kathy encouraged her. Kathy drove her. Comanche was very, very careful never to score higher than Kathy on anything.

☼

One day after graduation, Kathy said, "I'm emigrating to Io. They have dragons there." As if she didn't care at all what Comanche did.

But Comanche knew that if she didn't say, "I'm emigrating to Io too," that would be the biggest, shiniest ruby of all. So Comanche kissed her mother goodbye, and kissed her father, and packed up her few worldly things. Kathy gave Comanche Kathy's old datageneral, because Kathy's family had bought her a new one as a graduation present. Comanche couldn't use a lot of the functions because she didn't have the wetware, but it was better than the cheap one Comanche had bought with her grant. Comanche had planned to use the last of her stipend to purchase a ticket, but she surprised herself by applying for and getting a good entry-level technical job at the sulfur plant, so Iocorp paid her passage.

Kathy and Comanche took the elevator to Skypoint together, their duffels following obediently.

They couldn't sit together on the shuttle because Kathy was traveling first-class, but they used their datagens to text back and forth—no vids so the sound didn't annoy the other passengers, since Comanche wasn't wetwired. Once they disembarked on the *Activist*, Kathy let Comanche sleep in her stateroom. That way Comanche could run out for ice or whatever and Kathy would not have to wait for a steward when she wanted something.

The stateroom seemed luxurious by Comanche's standards, but Kathy seemed restless and disappointed in it. She wouldn't order in food, complaining that the ship charged premiums for cabin service, but Comanche couldn't coax her to go to the commons, either. Kathy paced the room, petted her jewels, refused to answer her phone, and gnawed on her cuticles until white streaks grew into her nails.

Often, Comanche brought back cheese and bread and fruit, and cups of coffee. Kathy could be a horrible person sometimes. But Comanche knew she had her reasons. And every time she looked at a screen or out a porthole, every time she kick-glided the length of the *Activist's* central gangway, Comanche was glad she'd come.

☼

Io was a world like dragonscale, vermilion and goldenrod mottled and crackled with white. Comanche had arranged to be at one of the viewports as they came up on it, and she drifted with her hands pressed to her thighs as her new home hove into sight. The arc of one of its sulfur volcanoes was visible against the jet-black horizon. Comanche could almost convince herself that those glittering sparkles she saw around the eruption's border were the dragons.

It took Comanche's breath away so thoroughly that she almost forgot to turn around and take in the round of Jupiter's belly as well, an echo of Io's colors so huge it was only partially visible through the port. Comanche held out her hands, imagining she could feel the fat world's tidal pull.

Kathy was back in the cabin, possibly watching the arrival on her wetware, possibly reading technical docs. She didn't have a job on Io yet, but it wasn't as if an out-of-the-way worldlet had a lot of competition for employment. She'd have to find something soon. True, Comanche had never seen her worry about money before—but it was probably just being so far from home and feeling insecure.

☼

They shared a room on Io, too. Comanche got one as a perk of her job, and it was taking Kathy longer to find work than they'd expected.

"I don't want to keep taking money from my parents," Kathy said. "And I need to save mine for something that will get me a job."

Comanche approved. Kathy needed to cut the apron strings.

Comanche paid for everything. Nearly everything; every few days, Kathy brought home some kind of a treat—imported food, beers, a video player. She was often gone. "Working on getting a job," Kathy said, and then gave her that look that meant, *Boundaries.*

Barter, then. The hidden economy. Even out here.

Kathy was working on a new cuff. The first stone was an emerald as big as a cat's eye, one Comanche hadn't seen before. She knew it wasn't hers, because Kathy would have told her. Kathy always told her when she made a mistake.

The work was hard but interesting, though Comanche struggled with Kathy's datagen. She liked her shift leader, Arachne Jericho, whose expectations never changed from moment to moment. Mary Manley said Jericho was wanted on Mars for a murder that was really a justifiable homicide; Comanche never quite managed to not believe it. But if Jericho had killed somebody, they probably needed killing. And this was Io, not Mars.

Comanche's job paid well and it used her brain; she did external science and maintenance in a suit. As she walked from place to place, her boots kicked up plumes of sulfur dioxide frost. They hung in Io's frail gravity for long seconds before drifting gently down again. Comanche tended to frolic around outside when she thought nobody was looking.

She also spent a lot of time watching the dragons, wired into their integral armor, looping overhead. Their jobs were something like hers, but they were doing the real observational science out there on the edge of the solar system. They glittered, their metal bodies paved with synthetic diamonds and sapphires that held massive amounts of survey data in a permanent holographic matrix. Some were gold, some white, some blue. One in particular was a shade of padparadscha orange that caught her eye every time it passed.

She found it hard to imagine that they had been human once.

Io was one of their waystations, but they traveled throughout Jupiter's solar-system-in-miniature at will: Ganymede, Callisto, Metis, Amalthea... If they could get a lift back out of the gravity well on a survey rocket, some of them even visited the upper atmosphere of the giant world itself. Some of them went farther out, too—there was a colony on retrograde Triton with its nitrogen geysers. She guessed some of them were indentured to corporations too... but some had to have bought off their contracts. They could go places only drones could, otherwise, and that made them valuable.

They might be the only free things in the solar system. Only Europa was off limits to them. Europa with its water ice and its primitive life. Nothing that had not been sterilized and resterilized was permitted anywhere near Europa.

Watching the dragons, Comanche was reminded that she needed better hardware—and the attendant wetware—if she ever wanted to be promoted past a certain level. She didn't want to be like them—human body lost forever in a shell of alloy, ceramic, and memory jewels—but she needed to skin, and she needed to link, and she needed to be faster on these repairs in the way she only could be if she were projecting a schematic immediately over the work.

She couldn't save money while she was taking care of Kathy, not unless she had a better job, and the wiring cost a lot more out here than it did back on warming, overpopulated Earth. Iocorp would pay to have her wired... but it was a loan, not a gift. She'd belong to them for thirty years after, mind—quite literally—and soul.

✿

Back inside, she found a note on her locker to talk to Jericho. Apprehension twisted her gut as she walked into Jericho's office—a broom closet, about the size of the room Comanche and Kathy shared. Jericho—a compact woman with Asian features and broad shoulders, her slick dark hair cut in a utilitarian bob—stood as Comanche came in, which wasn't a good sign.

But her words replaced Comanche's worry of personal failing and punishment with a different worry indeed. "Hey," she said. "Have you noticed stuff out of place on your rounds?"

"Stuff?"

"Tool kits," Jericho said. "Oxy backup. First aid. Anything that gets left in the lockers."

Comanche shook her head. "Shouldn't there be access logs for all those things?"

"Yep," Jericho said. She tapped her fingers on the desk. "You keep an eye peeled. Stuff is going missing; I'd like an idea how. And we have to replace it. Or somebody's going to get caught outside without enough ox."

✿

One night—not really a night, but the language wasn't adapted to the world—Comanche came back to the room to find Kathy home, and in bed already. She was curled up on her side, head resting on her fist. Her body under the sheets looked strangely lumpy.

She raised herself as the light came on, but only from the waist—pushing herself up on her arms like a sick dog. "Hey," she said.

"Hey." Comanche dropped her gear kit inside the door. Kathy would normally give her hell for not putting it away immediately, even though she left her own stuff all over the place. "What's wrong?"

"Give me a hand up," Kathy said. "And you'll see."

✿

Her long legs ended in perching talons, and glittered with memory jewels. All in different colors, arranged in rainbow belts—an angled spiral that peaked above her left hip in that big, green emerald. Her stabilizing tail ended in a hooked barb that put Comanche in mind of a safety knife, and which served the same purpose.

She was still a girl from the waist up.

"You're a chromatic dragon," Comanche said, even though she knew Kathy wouldn't get it. The look Kathy gave her told her that one wasn't quite enough for a jewel of its own, but she was adding it to the bank. "I didn't know—"

"My parents cut me off." Kathy's human hands sounded funny, tapping on her jewel-encrusted metal knees. "When I told them I wanted to emigrate here. My dad said he wouldn't pay for me to leave him. I had to save my money for this—"

"Of course," Comanche said. "It's expensive, becoming a dragon." She heard the aggression in her own voice, but for once Kathy didn't react. She sat down on the bed beside Kathy and sighed. "*I* couldn't afford it. I can't even afford the upgrades I need for my work. I'm going to have to sell out to Iocorp."

It was easier to say than she'd expected. It didn't hurt any less, though—she'd followed Kathy all the way out here, and Kathy was going to keep running. That's what it was, Comanche realized. Armoring up and running.

"I can pay for it," Kathy said.

"You need—"

Her armored lower body creaked as she stood up. "I'll be able to afford both. Just listen to me."

✿

I'll be able to afford both. I will.

Comanche heard it. Heard it, as she had heard what Jericho said to her. Heard it and put it away.

She'd be extra careful policing the supply lockers. She'd make sure everything was fully stocked, and nobody's safety was compromised. She wouldn't help Kathy—but it was Iocorp she was robbing, not a person, not a charitable organization. Iocorp that brought people out here and then controlled price and supply of everything.

Kathy was leaving her. Comanche needed to be able to take care of herself. She stroked her own soft arm with her fingers. She didn't want to be a dragon, though she thought she knew why Kathy might. The same reasons Kathy might want to come all the way out to Io to get away from her family.

Comanche wasn't naïve. She knew there were things Kathy had never told her.

Things she only told her jewels.

✿

It would be one procedure for Comanche and just one more for Kathy. Then she would be sealed into her untouchable armor shell. Bonded to it. It would become her body, forever.

Well, maybe not forever—Comanche supposed that some dragons, somewhere, must have changed their minds. But it was a tremendous expense to get that way. A commitment. Getting back out again would be worse, and you wouldn't be the way you had been.

✿

When Comanche awoke from her surgery, Kathy surprised her by being there. Her iridescent armor encased her in rainbow spirals to the delicate wings of her collarbones, which were framed by the attachment points for her helmet. Comanche tried to sit up, but her head seemed to be part of the pillow.

"Can you feel anything?" she asked, looking at Kathy's hands, one gold and one violet, and the way the light caught in the facets of her jeweled carapace and shattered.

"I can feel more than I want to," Kathy said. "Look, here's my new face."

She reached between her knees and lifted it from the floor. Comanche had never seen a dragon helmet up close before. The great glassy eyes were packed with sensors. The stone-crushing jaws could detect any number of chemical compounds. Comanche looked at Kathy's perfect porcelain geneshaped face, and thought she knew why Kathy might want to hide it forever.

Did your father tell you how pretty you are?

"I think I might go to Titan," Kathy said. The new interface points all around her shaved hairline shone when she tilted her head. "Did you know the atmosphere is transparent in the infrared?"

"When are you leaving?"

Her expression was trying to be a smile. "Soon. But not tomorrow."

✿

Comanche healed fast, and Kathy refused to leave before she was sure Comanche could take care of herself. It was as if the armor changed her, made her tender. Gave her the strength to be somebody who could care. But the spectral jewels that shimmered with every move were a constant reminder: Kathy would never forget.

And every time Comanche asked when Kathy was leaving, Kathy said, "I'm not ready yet."

There was work for dragons here on Io. Despite herself Comanche more or less began to hope.

I can't follow you this time, she whispered in the dark, when she could hear Kathy breathing. *This time you have to stay with me.*

✿

Comanche was one of the three inspectors on shift when Mary Manley's distress call went out. Suit breach. Comanche made rapid contact with Jericho, and Jericho gave her the go to make a run.

Comanche went bounding across the yellow-white frost, glittering sprays kicking away from each stride. She ran until she strained her suit respirator, the rasp of her breath drowning out Jericho's instructions and calm tone, and staggered and ran on.

Comanche was the closest help, but close was still halfway around the outside of the complex and the leak in Mary's suit was too big. It was one of those cascading errors where nobody should have died—but a suit seal gave way the same day an airlock failed to function, and when Mary tried to jam herself into the panic pod beside the failed airlock she found out the hard way that somebody had disconnected the ox and walked off with the bottle.

Comanche brought her body inside, all the way around the long outside of the complex to the next airlock. It wasn't heavy. Not in this gravity.

Inside, Jericho was waiting with a physician-coroner and a team of medics. There weren't enough people on Io for postmortem staff not to have other, primary jobs. Comanche's shift mates lined the corridor bulkheads. She felt like she was passing a court of judgment as she carried Mary over her shoulder to a gurney, frost flaking from the joints in her suit.

She stepped back and waited, chest heaving, eyes on fire. Not because carrying Mary was hard, not in this gravity. She had other reasons.

Jericho came up behind her while she watched the medics work. "She's cold and dead," Jericho said. "You're not dead until you're warm and dead."

Comanche nodded. "Cold comfort." It wasn't funny. She leaned a shoulder against the bulkhead and struggled with her helmet.

Jericho lifted it off for her. "Your half-dragonish friend was here," she said. "Looking for you. She ran off."

"Mary—"

Jericho put a firm hand on her shoulder. It kept her from turning around. The shift boss shoved the helmet under Comanche's arm. "You can't help here. I'll need you for debrief in a half hour, but right now you'd better go see to your friend."

Kathy curled up beside a condenser, small despite the armor. Her human body seemed thin and collapsed, like an empty fire hose run through the ar-

mature of her dragonish carapace. In this dark corner, even the glitter of her jewels was muted.

"Hey." Comanche crouched next to her. She knew better than to touch Kathy uninvited (that was the Tanzanite that lived at the small of her back now), but her hands hovered over her friend nonetheless.

Comanche waited. When Kathy didn't answer, she said, "I think you maybe owe Mary one of those stones now."

Kathy raised her head. She'd been huddled, hunched over her dragon helmet. Her eyes were rimmed red, her cheek cobbled with indentations that the stones had pressed. The armor could have been sealed across her face for all the expression it offered.

Flatly, mechanically, Kathy said, "You took the money."

"Yeah," Comanche said.

She turned around and slumped down against the wall where Kathy could see her. In her suit, sitting wasn't comfortable.

"You need to stop stalling, Kathy. Leave if you're going to leave. Because I have to tell Jericho. And then you won't be able to go. You're a free dragon. Get out of Iocorp jurisdiction, you'll find work. Resupply."

Kathy's cheeks were crimson spots in the center of bone white. "You'll lose your job. You might go to jail. Iocorp won't hire you again. How will you get home?"

"If they want to put me in a jail, Iocorp will have to ship me home." She snorted and looked at the back of her hand. She turned it over and looked at the palm.

Kathy started to her feet, talons clutching and skittering at the floor. "You're just threatening me because you're jealous!"

"Because you're going where I can't follow? Maybe. I followed you to the fucking end of the Solar System because... because you expected it. Because that's how things are with us. And now you're leaving me. And you always planned to be leaving me."

Comanche paused. She could have told Kathy that she had always been a dragon, really, even before she put the armor on.

But the truth was, Comanche had liked being the person who could walk with the dragon. Even if she got a little clawed or scorched. She'd made her choices. She was responsible too. And now she was making a different one.

She didn't need to hurt Kathy by explaining.

So she just said, "I'm not saying I'm innocent. But that doesn't change the fact that Mary is *dead*."

Kathy stared at her, wide-eyed. Breathless. "Come with me."

It could have been a punch in the solar plexus. "Kathy—"

"Come with me," she said. "You're the only one who ever wanted me for myself."

Comanche pressed her lips together. Maybe it would be good for Kathy to think that was what Comanche had wanted.

Kathy said, "You said I just expected, before. Well, I'm *asking* now."

"Kathy. You're a dragon. I *can't* follow."

Kathy's mouth opened. It closed. "I don't know how to—"

You should have thought of that.

"Five minutes," Comanche interrupted. "You can be here when she comes to get you, or you can be on your way to Titan."

"Comanche—"

Comanche turned her back. She put her helmet on. She squared her shoulders. She closed her eyes.

Eighty-seven seconds elapsed before the puff of displaced air told her Kathy had gone. Comanche still gave her the full five minutes lead before she went to Jericho.

Copyright © 2012 by Sarah Wishnevsky

J. R. Vogt has recently joined the ranks of the full-time freelancers. This constitutes his twentieth short story sale, though it's his first appearance in Galaxy's Edge. *In May of this year he sold a pair of novels,* Forge of Ashes *to Paizo and* Enter the Janitor *to Wordfire (which has since bought his* The Maids of Wrath*).*

ESCAPE MECHANISM

by Josh Vogt

"Found him," Rachel said, peering through the telescope. "Bastard couldn't hide forever."

Bryan glanced up from his beer. "Who? The man in the moon?"

She straightened and adjusted her pink earmuffs. "Idiot. I spotted God. And I was right. He's a space squid."

"I've...either had too much to drink or not enough."

"God. Is. A. Space. Squid. What part doesn't make sense?"

Bryan sighed. Date night had begun oddly enough when Rachel lugged her telescope along, chattering about fluxing gravitational tides. "The individual words are okay. All together? Not so much."

She pointed at the telescope. "Just look."

"Fine." He shuffled over and squinted through at the interstellar expanse. "It's...black."

She snorted. "Duh. God activated his escape mechanism. You're looking at a galactic ink cloud. Totally explains dark matter and black holes."

"Totally."

Her huff plumed white. "You never respect my beliefs."

"Since when have your beliefs included space squids?"

"I told you I study astronomy to find God in the stars."

"I thought you were being poetic!"

"You're so narrow-minded!"

"Seriously?" Bryan reached to the heavens. "Oh, Divine Space Squid! Accept this offering of cheap beer and hear my plea. Free me from this madwoman and I shall forever serve you!"

A writhing column obscured the stars; Rachel shrieked as a tentacle yanked her into the night.

As Bryan stared, another swooping tentacle snatched the can from his hand.

After time unfroze, he retrieved the pink earmuffs from by his feet.

"I'm guessing this means no more calamari…"

"While great writing, vivid scenarios, and thoughtful commentary outshine the scientific concepts, the stories will linger after the last page is turned."

—*Publishers Weekly* (Starrred Review)

Lawrence Person has been active in all aspect of science fiction, editing the Hugo-nominated Nova Express, writing dozens of reviews and essays, and selling short fiction, of which this is his twentieth sale, and his first appearance in Galaxy's Edge.

SAUL'S DIARY

by Lawrence Person

Dr. Crenshaw said keeping a diary might help me remember things better. No skin off my nose. I agreed to just to keep him off my back. One less thing for him to nag me about.

I asked when Bernice was going to come pick me up. He said Bernice has been dead for eleven years.

He's a liar, just like everyone else in this lousy joint. I wrote a letter to the paper complaining about it but they never published it.

My TV is still on the fritz so I went to the lounge. The old biddies were out in force again. I told them to turn on some baseball, but they were watching that stupid bug-eyed monster garbage they're always watching. Then they all come over and try to make googly eyes at me, since I'm still walking and every other yat in the place has a half a foot in the grave.

I wish Bernice would come and pick me up.

Dr. Crenshaw puts me through a bunch more tests. He pulls a sheet off a cage and there's a big tarantula sitting there. I shrug. I used to be scared of spiders, but not since Nam.

"Am I supposed to pet him and name him George?"

"No," says Dr. Crenshaw. He's just testing my amigawhatsit (I don't know the word, something like that) reaction.

I ask him if the VC bullet in my amigawhatzit is what's messing with my memory. He says no, that's the Alzheimer's. He asks me what tests we went over the day before, and I tell him he's screwing with me because we didn't meet yesterday.

Bernice should fire this quack.

The lousy chiselers finally get around to fixing my TV. They tell me not to break this one. Hell, I didn't break the last one!

I turn it on to watch the news, and what do you know, half the stations are showing that stupid bug-eyed monster sci-fi crap! It's the same goddamn thing every time, some slab of beefcake goes into this big black ship they got parked out in the bay, and as soon as he gets in, this monster rears up and the guy starts screaming his head off, then the thing eats him! Then the announcer starts talking about champions and fear-a-moans and some other made up gobbledygook.

I keep switching around until I find a baseball game.

Later on I try calling Bernice, but a guy answers and said he's had this number for seven years and hangs up on me.

The nerve of some people.

✿

Lot's of excitement today! Staff says a guy's come to see me and to be nice, not like last time. I've got no idea what they're talking about, since I'm always nice, except when people piss me off.

Tall, smug-looking guy in a suit asks me "Are you Saul Bednarski?"

"Yeah, what's it to you?"

"Did you write a letter threatening the President of the United States?"

"I wrote a letter! I told him he was a liar and crook and if I ever saw him I'm gonna punch him in right in his ugly, two-bit chiseler face!"

"Are you aware that using the U.S. Mail to threaten the President's life is a felony?"

"Ask me if I care! What are you, crooked boy's personal muscle?"

"You don't speak to a member of the Secret Service that way!"

"I'll speak to you any goddamn way I want, you putz!" I said. Then I whacked him right in the middle of his smug face with my cane.

Direct hit! Blood starts flying everywhere! It was glorious!

That's when Mac, the big orderly, grabs me so I can't whack him again. "Saul, you can't do that! Do you want to go to federal prison?"

"Why not? Maybe the food's better."

Dumbass actually has these handcuffs out in his hand, but can't cuff me because he's holding a hanky to his bleeding schnoz, when Crenshaw pulls him in the next room and has a half-shouted, half-whispered argument about yours truly. Crenshaw talks about the war, and my amgiawhatzit, and every other goddamn thing for like five minutes.

Finally they walk back into the room. Dumbass is still holding a hanky to his schnoz but not the cuffs.

"Want some more, tough guy?"

"I'm not going to fight a seventy-five-year-old man."

"Why, you afraid of telling your fancy Washington friends you got your ass kicked by a sawed-off yid geezer?" And I don't correct the seventy-five, even though I'm only sixty-something, but I lost count as to what.

He glares at me, then walks over to where my medal case is on the shelf.

"Is that a Distinguished Service Cross?"

"Yeah. Killed half a dozen VC and hauled my buddy out despite the bullet," I said, tapping my head.

"What's it to you?"

After that dumbass walks out without saying a single word.

I can't wait to tell Bernice how I clocked that clown, but she's not picking up the phone.

✿

Lot's of guys in suits today came to visit, including a general in full dress with a brace of medals. We talked about Nam for a few minutes. I was with the 82nd, he was in the 4th.

He asks me if I'm up for one last mission. I shrug. Beats the hell out of piddling around here waiting to die.

Then he starts talking about the bug-eyed monster garbage and how all the other champions have been killed, but I might still have a chance because of the bullet in my amgiawhatzit, and asks if I would fight it. I laugh at him.

"All due respect general," I say, trying to be polite cause he's a general and was in Nam too, "but that bug-eyed monster crap is fake is hell. I don't know what game they're playing, but I'm surprised they dragged you into this."

So he talks to Crenshaw for a few minutes, and he comes back and says its real, and I can fight it if I'm willing, but there's a good chance I'll get killed because everyone else has, but they're desperate and running out of time. I laugh and say I don't believe a word of it, but I'm game if it will get me the hell out of here.

So they give me a bunch of release forms and I sign them. And that's that.

It's all a crock. I don't know what sort of game they're playing, but I'll play along.

Beats the hell out of waiting around to die.

☼

Boy the city has changed!

I'm riding along and I feel like a million bucks because I haven't been out of the joint in forever, but everything's changed. I don't recognize half the buildings or the signs on them, and everywhere kids dress like morons.

I wish we had a chance to swing by Times Square so I could hassle the working girls for old time' sake, but they said I didn't have time.

I don't know what game they're playing, but they sure went all out! The ship in the bay looks enormous, just like it is on TV. Somebody's set up hundreds of flower displays on the shore, bouquets, crosses, even a few Star of Davids, which I take as a good sign.

We walk up to one of those shiny sci-fi robots and the general starts talking to it, holding up a piece of paper for it to read. After a few questions, the tin can rolls back and we start walking out on this weird stretchy material that moves with the waves. I'm worried I'm gonna get seasick and spew, but after a few minutes we get there.

Up close it's all fake and plastic looking; it's not even as good as *Star Wars*. I keep wondering when Alan Funt will jump out.

A big round door slides open and another tin can asks me if I'm there of my own free will. I say yeah. It asks me if I'm Earth's champion or some crap. I say why the hell not? Then it turns around and tells me to follow and the general wishes me luck.

We walk a ways and then we're in this big room with a bunch of bones on one side and swords and maces and stuff on the other, like some Hollywood prop room. The robot asks me if I want a weapon. I say I'll make do with my cane.

Then he leads me to a small room and it's showtime.

One side of the wall suddenly disappears, and I'm in this open space with one of those big black monster things. It slithers up to me like an eel and unfurls its top half like a cobra hood, the inside of which is covered by row after row of sharp teeth mixed with clusters of these weird scarlet eyes, screaming this annoying, high-pitched scream.

It looks fake as hell.

It screams again and starts moving toward me, so I whack it in the middle of its eye-clusters with my cane.

"Shut the hell up, your schmuck! You think I wanna listen to that?"

It screams again, a different sort of pitch, slithers back a few feet, then tries rearing up again. So I whack it again.

This happens a few more times, and suddenly this thing isn't liking it at all! I'm raining all over its goddamn parade! Soon instead of rearing up it starts backing away from me, making this sound like a two-ton kitten trying to cough up a hairball. Thing is, going backward it ain't nearly as fast as forward, so I just keep whacking it with my cane, and eventually it just curls up into a ball and stops moving.

I'll write more later. Right now I gotta take a dump.

☼

That night was great! Driving back everyone's out on the street cheering the car as it passes, chanting my name, waving homemade signs. It was crazy.

Back in the geezer joint everyone wants to kiss me or shake my hand. They all cheer when the TV shows the big ship taking off.

Finally, they give me a *real* meal, a big, fat, juicy steak, not all that soft bland crap, plus whisky and cigars! One of the biddies tells me not to smoke in here and I tell her to go to hell. Everyone laughs.

I get so drunk I forget to call Bernice, but I figure I can call her tomorrow.

Maybe now they'll finally let me go home.

☼

My head's killing me the next morning, and some jackasses start sawing and hammering right outside my window. I ask Mac to tell them to knock it off cause of my hangover. He tells me they're building a grandstand for my parade. They say the President is going to be there, and I tell them how I want to punch him right in his stupid, lying face. They tell me he's going to pin a medal on me, and make me promise not to punch him.

I ask them if Bernice is going to be there. They said she'll try to make it.

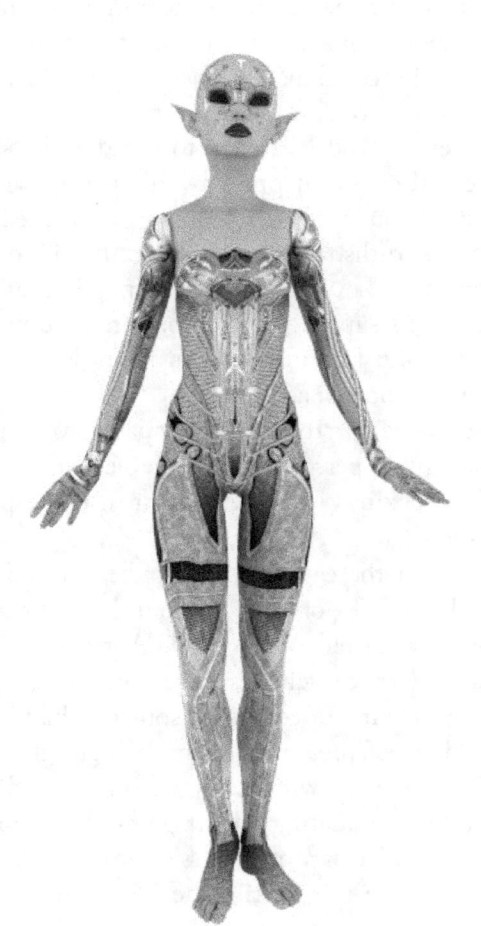

Robert J. Sawyer is the author of twenty-three novels including Hugo Award-winning Hominids, Nebula Award-wining The Terminal Experiment, plus Starplex, Frameshift, Factoring Humanity, Calculating God, and Wake, all of which were Hugo finalists. His novel Flash Forward was the basis for the television series. Canada's leading science fiction writer, he was recently given an honorary Doctor of Laws degree by the University of Winnipeg.

THE EAGLE HAS LANDED

by Robert J. Sawyer

I've spent a lot of time watching Earth—more than forty of that planet's years. My arrival was in response to the signal from our automated probe, which had detected that the paper-skinned bipedal beings of that world had split the atom. The probe had served well, but there were some things only a living being could do properly, and assessing whether a lifeform should be contacted by the Planetary Commonwealth was one.

It would have been fascinating to have been present for that first fission explosion: it's always a fabulous thing when a new species learns to cleave the atom, the dawn for them of a new and wondrous age. Of course, fission is messy, but one must glide before one can fly; all known species that developed fission soon moved on to the clean energy of controlled fusion, putting an end to need and want, to poverty, to scarcity.

I arrived in the vicinity of Earth some dozen Earth years after that first fission explosion—but I could not set down upon Earth, for its gravity was five times that of our homeworld. But its moon had a congenial mass; there I would weigh slightly less than I did at home. And, just like our homeworld, which, of course, is itself the moon of a gas-giant world orbiting a double star, Earth's moon was tidally locked, constantly showing the same face to its primary. It was a perfect place for me to land my starbird and observe the goings-on on the blue-and-white-and-infrared world below.

This moon, the soul natural satellite of was devoid of atmosphere, bereft of water. I imagined our homeworld would be similar if its volatiles weren't constantly replenished by material from Chirp-*cluck*-CHIRP-chirp, the gas-giant planet that so dominated our skies; a naturally occurring, permanent magnetic-flux tube passed a gentle rain of gases onto our world.

The moon that the inhabitants of Earth called "*the* moon" (and "*La* Lune," and a hundred other things) was depressingly desolate. Still, from it I could easily intercept the tens of thousands of audio and audio-visual transmissions spewing out from Earth—and with a time delay of only four wingbeats. My starbird's computer separated the signals one from the other, and I watched and listened.

It took that computer most of a smallyear to decipher all the different languages this species used, but, by the year—being a planet, not a moon, Earth had only one kind of year—the Earth people called 1958, I was able to follow everything that was happening there.

I was at once delighted and disgusted. Delighted, because I'd learned that in the years since that initial atomic test explosion had triggered our probe, the natives of this world had launched their first satellite. And disgusted, because almost immediately after developing fission, they had used those phenomenal energies as weapons against their own kind. Two cities had been destroyed, and bigger and more devastating bombs were still being developed.

Were they insane, I wondered? It had never occurred to me that a whole species could be unbalanced, but the initial fatal bombings, and the endless series of subsequent test explosions of bigger and bigger weapons, were the work not of crazed individuals but of the governments of this world's most powerful nations.

I watched for two more Earth years, and was about to file my report—quarantine this world; avoid all contact—when my computer alerted me to an interesting signal coming from the planet. The leader of the most populous of the nations on the western shore of the world's largest ocean was making a speech: "Now it is time," he was saying, "to take longer strides"—apparently significant imagery for a walking species—"time for a great new American enterprise; time for this nation to take a clearly lead-ing role in space achievement, which in many ways may hold the key to our future on Earth..."

Yes, I thought. *Yes.* I listened on, fascinated.

"I believe this nation should commit itself to achieving the goal, before this decade"—a cluster of ten Earth years—"is out, of landing a man on the moon and returning him safely to the Earth..."

Finally, some real progress for this species! I tapped the ERASE node with a talon, deleting my still-unsent report.

At home, these "Americans," as their leader had called them, were struggling with the notion of equality for all citizens, regardless of the color of their skin. I know, I know—to beings such as us, with frayed scales ranging from gold to green to purple to ultraviolet, the idea of one's coloration having any significance seems ridiculous, but for them it had been a major concern. I listened to hateful rhetoric: "Segregation now, segregation tomorrow, segregation forever!" And I listened to wonderful rhetoric: "I have a dream that one day this nation will rise up and live out the true meaning of its creed: 'We hold these truths to be self-evident: that all men are created equal.'" And I watched as public sentiment shifted from supporting the former to supporting the latter, and I confess that my dorsal spines fluttered with emotion as I did so.

Meanwhile, Earth's fledgling space program continued: single-person ships, double-person ships, the first dockings in space, a planned triple-person ship, and then...

And then there was a fire at the liftoff facility. Three "humans"—one of the countless names this species gave itself—were dead. A tragic mistake: pressurized space vehicles have a tendency to explode in vacuum, of course, so someone had landed on the idea of pressurizing the habitat (the "command module," they called it) at only one-fifth of normal, by eliminating all the gases except oxygen, normally a fifth-part of Earth's atmosphere...

Still, despite the horrible accident, the humans went on. How could they not?

And, soon, they came here, to the moon.

I was present at that first landing, but remained hidden. I watched as a figure in a white suit hopped off the last rung of a ladder and fell at what must have seemed to it a slow rate. The words the human spoke echo with me still: "That's one small step for man, one giant leap for mankind."

And, indeed, it truly was. I could not approach closely, not until they'd departed, but after they had, I walked over—even in my environmental sack, it was easy to walk here on my wingclaws. I examined the lower, foil-wrapped stage of their landing craft, which had been abandoned here. My computer could read the principal languages of this world, having learned to do so with aid of educational broadcasts it had intercepted. It informed me that the plaque on the lander said, "Here men from the planet Earth first set foot upon the moon, July 1969. We came in peace for all mankind."

My spines rippled. There *was* hope for this race. Indeed, during the time since that speech about longer strides, public opinion had turned overwhelmingly against what seemed to be a long, pointless conflict being fought in a tropical nation. They didn't need quarantining; all they needed, surely, was a little time...

✧

Fickle, fickle species! Their world made only three and half orbits around its solitary sun before what was announced to be the *last* journey here, to the moon, was completed. I was stunned. Never before had I known a race to turn its back on space travel once it had begun; one might as well try to crawl back into the shards of one's egg ...

But, incredibly, these humans did just that. Oh, there were some perfunctory missions to low orbit, but that was all.

Yes, there had been other accidents—one on the way to the moon, although there were no casualties; another, during which three people died when their vessel depressurized on reentry. But those three were from another nation, called "Russia," and that nation continued its space efforts without missing a wingbeat. But soon Russia's economy collapsed—of course! This race *still* hadn't developed controlled fusion; indeed, there was a terrible, terrible accident at a fission power-generating station in that nation shortly before it fell apart.

Still, perhaps the failure of Russia had been a good thing. Not that there was anything inherently evil about it, from what I could tell—indeed, in principle,

it espoused the values that all other known civilized races share—but it was the rivalry between it and the nation that had launched the inhabited ships to the moon that had caused an incredible escalation of nuclear-weapons production. Finally, it seemed, they would abandon that madness...and perhaps if abandoning space exploration was the price to pay for that, maybe, just maybe, it was worth it.

I was in a quandary. I had spent much longer here than I'd planned to—and I'd as yet filed no report. It's not that I was eager to get home—my brood had long since grown up—but I was getting old; my frayed scales were losing their flexibility, and they were tinged now with blue. But I still didn't know what to tell our homeworld.

And so I crawled back into my cryostasis nest. I decided to have the computer awaken me in one of our bigyears, a time approximately equal to a dozen Earth years. I wondered what I would find when I awoke...

✧

What I found was absolute madness. Two neighboring countries threatening each other with nuclear weapons; a third having announced that it, too, had developed such things; a fourth being scrutinized to see if it possessed them; and a fifth—the one that had come to the moon for all mankind—saying it would not rule out first strikes with its nuclear weapons.

No one was using controlled fusion. No one had returned to the moon.

Shortly after I awoke, tragedy struck again: seven humans were aboard an orbital vehicle called *Columbia*—a reused name, a name I'd heard before, the name of the command module that had orbited the moon while the first lander had come down to the surface. *Columbia* broke apart during reentry, scattering debris over a wide area of Earth. My dorsal spines fell flat, and my wing claws curled tightly. I hadn't been so sad since one of my own brood had died falling out of the sky.

Of course, my computer continued to monitor the broadcasts from the planet, and it provided me with digests of the human response.

I was appalled.

The humans were saying that putting people into space was too dangerous, that the cost in lives was too high, that there was nothing of value to be done in space that couldn't be done better by machines.

This from a race that had spread from its equatorial birthplace by walking—*walking!*—to cover most of their world; only recently had mechanical devices given them the ability to fly.

But now they *could* fly. They could soar. They could go to other worlds!

But there was no need, they said, for intelligent judgment out in space, no need to have thinking beings on hand to make decisions, to exalt, to experience directly.

They would continue to build nuclear weapons. But they wouldn't leave their nest. Perhaps because of their messy, wet mode of reproduction, they'd never developed the notion of the stupidity of keeping all one's eggs in a single container ...

✿

So, what should I have done? The easiest thing would have been to just fly away, heading back to our homeworld. Indeed, that's what the protocols said: do an evaluation, send in a report, depart.

Yes, that's what I should have done.

That's what a machine *would* have done. A robot probe would have just followed its programming.

But I am not a robot.

This was unprecedented.

It required judgment.

✿

I could have done it at any point when the side of the moon facing the planet was in darkness, but I decided to wait until the most dramatic possible moment. With a single sun, and being Earth's sole natural satellite, this world called *the* moon was frequently eclipsed. I decided to wait until the next such event was to occur—a trifling matter to calculate. I hoped that a disproportionately large number of them would be looking up at their moon during such an occurrence.

And so, as the shadow of Earth—the shadow of that crazy planet, with its frustrating people, beings timid when it came to exploration but endlessly belligerent toward each other—moved across the moon's landscape, I prepared. And once the computer told me that the whole of the side of the moon facing Earth was in darkness, I activated my starbird's laser beacons, flashing a ruby light that the humans couldn't possibly miss, on and off, over and over, through the entire period of totality.

They had to wait fourteen of Earth's days before the moon's face was naturally all in darkness again, but when it was, they flashed a replying beacon up at me. They'd clearly held off until the nearside's night in hopes that I would shine my lasers against the blackness in acknowledgment.

And I did—just that once, so there would be no doubt that I was really there. But although they tried flashing various patterns of laser light back at me—prime numbers, pictograms made of grids of dots—I refused to respond further.

There was no point in making it easy for them. If they wanted to talk further, they would have to come back up here.

Maybe they'd use the same name once again for their ship: *Columbia.*

I crawled back into my cryostasis nest, and told the computer to wake me when humans landed.

"That's not really prudent," said the computer. "You should also specify a date on which I should wake you regardless. After all, they may never come."

"They'll come," I said.

"Perhaps," said the computer. "Still..."

I lifted my wings, conceding the point. "Very well. Give them..." And then it came to me, the perfect figure... "until this decade is out."

After all, that's all it took the last time.

David Gerrold, this year's Worldcon Guest of Honor, is a Hugo and Nebula winner, a bestselling novelist, and a screenplay and teleplay writer. His Star Trek *episode, "The Trouble With Tribbles," was voted the most popular single episode of that series.*

A MILD CASE OF DEATH

by David Gerrold

Death—after the fact—feels just like a bell, like a great giant gong struck with a silver hammer. Bdooonnnggg!!

While I stood there wondering just what the hell had happened, a voice materialized beside me.

IT'S TIME TO GO, DAVE.

"Dave's not here, man—" I said it without thinking.

PLEASE DON'T MAKE TROUBLE, DAVE.

I turned to look at the intruder. "Who are you and what the hell—" The rest of the sentence died in my throat. Or what would have been my throat, if I had still had a throat. But yes, it died.

To tell the truth, I felt disappointed. I had expected, hoped that Death would appear as a tall sepulchral figure in a black hood and cloak, carrying a transparent scythe of mysterious power. If I squinted just right, I could sort of imagine Death as that kind of figure, but mostly he manifested as a polite blurry darkness.

IT'S TIME TO GO, DAVE.

"I already told you, Dave's not here."

The figure hesitated, appeared to check its PDA, or maybe a clipboard. I said it was blurry.

THE SCHEDULE SAYS DAVE. 11:37, SUNDAY EVENING.

"And I told you twice already, Dave's not here."

YOU'RE DAVE.

"No, I'm not."

YOU'RE HERE. IT IS 11:37, SUNDAY EVENING. 11:38 NOW.

"But I'm not Dave. Dave doesn't even live here. He was supposed to stop by earlier, but he never showed. He didn't call either. I don't know what happened to him. Tell you what, if he calls I'll tell him you're looking for him—"

THE SCHEDULE SAYS DAVE. 11:37, PACIFIC STANDARD TIME. AND HERE I AM AND HERE YOU ARE, SO YOU MUST BE DAVE.

"I'm not Dave."

ARE YOU SURE?

"I'm sure."

The figure hesitated. It's hard for a blur to look confused, but it did.

"What's the problem?"

YOU'RE TRYING TO FOOL ME, AREN'T YOU?

"No, I'm not. I'm not Dave. You made a mistake."

NO, I DIDN'T. YOU'RE DAVE.

"Listen, it's all right. Everybody makes mistakes—"

Death checked its clipboard again. I HAVE A SCHEDULE TO KEEP. I HAVE OTHER APPOINTMENTS. WHY DON'T YOU JUST PRETEND YOU'RE DAVE AND COME ALONG LIKE A NICE CHAP. THAT WILL SAVE US BOTH A LOT OF TROUBLE.

"No, I don't think so. That doesn't sound like a good idea to me."

BUT I'VE ALREADY COLLECTED YOU.

"You did *what?*"

LOOK DOWN.

"Eh? Is that me?"

NO. THAT'S YOUR BODY. YOU'RE RIGHT HERE. NOW IF YOU'LL JUST TELL THEM THAT YOU'RE DAVE, EVERYTHING WILL BE ALL RIGHT FOR BOTH OF US.

"No, wait a minute—! I know how Dave lived. He was a liar, a thief, a cheat, a fraud. He was a television producer, for god's sake. If I tell them I'm Dave, they'll send me to the bad place—"

IT'S NOT THAT BAD. IN FACT, IT CAN BE QUITE PLEASANT. EXCEPT FOR THE COMPANY, OF COURSE.

"You've been there?"

NO. BUT I'VE READ THE BROCHURES.

"It's full of lawyers, isn't it?"

NOT AS MANY AS MOST PEOPLE THINK. THEY DON'T LET LAWYERS IN, BECAUSE THEY BRING DOWN THE PROPERTY VALUES. BUT THERE ARE A LOT OF TELEMARKETERS, EVANGELISTS, USED CAR SALESMEN, AND BARRY MANILOW FANS.

"Barry Manilow?"

Death sighed. IT'S A LONG STORY.

"Like we don't have all eternity...? Look, can I ask you something?"

YES?

"Do you have to talk like that?"

LIKE HOW?

"Like that."

OH, THAT.

"Yes."

"Well, not really. But it's sort of expected, so—well, you know."

"That's better. Listen—you seem like a nice fellow, a hard worker, just trying to do the best job you can. I'm sure you call your mom regularly, floss your teeth every day, you don't jaywalk, right?"

"Well—"

"But you get my point. So, why don't you just put me back and let me get on with the rest of my life and I tell you what—if you'll give me your pager number, as soon as I can track down Dave, I'll beep you, okay?"

"I can't do that—"

"Sure you can—"

"No, I can't. I don't know how."

"You don't know how?"

"We don't do reinsertions. Once you're decanted, well—that's pretty much it."

"Decanted? Like you can't get toothpaste back in the tube, eh?"

"Actually, you can get toothpaste back in the tube. Would you like me to show you how it's done?"

"Toothpaste you can do. People, you can't."

"Yes, that's right."

I felt like I should sit down and sink my head into my hands and feel something. Anger? Outrage? Grief? Except I couldn't feel anything. Dead people don't have feelings. Great. Just great.

"Y'know, this is really crappy. All that exercise, all that healthy living, all those goddamn pills and herbs, look at me, I'm so goddamn healthy, vitamins take me. Look at what I missed. All those cheeseburgers and fries and Cokes, all the beer and pizza I never put away. All the booze and dope and fatty foods. This is not fair." I turned to the blur, realizing I towered over it, well maybe not *towered*, but I had at least a good two inches, maybe three. "Do you have a supervisor?"

"Yes, but it won't do you any good?"

"Why not?"

"He's on vacation."

"I'll wait. Right here."

"That's probably not a good idea."

"Why not?"

"Because, well—do you really think you'll want to be reinserted after two weeks?"

"This is a done deal, isn't it?"

"Pretty much."

"Somebody owes me, big time."

"You're very convincing, you know."

"Thank you."

"You even had me going there for a minute. Now, come along, Dave."

"I'm not Dave."

"Have it your way." The blur gathered itself together. IT'S TIME TO GO NOW. Then it added politely, DAVE.

"I'm not Dave."

DON'T BE DIFFICULT. YOU'RE DAVE NOW.

"I will too be difficult. I'll be any damn thing I want. I'm going to tell them I'm not Dave."

IT WON'T DO ANY GOOD.

"Why not?"

HUMANS SAY ANYTHING TO AVOID THE CONSEQUENCES OF THEIR ACTIONS. THEY WON'T BELIEVE YOU. IF I SAY THAT YOU'RE DAVE, YOU'RE DAVE.

"This isn't fair—!"

DEATH HAS NEVER BEEN FAIR.

"But I'm not Dave!"

THIS WAY, PLEASE. MIND THE STEP—

It was a long step. Down.

Down?

"Excuse me?"

WHAT?

"Down?"

YES, DOWN.

"This is really not right. I mean it. You got the wrong guy and now you're taking me to the wrong place."

THEY ALL SAY THAT.

"Would you please stop talking like *that?*"

IT'S PART OF THE JOB.

"Well, it's freaking me out, and I'm already freaked out enough."

EXIT THROUGH THE GIFT SHOP, PLEASE.

"The what—?"

Souvenirs

"Hello, welcome to the gift shop!"

The young man was as bright and smiley as a high school cheerleader, and every bit as cute—bubble-butt and all. He wore a crisp red and white uniform. The insignia was shaped like a Star Trek badge. His name badge identified him as Michael.

Great, just great.

"Where am I? Is this—?"

"This is the gift shop of course. There's always a gift shop at the end of the ride, so you can pick out souvenirs."

"Souvenirs—?"

"Of course!" he sparkled. "You don't want to leave life empty-handed. Take your time, look around. You'll find all kinds of wonderful mementos—"

"Mementos…?"

Michael gestured proudly, pointing with his whole hand. His posture, his smile, everything—he'd obviously been trained by Disney. "Over here, to your right, we have action figures. "And over here, to your left—" Another open-palm gesture. A wall of screens.

"Here we have a display of photos taken at all the most surprising moments in your life—here's where you pooped your pants in first grade, *that* was embarrassing, you look like you're going to cry, what a cutie you were. Oh, I like this—here's one of you learning how to masturbate, looks like you were having a lot of fun there, humping your pillow while watching the Mouseketeers. And here's that auto accident where you were almost killed, that was a close one, look at how scared you were, that's such a great expression! Oh, here's my favorite—your first time having sex with another person—oh my, he was handsome, wasn't he? Look at how amazed you were when he took off his underwear. Let me suggest that you order the whole collection, it comes in a beautiful red leather folder with your name engraved in gold, plus your birth and death dates,

no extra charge. Oh—and look, here's your death already—ooh, that's a much better expression than most people make. That's quite nice. You should have that one framed—"

"I, um—okay, this wasn't what I was expecting."

"Yes, I understand. You were on the ride a long time, longer than most—we're seeing that more and more these days, a lot of guests are staying on the ride for decades, sometimes as long as a century. Getting off so suddenly can be a little disorienting." He brightened. "Maybe you'd like to see the action figures—?"

He led me across the aisle, where the racks were filled with stacks and stacks of boxes, each with a different figure, each one appropriately dressed—each of them attached to a colorful cardboard backing, all of them posed and mounted behind form-fitted, stiff transparent plastic. "On this rack, most of these just have you typing, there's a lot of those—but over here, there's even more of you just sitting and staring out the window, I guess you were thinking, right?"

"So those are the *in*action figures….?"

Michael shook his head disapprovingly. "Oh no. We would never insult the guest. Those might have been your most interesting moments—that's when you did your best imagining—"

I was already moving to the next counter. "Hey? What are these—?" I held up a couple boxes. "I was never in the Navy. Not the army either. And what the hell is this? I was never a drag queen. I never did drag in my entire life—I would have looked like my mother."

Michael hurried over to explain, "Oh, those are your alternate lives—who you could have been, what you could have done. I'm afraid you were a disappointingly good person—okay, there's a little shoplifting when you were a kid, some tax evasion as an adult, but those hardly count. Some people, their alternate lives—they've been drunks, abusers, junkies, child molesters, thieves, televangelists, and a lot more murderers than you would believe—but that's a contextual possibility as much as a personality thing—"

Michael indicated the shelves with another of those professional gestures. "But you—the worst you'll find on the Bad Lives Shelf is lying to your parents, a little bit of early plagiarism—you covered that one well, I'll give you credit for that—and that time you went out driving drunk and stoned and whiplashed that old lady. Tsk tsk. But that's hardly very exciting, I mean, compared to some of the things you could have been—"

"So, all the bad things I've done are—?"

Michael waved it off. "Negligible in context. Compared to some people who've come through here—never mind, that would be tattling."

I looked around. "Is there a Good Lives Shelf? Are there better lives I could have had?"

Michael shook his head. "Well, yes and no—there are better lives you could have had, but you don't need to see them. Some people find them depressing. And in your case, oh my, yes. We don't want you breaking down and crying, collapsing in anguish, smashing things in rage—it disturbs the other guests."

"I'm not that kind of person."

"No, but you could be."

"Really? That's the first piece of good news I've gotten here—"

Michael said, "The whole point of the Alternate Lives Section—to show you some of the other possibilities of the ride. For the next time you do it."

"The next time?"

"Oh yes. Just go around to your right—"

"Uh, no. I don't think so. Not right now. Which way is the exit?"

Michael pointed to the left. "Right out there. Remember, the afterlife is the happiest place after life." He twinkled at me. "Would you like a pair of complimentary wings and a halo?"

"Not really."

"Well, some people expect it so, we make it an option—" He handed me a pair of sunglasses. "But do put these on. It can get pretty bright out there. It's full of stars."

After Life

Eventually, I found myself in a room.

Well, not a room. A space. Not very well defined. In fact, not defined at all. So I wasn't sure how I knew it was a *space*. But I knew.

There was a person here. Sitting behind a desk. There was nothing on the desk except a thin black vase with three white lilies sticking out of it. The person behind the desk was indeterminate, dressed in something that could have been white, or maybe gray, but wasn't quite enough of either.

"Please sit down. Be comfortable."

"Sit where?" I looked behind me. There was a chair there. Now. I sat. It was neither hard nor soft. Neither comfortable nor un-.

"Excuse me?" I said.

"Yes?"

"Is it necessary for this whole place to be so … so indeterminate?"

"Mm, yes. I see your point. Just a moment. Is this better?" The space was now identifiably a room. Bare blank walls. No door.

"Um, no. It isn't."

"Something wrong?"

"It's—it's very stark. Institutional. Not very comfortable."

"You think this place should be comfortable?"

"Is there any reason why it shouldn't be? And you did tell me to be comfortable."

"Point taken. How's this?"

I looked around. Now the space was defined by Grecian pillars that stretched infinitely upward. Long silky-white drapes wafted in a soft breeze. Beyond, summer-blue sky with soft cumulus pillows here and there. "Nice," I admitted. "A little bit of a cliché, very Warner Brothers, but—"

"I can change it, if you wish—"

"No, no thanks. This will do."

"You're sure."

"Quite."

"Can I get you something? Water? A soft drink? Iced tea?"

"No, I'm fine. Really."

"Good."

I waited. He waited. We waited. He still seemed indeterminate.

Finally, I asked, "Are you God?"

"I'm an aspect of the universe."

"You don't look like an aspect."

"Oh? How do you think an aspect should look?"

"I don't know. Like God, I guess."

"And what does God look like?"

I shrugged. "Like God. Unmistakeable."

"I see. Do you prefer the George Burns or the Morgan Freeman iteration? Or perhaps something more in the Charlton Heston or Michelangelo mold? Or maybe Hattie McDaniel?"

"Hattie McDaniel?"

"A very popular aspect."

"Um, no. I just—"

"How's this?" Gregory Peck. The Atticus Finch version. "Will this do?"

"Yes. That's fine."

Gregory Peck looked at me across the desk. "Is there anything else?"

"Is this where I get judged?"

"No."

"I get judged somewhere else?"

"No."

"Well, where *do* I get judged—?"

"Being judged is important to you?"

"No. Yes. I mean, I thought it was part of the deal."

"No, it isn't."

"No judgment at all?"

"No. Are you disappointed?"

"Well, sort of. I thought I did pretty good. Didn't I?"

"I don't know. Why don't you tell me—"

That stopped me for a moment. "I have to tell you?"

"It's a start."

"Oh, I see. This is all self-service. Like a cafeteria. I'm supposed to sort it out for myself, argue both sides of the case, all my good works versus all my sins, right? I get to undertake a self-examination of my entire life, however long as it takes, and then finally pronounce my own judgment. Right?"

"No," said Gregory Peck.

"No…?"

"No."

We waited some more. He waited while I sorted it out in my head. No judgment. But if there's no judgment, then what is this place? What am I doing here?

"Is this Heaven? Or Hell?"

"What do you want it to be?"

"Look, you're the aspect. You're the one who knows what's going on. Not me. So could we just get on with it?"

"We are getting on with it. This is it."

"This is it? *This* is it? This is *it?*"

"Yes."

"What about eternal reward? Eternal punishment? Judgment day? Heaven? Hell? God? St. Peter? Pearly Gates? Satan? Fiery pits of agonizing brimstone? Demons? Pitchforks? Are you telling me none of that is here? If it's not here, where is it?"

"Is that what you want?"

"No, I don't—"

"What is it you want?"

"I want an explanation. I think I deserve an explanation, don't you?"

"What I think is irrelevant. This is *your* space."

"Did I end up in some kind of purgatory? Limbo? Is that it? This is a waiting place, isn't it? How long do I have to wait? Ten thousand years? A million? That really doesn't seem fair. I only had seventy two years on Earth. Why should all of eternity be determined by a mere flick of time? I didn't even have enough time to—to live a whole life, to learn enough to—to be wise. I didn't have enough time to do all the things I planned to do."

"You had seventy two years, four months, three days, twenty two hours, fourteen minutes, thirty three seconds. Wasn't that enough?"

"No, it wasn't."

"It was a lot more than most people get. And you had your health."

"Fat lot of good that does me here."

We waited some more.

"So okay, fine. I get it. What happens next?"

"Nothing."

"Nothing?"

"That's right."

I inhaled. I exhaled. Mostly for effect. That was interesting. I could breathe here. I did it again. "Nothing," I repeated.

"That's right," said Gregory Peck. "Is there something you would like to have happen?"

"Can I ask you something?"

"Ask anything you want?"

"Will you answer honestly?"

"Of course."

"How long does this go on?"

"As long as you want."

"Where is God?"

"God is here."

"Here?"

"Yes."

"Where?"

"Here."

"Do I get to meet God?"

"If you wish."

"When?"

"Whenever you wish."

"How about now?" I said.

"All right."

Nothing happened.

I looked across at Gregory Peck. He did not seem antagonistic. In fact, he seemed very nice. He wasn't doing this deliberately.

"So, where is God?"

"God is here."

"Are you God?"

"I'm an aspect."

"Yeah. I got that part. So, let's see. There's no Heaven. There's no Hell. There's no Day of Judgment. There's no reward, no punishment."

"Do you want any of those things?"

"No, I don't." I got up from the chair, went to the edge of the room—the *space*—and stared out into the eternal blue. I scratched behind my ear.

"Is it this way for everybody?" I asked.

Behind me, the aspect answered. "No. It's this way for you."

"Hm." Well, that was useful. The afterlife was a personal experience. A puzzle that each person had to solve for himself. "So how much time do I have here?"

"As much as you want. We create it as we need it."

"Yes, of course. I should have known. Thank you."

"You're welcome. Are you sure I can't get you anything? Water? A soft drink? Iced tea?"

Something went click. Or *klunk*. Or whatever sound a small epiphany makes inside your head—if you have a head.

But I was starting to figure it out. I walked back to the chair and sat down at the desk. The aspect sat across from me. He waited patiently.

"You work for me, don't you?"

"Yes, I do."

"You didn't tell me that."

"You didn't want me to. You wanted to see how long it would take for you to figure it out for yourself."

"Well, this is embarrassing."

"Every time."

"Right." I scratched behind my ear again. An interesting sensation. I'd have to remember that one.

"I like playing jokes on myself, don't I?"

"Yes, sir, you do. Who else do you have to play jokes on?"

"Yes, there is that."

"That was a good one with the redhead, though. Nicely orchestrated."

"Yes and no. It didn't seem like fun from the inside."

"I guess not."

"I'll have a cappuccino, please."

"Right away—"

And there it was. Coffee was one of my better ideas. Almost as good as sex. I put the mug back down on the desk. "So," I said. "I guess I'm ready for the next life."

"Very good, sir. What would you like to try this time?"

"Well, I'm just brainstorming here, but how about this—"

Copyright ©2015 by David Gerrold

Jody Lynn Nye is the author of forty novels and more than one hundred stories, and has at various times collaborated with Anne McCaffrey and Robert Asprin. Her husband, Bill Fawcett, is a prolific author, editor, and packager, and is also active in the gaming field.

BOOK REVIEWS

by Bill Fawcett and Jody Lynn Nye

It is Hugo Awards time and the nominees are out. This gives us the opportunity to enjoy and review many of the nominees. There has been a good bit of controversy this year's nominees and the obsolescence of the nomination process, but that takes nothing away from the several well-written books that have been nominated.

✧

Skin Game
by Jim Butcher
Penguin/Roc, 2014
ISBN: 978-0451464392

A "skin game" is the name of a type of confidence trick where you use something agreed to in order to accomplish something else the other party would not accept. This Hugo-nominated and fifteenth *Dresden Files* novel involves just that, a game within a game with a twist. Harry Dresden is a professional wizard who lives on the near north of today's Chicago. Due to some rather extreme situations and compromises he has become the champion for Mab, a Faerie Queen and power player in magical politics. Failing to act faithfully to her when any reasonable

request is made has dire consequences, but Harry is tempted when he is loaned out to one of his worst enemies by Mab. He is needed to help steal the Holy Grail from the ancient treasure horde of the still-powerful deity Hades. But Harry is also expected to thwart the same theft even as he is honor bound to faithfully accomplish it. Complicating it all is the desire of most of the rest of his forced allies to make sure he does not survive the effort. The result, along with complications caused by old friends and older enemies, leads to a true page turner and great reading. Harry has to double and triple deal, endure his worst battering yet, come to some understanding of himself, and break into and out of the Chicago Mob boss's personal safe.

If you have not yet discovered the writing of Jim Butcher, or thought you would enjoy contemporary fantasy novels, the *Dresden Files* series is a must. It remains one of the best. If you have already read some of the series, this book is also a must read because it is not only a compelling story and mystery, but it resolves a number of questions and side plots from earlier novels. This is a "page turner" with the best of them and it will keep your interest from the first line. Yep, *Skin Game* really is that good, and that much fun to read, right down to a wonderfully contemporary manifestation of the Holy Sword.

✧

Ancillary Sword
Ann Leckie
Orbit, 2015
ISBN: 978-0316246651

This Hugo-nominated novel is the sequel to *Ancillary Justice*, which was widely nominated for awards.

Ancillary Sword takes us to the next stage in the career of Fleet Captain Breq Mianaai, who had spent the last several centuries as the living brain and commander of a heavily-armed troop carrier and two thousand robot-like Ancillaries. Ancillaries are human in form, but basically emotionless and fearless soldiers controlled by implants. In *Ancillary Justice* the fleet captain's involvement in a civil war, with multiple versions of a cloned leader battling for supremacy, meant he was returned to a human body. Now, still barely adjusted to his new form, he commands a new ship manned by normal humans and has to control a system and solve a murder and assassination attempts, and deal with other humans unaware of his background. Since it is rarely clear whose side someone is on, mostly because they all took an oath to the many bodied leader, now factions of that leader are battling with one another for control.

While the concept of merging man and machine goes back to Anne McCaffrey's Brainship stories, this is a far different and darker approach. *Ancillary Sword* will appeal to readers who like a story where most things and people are not as they appear. It is a highly internal novel, in which a highly structured and traditional culture comes apart around the point of view character, Breq Mianaai, who is struggling to understand his new role and self as well. This is not an action novel. It is a novel that makes you think and puts you inside a fascinating culture combining oriental traditions, high technology, clones, brain-controlling implants, and tea. Lots of tea.

The Goblin Emperor
by Katherine Addison
TOR, 2014
ISBN: 978-0765326997

This Hugo-nominated novel may be the most fascinating and exciting coming of age story this reviewer has read since I discovered Robert Heinlein in the 1950s. Not only that, but is stands out also as very well written. It is the story of a young man torn from forced isolation and thrust into the role of emperor of a tempestuous land where noble families vie for control. Not only is he unprepared, but he also is of mixed race… elf and goblin. The fantasy setting supports the story and mixes well with dirigibles and steam engines without intruding on the narrative. His father, the former emperor, has been murdered and with him his two elven sons. The result of a loveless and somewhat embarrassing political marriage, upon the death of his mother Maia was banished at a young age to a small lodge in the most distant reaches of the Empire. But with the death of his family, the empire needs continuity, and the eighteen-year-old boy is rushed back to the capital and plunged into the intrigues and politics of the court. His adjustment is complicated by the likelihood his family was assassinated and the man investigating it may be their murderer. He knows that it is likely that he is next, and just to complicate it all further, he must rush into a marriage to ensure there is an heir.

There are no armies sweeping or dragons plunging with fiery breath. The magic is integral, but does not dominate the plot. This is not a high fantasy. *The Goblin Emperor* is a really good story full of characters with motives, and failings that bring them alive. A book where it is easy to empathize with the characters. The writing itself is excellent, the plot keeps you reading (me until 2 am), and the unexpected twists work. The story, the characters and the skill with which this is written combine to make *The Goblin Emperor* a great read for teens and adults. Katherine Addison also writes as Sarah Monette.

✿

The Grace of Kings
by Ken Liu
Saga Press, 2015
ISBN: 978-1481424271

We had a bit of a friendly rivalry going this month. "My epic's longer than YOUR epic," each of us said to the other. "No, mine is!" "No, mine!" (Bill's won by 70 pages.)

The truth is, we each like a great big chunk of book. When one is worth reading, we don't want it to end. For this month's issue, we each had a massive tome. Mine was *The Grace of Kings*, by Ken Liu. Mr. Liu was not nominated for a Hugo this year, though he was the translator of one of the nominees (*The Three-Body Problem*, by Cixin Liu). The more of it I read, the more I wanted to read. This grand saga, beautifully drawn, with layer upon layer of intrigue, comes from a writer celebrated for his short stories. Finally, Liu has the page count to indulge in lush description of his setting and the complex histories of his characters. Six provinces of Tiro, all previously autonomous and equal, were conquered by the king of the seventh, who set himself up as emperor. Such a situation proves to be against not only the will of the people, but of the gods who protect the islands. As the empire collapses, heroes arise to re-

build the conquered nations. I conceived great affection for the charming rogue who fell so in love with the brilliant and well-born herbalist that he had to make something of himself in order to win her, and continued to rise to greatness. The reader will come to care deeply about these wonderful, complex, and interesting personalities whose lives become tied together. Gods, magic, steampunk technology, and a Seven Kingdoms cast all intertwine in a plot made complex by the machinations of human nature.

✿

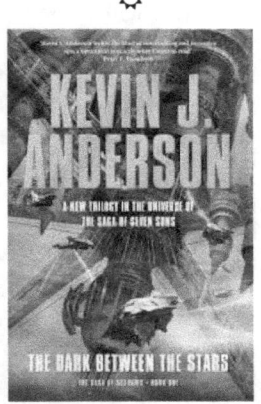

The Dark Between the Stars
by Kevin Anderson
TOR Books, 2014
ISBN: 978-0765332998

This novel is the first of a trilogy. The *Dark Between the Stars* is set in the same universe as the best-selling *Saga of the Seven Suns*. This Hugo nominee is a sweeping novel showing from almost a dozen points of view at the beginning of humanity's new and even more desperate struggle for survival. This time the enemy is the Shana Rei. These are lightless and appropriately formless creatures from another dimension that thrive on entropy and find all existence, and particularly intelligence because they create order, literally painful. They are the dark between the stars. These entities had attacked the spiral arm thousands of years ago, wreaking havoc so great that even after being driven away, the race that fought them off is still congenitally afraid of the dark. Allied with the Shana Rei against all life are the last of the desperate few remaining killer robots, defeated in the *Seven Suns*. The threat grows throughout the book, culminating with a desperate space battle to protect the worldforest that allows FTL communications. The characters are well painted and emotionally deep. The worlds vary from alien Imperial courts, schools of academics trying to recover a lost history after millennium, to the habitats and ships of the Gypsy like Roamers. Other complications add to the suspense, including a plague, politics, and love. This is a true space epic by every definition. It is full of action, personal conflict, unexpected turns, and fleets of warships. A long book, it keeps you reading and never disappoints. This is Kevin J. Anderson's first Hugo-nominated novel.

☼

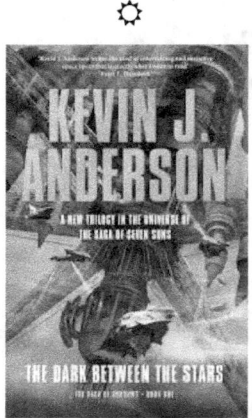

Running From the Night
(Hunter's Moon #1)
by R.J. Terrell,
WordFire Press, 2015
ISBN: 978-1614753094

Not a Hugo nominee, but an interesting read nonetheless.

With the enormous quantity of vampire books out there, it's difficult to find a way to introduce hemophagic humanoids without falling into the familiar and trite. R.J. Terrell manages to walk this tightrope well. In the first of his Hunter's Moon series, he plunges his characters into the action and drives them through the landscape around Vancouver, B.C. from terror to terror until the reader is breathless, trying to see any way for Jelani and his friends to survive another day. His vampires are dangerous, relentless, and pitiless, subject to an ironclad hierarchy. Terrell still finds time to present well-rounded, diverse, and engaging characters with jobs, hobbies, and love lives, the latter sometimes as complicated

and inescapable as the vampires on their trail. A good read, although *Running From the Night* doesn't stand alone. The action only pauses at the conclusion of this volume, but doesn't resolve. I'm looking forward to reading more.

Copyright © 2015 by Bill Fawcett and Jody Lynn Nye

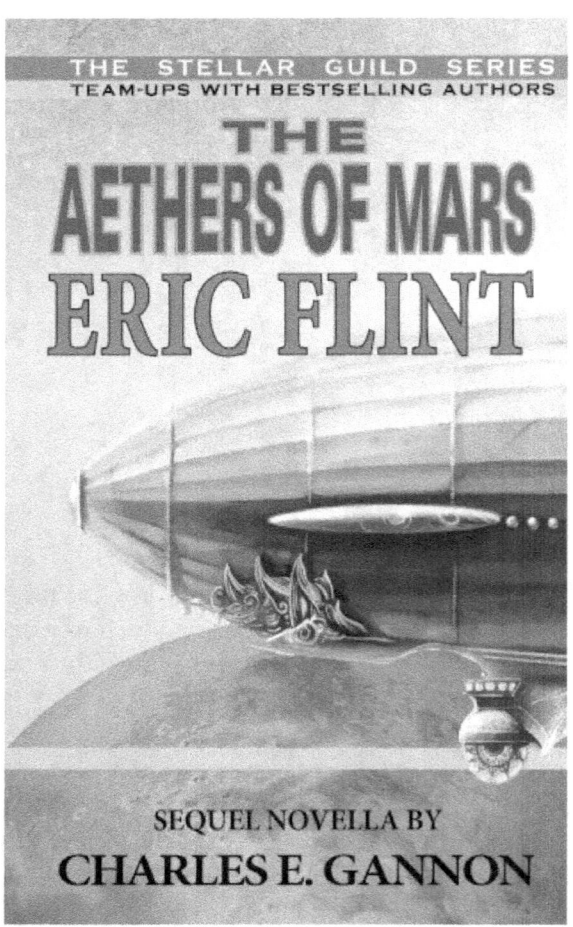

Welcome to Mars…circa 1900. Cecil Rhodes rules Mars and is on his way to transforming the British Empire into his vision of a powerful force, managed by the "right" type of people.

But what of Savinkov…presumably on board the British aethership Agincourt, travelling from Earth to Mars? Savinkov is a legendary revolutionary and assassin and, with Russian secret agents hot on his heels, is reputedly planning something truly dramatic and Mars-shattering.

Views expressed by guest or resident columnists are entirely their own.

Gregory Benford is a Nebula winner and a former Worldcon Guest of Honor. He is the author of more than thirty novels, six books of non-fiction, and has edited ten anthologies.

LAST THINGS: COLD COMFORT IN THE FAR FUTURE

by Gregory Benford

…the use, however haltingly, of our imaginations upon the possibilities of the future is a valuable spiritual exercise.

J.B.S. Haldane, 1923

How did it all begin?

This is a very old obsession. Less often fretted over is the symmetric question: How will it all end?

Robert Frost's famous imagery—fire or ice, take your pick—pretty much sums it up. But lately, largely unnoticed, a revolution has unwound in the thinking about such matters, in the hands of that most rarefied of tribes, the theoretical physicists. Maybe, just maybe, ice isn't going to be the whole story.

Of course, linking the human prospect to cosmology itself is not at all new. The endings of stories are important, because we believe that how things turn out implies what they ultimately mean. This comes from being pointed toward the future, as any ambitious species must be.

There are three forms of chimpanzees: the common chimp, the bonobo, and us. We are the only chimp who got out of Africa. That experience reflects and probably laid down the deep human urge—indeed, our signature: the urge to restlessly move on, explore, exploit. Natural selection gives us a gut imperative that plays out physically and culturally, in pursuit of our goal: the expansion of human horizons.

On Earth, horizons worked for many millennia. But that time is over, the skies beckon—and it is natural to think in terms of our horizons in time. We have cosmology to aid us now, unlike people only a century ago. Most of us believe that physics can tell us more about our prospects than religion. Still, we do think long, and often with theological implications. The far future matters for very basic reasons.

Our yearning for connection explains many cultures' ancestor worship: we enter into a sense of progression, expecting to be included eventually in the company. Deep within us lies a need for continuity of the human enterprise, perhaps to offset our own mortality. Deep time in its panoramas, both past and future, redeems this lack of meaning, rendering the human prospect again large and portentous.

We gain stature alongside such enormities. But this flattering perspective sets an ultimate question: will a time come when humanity itself will not be remembered, our works lost and gone for nothing?

Of course, SF has always looked long, from Wells' dying crab on a red beach, and onward. Freeman Dyson suggested that spheres around stars could be technology's distant goal, and inspired many SF novels—but such ideas only worked as long as stars burned, which means about 100 billion years. One could look longer, and some did. In this spirit I edited *Far Futures* in 1995, looking at the long view. Two of the five novella authors therein have died—Poul Anderson and Charles Sheffield; alas, mortality vs. the abyss. There are myriad other literary examples of writers and scientists confronting a truly ultimate question—of Last Things.

The Final Dark

A major change in our ideas of cosmology occurred only fifteen years ago, with the discovery that the expansion of our universe is *accelerating*. To reach such an astonishing conclusion demanded new measurements of supernova brightness in far-away galaxies, meanwhile eliminating many possible sources of error, combined with precise calibrations of their distances. Together, these showed that the further away, the faster others were fleeing from us, and us from them, as we share a quickening expansion.

This acceleration overthrows half a century of conventional wisdom. For eighty years, even since Einstein began modern cosmology, we thought that deceleration held sway. Gravitation would slow the swelling that began with the Big Bang. Around

1950 it even seemed that the universe might cease expanding and implode into a final crunch, and that perhaps this had happened before.

This finding, that space-time is opening ever-faster, relies upon a fairly tricky measurements. It is not easy to study whether the momentary luminosities of supernovas in very distant galaxies, fit a pattern. It remains to be extensively checked, but for the moment suppose we take it as given.

Ancient Ideas

Acceleration implies an ever-bigger cosmos. Some feel repulsed by the entire notion. Cyclic universes have great appeal, as every public lecturer on cosmology knows from the audience questions. Evolution may have geared us to expect cycles; the seasons deeply embedded this in our ancestors. The ancient Hindu system embraces it especially, holding that we are already uncountably far into the oscillations, and the universe is unknowably old.

Love of cyclic universes may come from a deep unease with linear time, one that predates our modern ideas. At least the periodic supplies some rhythm, a pattern, rolling hills rather than just a flat plain stretching to infinity.

This feeling finds an echo in other common audience questions. *Doesn't all this have a purpose, an end? Does the drama go on forever, really?*

But then, genuinely endless repetition also seems to revolt most of the cyclic devotees—they still want to avoid the abyss of infinite time. The Hindu time scale is immeasurably long but not infinite.

Aristotle was an exception. He thought there had been an infinite number of generations, since there had been no beginning. He believed that despite some ups and downs, by and large things stayed on average the same, throughout all time. There were no changes of species or in nature's overall arrangement, or of the basic options in life. So even though the universe is eternal, it stays familiar. Aristotle felt that this made studying nature have a point. Nature provides regularities and we can know them, so science is at least possible.

Aristotle was a man of the West. Not all faiths or philosophies worry about time. Confucian and Taoist beliefs do not comment or care about how the universe began or will end. Chinese thought does spend a lot of energy on history and on the memory of the great ages in the past. There is a much concern with social beginnings and endings, golden ages and collapses. But even very long stories have a beginning and end.

For these faiths there is no far-off divine come-uppance, "to which the whole Creation moves," as Tennyson put it. As the *Bhagavad Gita* says, "There never was a time when I was not…there will never be a time when I will cease to be." Since time and space together began creation (as both St. Augustine and the Big Bang attest) the Bhagavad Gita has a point. The chicken and the egg arrived at the same time.

The Abrahamic faiths "of the book"—Jews, Christians and Islamites alike, envision linear, not cyclic time. This reflects a big conceptual shift from the unchanging atmosphere of the far ancient world, when little changed. Indeed, modern science needs the possibility of change, because Newtonian forces do not have to return everything to the status quo.

Christian scripture says that this is a suffering world, addicted to attachment, to be ultimately transcended. The far future then lies beyond that goal. God's agenda is then rigorous—creation, fall, incarnation, redemption, final judgment, then the ultimate fate, Last Things. But how far can this sequence go? Forever?

Newton founded his mechanics on the linear flow of time, inventing his "theory of fluxions" (differential calculus). But his cosmology is static, eternal, shadowed by the ever-threatening catastrophe of gravitational collapse. Given enough time, this fate would come through stars colliding and coalescing. This fate prefigures the black hole disaster, when mass colludes to escape our space-time entirely by collapsing to a singular point.

This, Newton thought, could be avoided by occasional divine intervention, as needed—a fix-up universe.

As for the beginning, Christian theists seem most comfortable with the Big Bang, since it says Creation is a fact. St. Augustine's doctrine that God made both space and time *ex nihilo* was never supposed to carry great weight as the crucial moment in all time; it was just a beginning, not the whole point of the matter.

When Aristotelian science became widely known, the medievals thought of that first moment as the establishment of the Aristotelian average sameness, as far as nature was concerned. There might be a social linear narrative, but no natural one.

Aristotle does have an argument that time cannot have a beginning or an end. Changes happen for Aristotle when the appropriate items are in the right situation—the pot on the fire, the seed in the ground, and so on. If a purported first change happens, suddenly, in a universe that was previously unchanging, then there had to have been a still earlier change that brought the items for the supposed first change together. Otherwise it would already have happened. But that new first change is subject to the same argument, so there cannot be a true first change. An analogous argument shows that any supposed last change must be followed by a further change, that then disposes things so that they won't be in a position to change further. But that change needs a later shoring up, etc.

It's a good argument. But Aquinas then claimed that it doesn't consider creation, which is not strictly speaking a change, just a beginning, a coming into being of the whole. This allows for a Creation finite in time.

But little rigor got invested in the eventual *fate* of our universe. That became the domain of modern science. Many are horrified by a universe that lasts only a finite time, ending in cold or heat. Even placing the event in the very far future, long after our personal deaths, carries the heavy freight of making what we do now meaningless, because it does not last. Recall the scene in *Annie Hall* when young Woody Allen refuses to do his homework because the universe is going to end anyway.

Will Shakespeare endure literally forever? As Bertrand Russell put it in *Why I am Not a Christian,* All the labours of the ages, all the devotion, all the inspiration, all the noonday brightness of human genius are destined to extinction in the vast heat death of the solar system, and…the whole temple of man's achievement must inevitably be buried beneath the debris of a universe in ruins.

So Russell doesn't believe in God because nothing lasts. At first this seems an odd argument, but it goes to our deep questions. If nothing lasts, what is our purpose?

Some fervent believers attack the second law of thermodynamics (the heat death) for exactly this reason. Ironically, these Christians join company with atheist Friedrich Engels, who disliked entropy because it would destroy historical progress in the long run.

Suppose we could create a heaven on Earth, or at least somewhere. Permanent, unchanging paradise seems boring to many, at least if it means mere joyful indolence. Is perpetual novelty even possible, though? Can we think an infinite variety of thoughts?

Christian theology solved this dilemma by putting God outside time, so that holy eternity was not infinite duration but rather not time at all. This belief is long-standing, but it need not stay in fashion forever. Faiths may arise which long for the heat death, or embrace the (apparently not coming) big crunch—cosmological cheerleaders for cleansing ends.

Theology has responded to cosmology, but the pace of discussion is now quickening so much that the connections between the two need fresh thought. Luckily, this is now coming mostly from the cosmologists themselves.

✿

In 1979 the celebrated Princeton physicist Freeman Dyson brought this entire issue to center stage for physicists and astronomers. He already had his prejudices: he wouldn't countenance the Big Crunch option because it gave him "a feeling of claustrophobia". Still, must all our revelries end? Science, he thought, might be able to settle whether a Last Day is ever going to arrive.

He knew of the threads in theological thinking. When I discussed these matters with him in the 1970s, he knew that theology faced a paradox. We seem to harbor twin desires—purpose and novelty, progress and eternity alike.

When physicists ask questions, they do a calculation to clarify matters. Dyson discussed the prognosis for intelligent life. Even after stars have died, he asked, can life survive forever without intellectual burn-out?

The BEST OF GALAXY'S EDGE
2013-2014

Larry Niven
C. L. Moore
Nick DiChario
Robert T. Jeschonek
Tina Gower
Mercedes Lackey
Ralph Roberts
Ken Liu
Marina J. Lostetter
Andrea G. Stewart
Eric Cline
Tom Gerencer
Nancy Kress
Sabina Theo
Gio Clairval
Steve Cameron
Brad R. Torgersen
Eric Leif Davin
Kary English
Lou J. Berger
Brian Trent
K. C. Norton
Leena Likitalo
James Aquilone

*Edited by
Mike Resnick*

ROBERT A. HEINLEIN

PODKAYNE

of

MARS

Energy reserves will be finite, and at first sight this might seem to be a basic restriction. But he showed that this constraint was actually not fatal. He looked beyond times when any stars would have tunneled into black holes, which would then evaporate in a time that will be, in comparison, almost instantaneous. As J.D. Bernal foresaw in *The World, the Flesh, and the Devil* (1929):

…consciousness itself may end…becoming masses of atoms in space communicating by radiation, and ultimately resolving itself entirely into light…these beings…each utilizing the bare minimum of energy… spreading themselves over immense areas and periods of time…the scene of life would be…the cold emptiness of space.

Dyson's answer was positive. He thought that by hibernating, life could endure eternally. But in the decades since Dyson's article appeared, our perspective has changed in two ways, and both make the outlook more dismal.

First, most physicists now strongly suspect that atoms don't live forever. The basic building block, the proton, will decay into lesser particles. White dwarfs and neutron stars will erode away in about 10^{36} years, sputtering into wan energies and small sprays of electrons and positrons. The heat generated by particle decay will make each star glow, but only as dimly as a domestic heater—no real help against the pervasive cold.

Dyson originally assumed matter would last for eternity. Though the proton lifetime remains unmeasured, current particle theory predicts protons should decay in about 10^{34} years.

Our universe is about 15 billion years old, or a little over 10^{10} years. In principle, everybody agrees that despite the steady cooling, order could persist even up to 10^{34} years. Here we speak of *unimaginably* long times—except that science fiction writers, and now physicists, have imagined them, guided by the gliding calculus of theoretical physics. But writing down numbers is a dry way of gaining what we really mean by imagining, i.e., having a gut feeling. Still, calculation is all we have to go on.

After protons fade away, say 10^{34} years, our Local Group of galaxies will be just a swarm of dark matter, electrons and positrons. Thoughts and memories could survive beyond the first 10^{36} years, if downloaded into complicated circuits and magnetic fields in clouds of electrons and positrons— maybe something that would resemble the threatening alien intelligence in *The Black Cloud*, the first and most imaginative of astronomer Fred Hoyle's novels, written in the 1950s.

"An austere mode of existence," Dyson felt. And with classic understatement, "…even if this assumption is wrong, it is certainly good for the next 10^{34} years, long enough for life to study the situation carefully."

The second bit of bad news is that the accelerating expansion means the universe cools even faster. There is less time to avert the cold, and less room, too.

Why less? Characteristically, Dyson was optimistic about the potentiality of an expanding universe because there seemed to be no limit to the scale of artifacts that could eventually be built. He envisioned the observable universe getting ever vaster. Many galaxies, whose light hasn't yet had time to reach us, would eventually come into view, and therefore within range of possible communication and "networking." Interactions will matter. We could gain knowledge from distant brethren, for use against the encroaching night.

But an accelerating expansion yields a more constricted long-term future. Galaxies will fade from view ever faster as they get more and more redshifted—their clocks, as viewed by us, will seem to run slower and slower. Then they will seem to freeze at a definite instant, so that even though they never finally disappear we would see only a finite stretch of their future.

This is analogous to what happens if a cosmologist falls into a black hole: from a vantage point safely outside the hole, we would see our infalling colleague freeze at a particular time. We'll have only a last snapshot, even though they experience, beyond the horizon, a future that is unobservable to us.

Well before 10^{34} years, our own Galaxy, its identical twin neighbor Andromeda, and the few dozen small satellite galaxies that are in the gravitational grip of one or other of them, will merge together into a single amorphous system of ageing stars and dark matter. Then the universe will look ever more like an 'island system' (the kind of universe originally proposed by Laplace). In an accelerating universe, everything else disappears beyond our horizon. If the acceleration is fixed, this horizon never gets much further away than it is today.

So there's a firm limit—though of course a colossally large one—to how large any network or artifact can ever become. This translates into a definite limit on how complex anything can get.

Still worse, one important recent development has been to quantify this limit. Space and time cannot be infinitely divided.

The inherent quantum 'graininess' of space sets a limit to the intricacy that can be woven into a universe of fixed size. Life has to work within boundaries.

Even if the problem of limited energy reserves could be surmounted—a big order in itself, and the main issue Dyson addressed—there would be a limit to variety and complexity. The best hope of staving off boredom in such a universe would be to construct a time machine and, subjectively at least, exhaust all potentialities by repeatedly traversing a closed time-loop. This appears to be possible, within general relativity, but Dyson and others found it also claustrophobic.

There is other theoretical hope, too, though it is a bit abstract. Kurt Godel's famous theorem showed that mathematics contains inexhaustible novelty, i.e., true theorems that can't be proved with what has come before. Only by expanding the conceptual system can they be shown to be true, in a larger view.

Most people would not turn to mathematics for a message of spiritual hope, but there it is.

☼

As this darkened universe expands and cools, lower-energy quanta (or, equivalently, radiation at longer and longer wavelengths) can store or transmit information. Just as an infinite series can have a finite sum (for instance, $1 + 1/2 + 1/4 + \ldots\ldots = 2$), there is perhaps, in principle, no limit to the amount of information processing that could be achieved with a finite expenditure of energy. Any conceivable form of life would have to keep ever-cooler, think slowly, and hibernate for ever-longer periods.

But there would be time to think every thought, Dyson believed, even in the face of the heat death. As Woody Allen once said, "Eternity is very long, especially toward the end."

Life that keeps its temperature fixed will not make it, though. It will eventually exhaust its energy store. The secret of survival will be to cool down as the universe cools. Being frugal means you could dole out in ever-smaller amounts the energy necessary to live and think.

Silicon or even dust could form the physical basis of such enduring life, at least until the protons decay. After that, there is no fundamental reason that information cannot be lodged in electron-positron plasmas, or even atoms made from them. "Positronium" is an "atom" of a positron, an anti-electron, orbiting with an electron, much like a hydrogen atom. In September 2002 a European group succeeded in producing tens of thousands of them in a magnetic bottle, so they could conceivably be used to build solid structures of a wholly new sort.

No matter what the basis of life is, the crucial distinction for far-future thinkers is their method of storing information. In our computer-saturated world, using information defines life—active flow, not mere passive storage.

Life tends to be defined in terms of the reigning paradigm of the time, so in our computer age we make a crucial distinction. There are two choices: analog or digital.

Old fashioned LPs are analog; CDs are digital. Cosmologist Fred Hoyle's ominous Black Cloud, imagined in a novel in the 1950s, was analog, storing its memories in magnetic fields and dust particles. A human mind uploaded into a computer would be digital life.

Are our brains analog or digital? We do not know, as yet. But this point became the battleground between Dyson and a bevy of physicists, including Larry Krauss of Case Western University. In *The Physics of Star Trek* Krauss tried to make sense of the mangled science in Trek. Many of his colleagues suspected his motives were less that of informing the masses than making money, and his challenge to Dyson had the quality of a young buck butting heads with an aging bull. The debate got rarefied right away, including lengthy calculations on the thermodynamics of ultra cold, with quantum mechanics for dessert.

Our genetic information carried in DNA is clearly digital, coded in a four-letter alphabet. But the active information in our brains remains mysterious. Memories live in the strengths of synaptic connections between billions of neurons, but we do not fathom how these strengths are laid down or varied. Perhaps memory is partly digital and partly analog; there is no reason the methods cannot blend.

If we are partly analog, then perhaps the hope of the brain-downloading method will be only partly fulfilled, and some of our more fine-grade thoughts and feelings will not make it into a digital representation.

Actually, the analog/digital divide may not be the whole story. Some theorists think the brain may be a quantum computer, keeping information in quantized states of atoms. But since we know little about quantum computers beyond their mere possibility, the argument over in-principle methods has fastened upon analog vs. digital.

Interestingly, the long term prospects of digital intelligences are not the same as analog forms. Krauss leaned heavily on a digital determinism, which shaded quickly into pessimism. Dyson stood his analog ground.

That there is any contest at all may surprise some, since we are so used to analog tools like slide rules giving way to digital ones like hand calculators. The essential difference is that analog methods deal with continuous variables while digital ones use discrete counting.

Surprisingly, analog wins, digital loses. It turns out that the laws of physics allow a thrifty, energy-hoarding information machine (life) to persist, but not a digital one.

The reasons are fairly arcane, involving the quantum theory of information storage. Still, one can think of a digital system as having rachets that, once kicked forward, cannot go back. As the universe cools, you eventually can't kick the rachet far enough forward. But a smooth system can inch up as much as you like, storing memories in smaller and smaller increments of energy.

Life can use hibernation to extend its analog form indefinitely. Like bears, it can adapt to falling temperatures by sleeping for progressively longer cosmic naps. Awake, it spends its energy reserves at unsustainable levels. Asleep, it accumulates.

It turns out further that such life can communicate with other minds over the great distances between galaxies, too. Energy reserves can dwindle, but so does the noise background in the universe, as expansion cools the night sky.

Communication depends not on signal strength (energy) but on the ratio of signal to noise. A cold, expanding universe is friendly to the growth of intergalactic networks. Life will have ample time to wait for an answer from, say, the Andromeda galaxy, without worrying about being able to hear the reply.

But not all is well for analog life if the universe continues to accelerate forever. At some distance, the repulsive force that causes this acceleration must win out over gravity's attraction. So galaxies further away than this critical distance will accelerate beyond view, setting the limit on the size of structures that life can build. This ultimately dooms it.

So to persist forever, life needs to be analog and the universe must not be accelerating forever. The first is an engineering requirement, and presumably savvy life forms will heed it. The second we can do nothing about, unless somehow life can alter the very cosmological nature of our universe—surely a tall order.

We do not yet know (and may not for quite a while) whether the acceleration will slow, because we do not know its cause. This is the biggest riddle in cosmology, and many are pursuing it. The Dyson-Krauss dispute rages still in the hallowed pages of *Physical Review*. Dyson's own vaguely optimistic theology clashes with Krauss's apparent atheism. They are reprising an ancient difference in tastes over the deepest issue: is there any discernible purpose to the universe? And does human action mean anything on this vast stage?

✧

These long-range projections over zillions of years involve fascinating physics, most of which is quite well understood...but not all of it.

First, we can't be absolutely sure that the regions beyond our present horizon are like the parts of the universe we see. Just as on the ocean, there could be something amazing just over the horizon.

Physicists John Barrow and Frank Tipler have pointed out that a new source of energy—so called 'shear-energy'—would become available if the universe expanded at different rates in different directions. This shearing of space-time itself could power the diaphanous electron-positron plasmas forever, if the imbalance in directions persists. To harness it, life (whatever its form) would have to build "engines" that worked on the expansion of the universe itself.

Such ideas imply huge structures the size of galaxies, yet thin and able to stretch, as the space-time they are immersed in swells faster along one axis than another. This motor would work like a set of elastic bands that stretch and release, as the universal expansion proceeds. Only very ambitious life that has mastered immense scales could thrive. They would seem like Gods to us.

As well, our universe could eventually be crushed by denser material not yet in view. Or the smoothing out of mass on large scales may not continue indefinitely. There could be a new range of structures, on scales far larger than the part of the universe that we have so far seen.

Physics can tell us nothing of these, as yet. These ideas will probably loom larger as we learn more about the destiny of all visible Creation.

Or... Even more fundamentally, maybe time itself is a hominid illusion, not fundamental at all. It might rather be an emergent property of some deeper structure to be revealed. Our human temporal anxiety would then be a passing fashion, not a feature of the universal destiny. This idea may be more sobering than even the cold comfort awaiting us 'way up ahead.

Finally, what can one infer from physics about theology?

It is tempting to suppose that a God who made such a universe might, as narrative-addicted humans do, think that the end of a story tells its meaning. If all order is to be leached away by eternal cold, what did the building of such structure by intelligence amount to? Put differently, what is the meaning of human action?

Perhaps nothing, if the fate of all order is mere ruin. If it is not, and Dyson proves right, we might turn to another Dyson idea: that the universe has been designed to be the most interesting possible. This means that variations arise and abound, then evolve and finally aspire to greater heights.

So in the end our choice of endings implies a choice of the Designer behind it all.

One wonders if, once the theoretical physics is settled, the outcome will provoke fresh theological thinking. If intelligence can persist forever in principle, will this result be used in a new form of the Argument from Design?

Conversely, if life cannot survive, will atheists make this into an argument for no God, or for a God with a perverse (to us) purpose?

Either way, the debate will be made more interesting by the injection of a new set of physical facts. Science fiction's role is to explore the human implications. Hot topics like the possibility of other dimensions in which different universes dwell ("branes" for membranes; not a great scientific shorthand) will be experimentally checkable within perhaps five to ten years.

Such exotic notions will provoke much fiction—already has, in my *Beyond Infinity*. The accelerating expansion might itself accelerate, leading to the "big rip" which shreds atoms, erasing all information—truly a horrifying prospect, if you think Shakespeare's works should live forever. Surely this is a grand, Wagnerian struggle worthy of life in the far future.

So I end by quoting James Gunn: "Fiction, I think, is humanity's way of seeking justice in an uncaring universe."

Copyright © 2015 by Gregory Benford

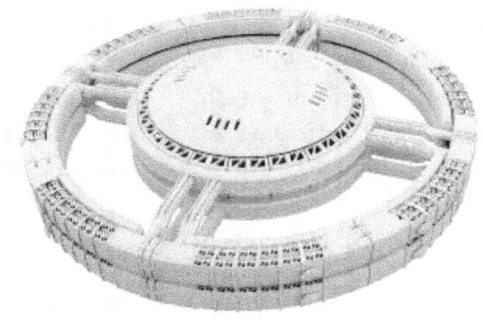

Views expressed by guest or resident columnists are entirely their own.

FROM THE HEART'S BASEMENT

by Barry N. Malzberg

Barry N. Malzberg won the very first Campbell Memorial Award, and is a multiple Hugo and Nebula nominee. He is the author or co-author of more than 90 books.

Yet More People, Places, and Things Which Will Not Appear in a Future Column

F. Scott Fitzgerald, 1896-1940

"If a great Hollywood novel ever were to exist," he wrote his daughter in the last year of his life, "it would have to deal with technique, with process, with the actual mechanics of making movies. The problem with all Hollywood novels to date were that they did not come from inside the industry, nor did they show command of these matters. They were manufactured gossip; they were at best slightly heightened examples of fan publications. The real novel of Hollywood would have a command of the dialectic of film and it would also deal by inference with the effects of movie-making upon its creators."

The Last Tycoon, which exists as little more than disconnected chapters and some detailed notes, was an attempt at that novel. There is no question that the dying Fitzgerald was on his way to a serious attempt, but not enough of it exists to make judgment possible. Monroe Starr, his dying protagonist (allegedly based on the dying Irving Thalberg) had a novelist's self-pity and angst rather than a producer's insistence. This might have been part of the problem—but another is that he loved Celia, the young woman who tried to touch Monroe Starr more than he could justify. That she gets in the way was only an obstruction on the road toward his soul.

Fitzgerald felt about Hollywood the way that Jonathan Herovit felt about science fiction, and in neither case could much good come of it.

Daniel Fuchs, 1909-1995

Fuchs might have come closest, because of all those who attempted the Hollywood novel; he had the greatest clarity and the ability to apply it. Hollywood ran and worked and hustled and dreamed and shed its light in the kingdom of fear, Fuchs understood. It was a fear beyond the simple insecurity to which the colony had always been willing to admit. (Dorothy Parker and "the Garden of Allah".)

Just as Marilyn's terror was evident from her earliest public presentation (as I have noted in the eleventh column of this series), just as that terror was the engine of her talent, her despair, her frail, whispering, penetrating little voice, so terror permeated the lives and deaths and everything in between for the Hollywood apparatus. In his novel *West of the Rockies*, published in 1989, Fuchs almost got it all: the famous, multiply-married actress in early career decline and on the run from everything, wrecking the big production in progress, her occasional lover, the hapless publicist assigned to keep her somehow functioning in an expensive film which documented her unraveling and her piteous terror. The publicist once enchanted and now entrapped no longer loves her but knows that he has been targeted as her salvation. The actress trying to bolt to the continent is holding desperately to memory and desire, the distant studio executives want to fire the actress and cast the publicist from a balcony, but they are wholly entrapped and can do neither.

Most of this short novel occurs at parties reminiscent of the famous Party at Jack's which centers Thomas Wolfe's *You Can't Go Home Again*; at these parties into which the actress and publicist separately flit and greet and clutch and depart, all of the guests know every horrid truth about one another and collaborate in their lies the way that film, the most distant and immediate of all mediums, collaborates from scene to scene with the lie of consequence.

Fuchs, one of the great writers of his first generation of American Jewish writers, published his Williamsburgh Trilogy in the 1930s, sold a total (he noted in an essay to a reissued collection three decades later) of twelve hundred copies, and using the few connections afforded him by the adaptation of a *Saturday Evening Post* story, decamped to Hollywood at the end of the decade. He got a little work, hung on, found that he liked it much more than struggling in Brooklyn and in collaboration shared a scriptwriting Oscar for *Love Me Or Leave Me*. (Perhaps his tortured actress in *West of the Rockies* owes a little to Doris Day.) In late Asimovian youth he returned to fiction and essays, placed a couple of "Letters From Hollywood" in *The New Yorker*, and finally got out *West of the Rockies*, which comes close to that illusory gonfalon of greatness—although it is barely known now. Fear as the engine of desire. The publicist marries the ruined actress on the stipulation that she will finish the picture. In some Williamsburg Summer, they may still be working on it.

Harlan Jay Ellison

He never wrote that true Hollywood novel but in the wretchedly-titled "The Resurgence of Miss Ankle Strap Wedgie" (1968) he probably wrote the great Hollywood novella and interestingly he published that 25,000-word work in a collection (*Love Ain't Nothing But Sex Misspelled*) in 1968, some years before *The Golden West*. His plot: a long washed-up actress is found in a diner and for publicity is signed for a minor role in a big-budget film. She is in the charge of a publicist, Handy, to whom Fuchs' man bears a stunning resemblance. She and Handy become lovers through the course of a film comeback to which she is obviously unequal. Handy knows that she is failing and knows that as hope turns to ash she will be entirely destroyed...but, hey, he just works here. The daily rushes are no good, but the director thinks that he and the editor might be able to make something from the wreckage. The film is completed, barely, and finally the preliminary version is screened for the studio. In one of the great scenes it becomes apparent to everyone in the room that the actress (clearly modeled on Veronica Lake whose story and "comeback" were similar) is no good, that the process cannot save her. She lands—like the Uncle in the film *Goodbye, Columbus*—on the cutting-room floor. Handy, wrecked by guilt and fear, allows fear to win. The studio, under pressure from the actress, pays her off. ("I can't go back to the diner. I was at peace but you stole even forgetfulness from me.") Handy goes to the diner, tries to take her away,

but she will not go with him. The publicist takes a long look in the mirror. Like the perished souls in *West of the Rockies* he is still looking.

Harlan Ellison wrote this novella at age thirty three, the kind of work about whom a reader—at least *this* reader—must say: "He is capable of anything in the decades to come." He did not disappoint ("The Man Who Rowed Columbus Ashore"), of course. But this novella like *The Golden West*, like Marilyn's slammed bureau drawers in *Some Like It Hot*—they were the fire which lit the century. Fitzgerald can rest. The job was done.

Copyright © 2015 by Barry N. Malzberg

Joy Ward is the author of one novel. She has several stories in press, at magazines and in anthologies, she conducts an interview for every issue of Galaxy's Edge, and she has also done interviews, both written and video, for other publications. This issue she interviews 2015 Worldcon Guest of Honor David Gerrold, and what could be timelier than that?

THE *GALAXY'S EDGE* INTERVIEW

Joy Ward interviews David Gerrold

David Gerrold, the 2015 Worldcon Guest of Honor, has had a long and fascinating career. Trekkers know him from his years as a writer on the original *Star Trek* television series. The rest of us know him from his hard science fiction writing or the magical realism of his *The Martian Child*. Always outspoken, never boring, Gerrold is a writer consistently ready to share his thoughts and feelings.

Joy Ward: How did you get started writing?

David Gerrold: It was almost accidental. I wanted to act and direct and produce, and it was very clear to me from the beginning that you have to know story structure, you have to know character, especially if you're going to direct, you have to know how to tell a story. And the writing was easy. It was fun, and one day they were paying me for it. So I said, all right, if they're going to pay me for it I'll just keep doing it.

Everybody else tells these stories of, "Oh God, I sent story after story, rejection slip after rejection slip." I didn't have that. I sent in a story, they said here's some money, kid, write the script. So I'm absolutely the wrong person to talk to about determination and discipline and stick-to-itiveness and stubbornness and all that commitment stuff because I've been very lucky to have it very easy.

JW: You've collaborated with a number of others. What do you get from collaboration?

DG: There are scenes you don't want to write. You get to be lazy. I don't want to write this one. I never said it this way. And there was stuff Larry (Niven) didn't want to write or couldn't write. Larry is brilliant on a lot of stuff, but at that time neither comedy nor characterization were his strongest suits. I never thought I was good at punch lines, but a lot of people think my work is funny so I must be good at punch lines.

What happens is I look at a line of dialogue and I say what's the obvious thing that someone is going to say next, and I don't say that. What's the opposite of the obvious? What's the punch line here? I don't think in terms of the punch line. What's the most interesting thing to say next?

I have certain strengths, and the reason they are strengths is because I know they're weaknesses. I always thought I was terrible with characterization, so I worked a lot on characterization. I thought I was terrible with dialogue, so I worked hard at it. I always thought I was pretty good with plot and structure, so I don't work too hard at it anymore. That's why my plots and structures are sloppy. So I have to work on that. I was taught to find your weakest aspect of your strength and concentrate on that to make it get stronger. Develop that writing muscle and that has always been my goal. What do I not know how to do? Okay, that's my next challenge.

Here's a half century later and I look at people writing reviews of my work and they say, "David is versatile." That's interesting because there's a thing that the Beatles always said. They never wanted to do the same song twice. I have that same feeling. I never want to write the same story twice. So every story I do is different from the others. This is kind of self defeating. I don't have a unique voice like Jack Vance did. I love Jack Vance. I don't have a unique voice like Harlan Ellison. Everything has to be a different voice. It's an acting trick really because I'm playing a different character each time I sit down to type. Because I'm playing a different character each time I sit down to type I get different voices.

I'll give you an example. Robert A. Heinlein, who I admired a lot, had a very distinct writing voice. So he writes *Glory Road*, which is a fantasy and reads like *Starship Troopers*, which is a military book, and it reads like *Farmer in the Sky*, which is a young adult book. They all have the same voice so you tend to feel it's all the same character. But if somebody is versatile in voices, for instance take Theodore Sturgeon. He did a story "Mr. Costello Hero" which I just reread because I just wrote a sequel to it. He wrote the story from the point of view of a not very intelligent person. He's not an imbecile; he's an idiot savant. He knows numbers, but he doesn't know people. Sturgeon conveys that very well, and you read that whole story through the character's eyes. In the sequel I did, I also looked at Mr. Costello, but through another character's eyes. That person has a whole different attitude about life. It's a very frontier, Western kind of attitude. The reason you want to do that is you want your reader to get into the soul, the heart of the narrator, the protagonist, and feel that viewpoint. When you write first person you're becoming the character, and you're saying this is how I experienced it, this is how I perceived it. So the "Jumping Off the Planet" trilogy—I wrote that from the point of view of a very angry thirteen-year-old in a very dysfunctional family. I succeeded so well that I had reviewers saying, "Obviously David comes from a dysfunctional family, he's a middle child, his parents were divorced, it was an ugly divorce and that's why he hates lawyers." All five of those are wrong.

My family was so white bread you could have put mayonnaise on us. My parents never divorced. We were not dysfunctional. I think the biggest dysfunction we had was whether I could buy a motorcycle, and I did anyway.

JW: You've had quite a journey in the human potential movement. How has that played out in your writing?

DG: I was living with a wonderful partner, a man named Dennis, and Ted Sturgeon invited him to do an EST (Erhard Seminars Training) seminar and didn't invite me. So Dennis signed up for EST. Then Ted and Jane (Sturgeon) kind of monopolized Dennis's time after that. Dennis came out to me and said, "I would like you to do the training." "All right, fine." Part of my reasoning was I was going to be damned if I was going to let anyone be more enlightened than me.

Dennis and I stayed with EST for two, maybe three years. We went through every possible program they offered. We did the communication workshop.

We did the seminar leadership program, which is I think the entire reason for doing EST would be to do that course because it is about enrollment. Now most people hear enrollment as please sign up for something and give me your money. It's not. Enrollment as I see it is inviting people—you want to go to the movies, you want to get married, you want to be my playmate, you want to hang out, you want to go to dinner—that's all enrollment. You want to share my space? Learning how to be an enrolling person is probably the greatest human condition of all. It is learning how to be open and vulnerable and generous and giving so that people want to be around you.

How does it affect my writing? This goes back to EST. Bullshit is everything you explain to allow yourself to evade responsibility, so once I started taking out explanations and started focusing on experiential, focusing on what is the person experiencing, the writing shifted dramatically. Now I had already been sort of moving in that direction, but now I had a clear context of don't explain, just show. Don't explain, just experience it. Give the reader the experience. Evoke the emotions. What does it smell like, taste like, feel like, look like, sound like? What is the reader experiencing? What is the character experiencing viscerally, stomach, heart, hands? What's the experience? Once I was writing from the experience and not explaining then there's room to do a lot of storytelling without bogging down. The story moves a lot faster. There's more impact.

What happens is that it's easier to get inside the character's head. My characters get didactic. There are long, long sections of dialogue I don't apologize for. I'm interested in this conversation. I want to hear what these people say. Most of my stories are conversations because a really great conversation is a connection between two people.

As a writer you're having a conversation with the reader. He just doesn't get to answer back. He just gets one option—whether or not he's going to turn the page. So my job is to make sure that it's so interesting the reader wants to find out what's going to happen next.

JW: What is your favorite high point of your career?

DG: My favorite high point isn't a career thing, as much as it's a personal. Adopting Sean and the day I met him. There was the day he was placed in my home. There was the day the adoption was finalized. They asked me, I had this wonderful caseworker, and she said are you planning to write a book about adoptions? I said, "No." One day after he moved in I just started writing a story about how much I loved my kid. It was rejected by the first six editors. It was editors who knew me too well. So I gave it to an editor who didn't know me very well at all, Kristine Katherine Rusch. She bought it for *Fantasy & Science Fiction*. We started getting the weirdest, most amazing fan mail on it and it brought home a Hugo and a Nebula and a Locus award and some other stuff, and then we got a movie offer and I expanded it into a novel. So I think *The Martian Child* would have to be the career high point.

JW: What made you decide to adopt a child?

DG: It seemed like a good decision at the time. They asked why do you want to adopt a little boy, and I couldn't answer the question. I said I don't know why. I just want to. I think even after all these years I'm not sure I can answer it completely. I think there's a biological, instinctual urge, your mommy clock goes off. Rrrring! Time to be a mommy!

We've had adoptions in my family starting with my grandmother who took in foster kids, and my aunts and uncles adopted kids. We have more adopted kids in our extended family than handmade ones.

I finally recognized that the only way to get love is to create love, and I get to create something that couldn't be created any other way. So I think it was just there's a thing about being complete, about having a family, and not being alone, but that wasn't the goal. The goal was I want a family of my own. Everybody else gets to show off pictures of their kids so I want to show off, there he is right there. I want a picture of my own kid to show off. Course I

got a late start. Everyone else was showing off their grandkids.

JW: Any advice for young writers?

DG: Quit. Quit. If you can be discouraged, quit now and save yourself all that time and anguish and energy and beating your head against the brick wall and the frustration and the anguish. Now if that sentence makes you pissed off then maybe you have enough determination and stubbornness and commitment to make it but most of the writers I know who have succeeded I know have done so because they are either too stubborn or too stupid to quit. I have seen writers of enormous talent give up because there's no push and I have seen writers of, I hate to phrase it any way that is negative, but let me say, writers of lesser ability or writers whose work does not interest me manage to have very successful careers because they don't quit.

You can learn almost all the skills of writing. You can take acting classes, read all the good books by Ray Bradbury and *Elements of Style* and John Gardner and Rita Mae Brown and Nora Ephron and read all the great books about writing. All these great, great books on writing give you some insight, but it's really experiential. What can you experience? Then just be too damn stubborn to quit. I think the best advice I could give any new writer would be always look at what you don't know how to do and do that next.

JW: How do you want to be remembered?

DG: Well, anything other than the Rodney Dangerfield of science fiction. And I loved Rodney Dangerfield! But every so often someone comes out with this Encyclopedia of Science Fiction and so of course I look myself up. Its like, wait a minute, half a paragraph? A footnote?

Yeah, if somebody said, "here is your Grandmaster trophy," that would be very nice, but that is not the goal. I would love to have it, but the real goal is the keyboard. What comes out of the keyboard next? What am I going to write next? What's the next story? What's the next thing I can accomplish?

There's a wonderful movie "Personal Best." It's not about winning. It's about what is your personal best? What are you capable of doing? My personal best is I once wrote ten thousand, three hundred words in a single day. I averaged six thousand words a day for a week. That's a personal best. And it was good stuff. A personal best is I've never done this kind of story before. A personal best is I've gone somewhere, I know where I've succeeded. I know when I've pushed the limits. Going back to your question, how would I like to be remembered? I would like people to remember me saying, "you pick up a story by David Gerald you're going to have a good time with it." I think that would be a fine epitaph or eulogy. "Read this, you'll have fun." That would be good.

I am still a student. I know some people consider me a master. But a master is still a student. That's why he's a master. He's still a student of the craft. Yeah, I know a lot about writing, and I know that I know a lot more about it than a lot of people. But I know how much I still don't know and still want to learn.

What is important for me is to not be arrogant. It's very hard to not be arrogant when you're a writer because the mere act of writing is arrogant. I have something to say. I have something to say that is so important that it justifies chopping down a tree. That is arrogant. I have something to say that is so important that you should pay for the privilege of listening to it. That is arrogant. One of the things I have constantly been called out on in all of the courses I have done is "David, you are very arrogant." No I'm not arrogant or aloof. I'm trying to figure shit out. But it shows up as arrogant, so I think being a student is about staying open and vulnerable because the minute you say I know all this crap, the minute you say I know how to do this you start the process of dying.

There was a writer, I won't mention her by name, she attended a lot of conventions, went to all the panels, she took notes, practiced, and her first book was ambitious and sold well. Her second book was better because she was learning. Her third book was a little better, but somebody asked her to be on the panel. She became pretentious and she stopped listening. Well. I'm an expert now and here's what I know about writing. I don't even know if she got to a fourth book. Her writing went downhill very, very fast because now she believed she knew it all. She's long forgotten, which is why I haven't mentioned her name. Long, long forgotten because she stopped challenging herself. I figure if I ever stop challenging myself I will have peaked. There's always another rung on the ladder.

There's another part to it which comes back to Ted Sturgeon. As much as I loved and admired Ted, one of the things I would never want to be is Ted. I don't want to be Harlan. I don't want to be Heinlein. I want to find out who I am sometime before the next half-century is over and be comfortable being me. Right now it's still a learning process as I've had the longest case of prolonged adolescence in history. I'm thirteen with a half century of experience. The golden age of science fiction is thirteen and that's exactly who I want to be. I don't want to lose my sense of wonder.

If you lose your sense of wonder you're dead. Your sense of wonder makes it worth getting out of bed in the morning. What am I going to discover today? What's interesting today? Sometimes it's what bad thing happened today, but even what bad thing happened is part of the learning experience. Life is not all about one great wonderful adventure after another, because an adventure means there's something at risk. So sometimes life is about being at risk. Sometimes life is the avalanche is headed your way and it's all bad news. So sometimes you have to say, and I have said this more than once, I've been through worse; I can handle this. So far the universe has not thrown anything at me that I haven't been able to handle one way or another. So I guess I'll get out of bed tomorrow morning, too.

We have fallen into a terrible trap of judging our worth or our success by how much money we have, and I don't do that. Which means money around here comes and goes in the strangest ways. My energy goes into the keyboard. The four or five years I was working with the training company I took a sabbatical from my writing. This past year I've turned out a lot of work because I'm on a writing binge. I will go away from writing for a while and learn something. I'll go drive cross country. I spent a month touring around, staying off interstates, doing the back roads. When I get on the back road I end up with a story. So sometimes not writing is part of the job.

I tell people ninety percent of what I do is research and the other ten percent is plotting revenge because most writing is about revenge of some kind. Sometimes the research means that you stop, you walk away from the keyboard, and go and live a life. Because how can you write about life if you haven't lived one? So go fall in love. Go adopt a kid. Go climb a mountain. Go do something that requires you to stretch yourself.

I think when I'm not writing I'm stretching. Okay, where's the stretch here? What am I going to learn? That's why I spent so much time with doing the trainings, and I loved being a trainer. I heard so many great stories from people sharing. But I also got to make a difference for them by being a good coach. So how do I get to be a better coach? By being a better coach how do I get to be a better human being? How do I get to be a better dad for my son? How do I get to be the person I want to be? And the person I want to be is insightful, introspective, thoughtful, generous, open, vulnerable, giving, powerful, loving. That's the person I want to be.

Copyright © 2015 by Joy Ward

Zombies and Werewolves in space
What could possibly go wrong?

SERIALIZATION
REBOOTS

Part 1

by Mercedes Lackey and Cody Martin
Phoenix Pick, 2012
Trade Paperback: 162 pages.
ISBN: 978-1-61242-059-2

Mercedes Lackey is the author of more than one hundred novels, many of them bestsellers, including the fabulous Valdemar series. She has collaborated with Marion Zimmer Bradley, Anne McCaffrey, C. J. Cherryh, Eric Flint, and Piers Anthony, among others. Cody Martin is a relative newcomer who, along with his writing talent, is, according to Ms. Lackey, "an incredibly fit climbing instructor, camping enthusiast, gun enthusiast, witty, good-looking, and unmarried."

Introducing Cody Martin

I first "met" Cody Martin in an online game.

The game is *City of Heroes*, an MMORPG (massive multi-player online role-playing game). We both belonged to one supergroup (aka guild for you WoW players) in a loose organization of role-playing groups on the Pinnacle server. For the uninitiated, role playing is very much like partially-scripted improvisational theater. The folks we were with were very much involved in storytelling (as opposed to "grinding" their characters to the highest level possible in the shortest amount of time), so it was pretty natural for me to gravitate towards them.

It turned out that he actually *had* been part of a "grinding" group of friends and was about to kill off his character and quit when he ran into us and got intrigued. Our characters meshed well and he quickly got involved in a couple of my story lines; I liked the introduction he had written and posted on the group's website (we heavily encouraged people to write prose as well as role-play) and as the people behind the "toons," we hit it off.

At the time I thought he was a college student or even in his mid-twenties. I had no idea he hadn't even graduated from high school. He was that good at character development.

We came up with a way to "save" his character once John Murdock hit the endgame, and about five books' worth of posted stories later, he, I, Dennis Lee, Steve Libbey, and later Veronica Giguere created The Secret World Chronicle, using some of the same characters, but a vastly different setting, and with some interesting personality or background changes for some. That started (and is ongoing) as a podcast (Podiobooks and www.secretworldchronicle.com) and is now a series from Baen Books.

But meanwhile, Cody wanted to try his hand at something else, too. We've had some ideas for a couple of things, but this is what took off first.

It all started with another writing acquaintance, Mike Williamson, asking if I'd commit to an anthology proposal, "Zombies in Space." Now…I'll be honest, that sounded like the most idiotic proposal I had ever heard, and I said, basically, "are you insane?" But as I was talking to Cody about it, and he (who like most men seems to be zombie-obsessed) suggested things, suddenly, it didn't seem quite so insane. In fact, it had a lot of comic potential. In fact….

In fact, it became what you are about to read.

Mercedes Lackey

REBOOTS, PART I

Bad Moon Rising

by Cody Martin

You know what they said in that ancient movie, about being in space? Well here's a news flash for you: in space no one gives a shit if you scream. Especially not your shipmates. Oh, you'd think your shipmates would care, right? I mean, it's just all of you against all of the dark and vacuum and whatever crap the universe has dreamed up to kill you? Another news flash: no. Especially if your shipmates are a bunch of sociopathic dirtbags that think dead puppy jokes are a laugh riot.

So the screaming and cursing in the aft drain-chamber was pretty much "Tuesday."

So much for the glamor and excitement of interstellar travel.

We'd strapped Fred down for the blood-drain again, and since he was human, it was going well aside from all the noise. That would be me, standing in the corner, doing my best to look like an appliance, while Fred screamed and ranted. That would be the High and Mighty, watching, and occasionally

changing out a blood-bag, since I wasn't to be trusted with something as important as their property. Three pints down, two to go, and Fred was still in fine voice. That was the thing about Fred being a Fur (ah, excuse me, I should be more sensitive, a "Were-person"); he regenerated the blood he was losing almost immediately. A couple spinach salads and a slab of beef and he'd be fine. Turn him loose under this planet's moons to let him feast on whatever he could catch and kill and he'd be more than fine. I never could figure out how it was that he could eat anything remotely living and carbon-based when he wolfed out, even if it would have poisoned him in human shape. Miracles of Were physiology, I guess, but hey, no one pays me to be the brains—hardy har har. Come to think of it, no one pays me at all.

"We" had him strapped down, by which I mean "me," since the Fangs (and I will be damned all over again if I call Our Vampiric Lords and Masters anything but Fangs) never got their lily-like hands dirty if they could help it. They were the "mission specialists." Meaning they had an excuse to be divas, or figured they did. It was up to me and the others to do all the work. And Fred, because he was lowest on this particular food-chain. So yeah, that's the shipmates. four Fangs and a Fur, and the hate and contempt is so thick most of the time it's like a fog in the air.

Barnabas was in charge today. Oh Barnabas, who really got the short end of the vampiric stick. Someone had bit him late in life, and as you are when you get Turned, so you stay. So there he was in all his sagging, jowly glory, looking like a basset hound in a tailored jumpsuit. Can't really wonder why he's a douche; he has to look at the others, who may not be the supermodels of the Fang world but certainly are not coyote-ugly, and at himself, and grind his fangs. Even their jumpsuits look good on them, while his looks…like a janitor uniform. Yes, here we are, hopping stars, and the attire de rigueur for space travelers is still the jumpsuit, go figure. Must drive the Fangs crazy, with their obsessive-compulsive fashion sense; kind of hard to get designer labels hundreds of light years from the nearest retailer.

The rest of the Fangs were lined up, waiting for their liquid lunch, and Barny was making them wait, which was not exactly quelle surprise. Barny was his usual patronizing self. He smiled snarkily down at Fred, who glared up at him. "Good boy, Fred. Nice doggie." He patted the top of Fred's head, then quickly pulled his hand out of reach when Fred snarled. Granted, he was in human form, but some of the wolf carried over, and he'd been known to bite.

"Shut up, Barnabas," Fred said, then told Barnabas what he could do with himself and where he could put that hand in long, loving, and profane detail, using only Barnabas's full name. Ol' "Barny" hated his full name; believe it or not, in the Before time there'd been some sort of soap opera with a vampire in it by that name, and…well, let's just say for the aristocratic Fangs, a soap opera was to the Grand High Literature of their kind (snork) as Mexican lucha libre wrestling was to the Olympics. Fred and the others chose to use Barny's full name as often as the occasion warranted to get under his skin, which happened pretty often, because he was really easy to aggravate. But with Barny sticking the verbal knife in and rotating it, as well as being none-too-gentle about the drain, *and* being parked on a world where he mostly couldn't go outside the ship, Fred was not happy at all and he was really heaping on the verbal abuse today. Not that I blamed him.

This particular dirt-ball must have had a dozen moons, maybe more, I hadn't counted. It wasn't my job to count things, just like it wasn't my job to think. I was just the guy they got to sweep up the shed fur and whatever else the Fangs discarded, strap Fred down in case he wolfed out in the middle of a drain, fix the ship's systems occasionally under strict supervision, and rehydrate the dehydrated cattle brains the zombies ate so they wouldn't waste away to nothing but bones. Of course, they could still do the job as bones except they tended to fall apart when they tried to pick up anything heavy, or when they were backhanded by a pissed-off Fang-face. Inconvenient. God knows the Fangs shouldn't be inconvenienced by anything. Dicks. Oh, had I not mentioned this before? Yeah. I'm a zombie too, which is why nobody gives a shit what I think, because I'm not supposed to be able to think. More on that later. Everybody has rude names for us. Reboots. Shambler. Dead Head. Bone Bags. Rot-pot. Corpsicle. Mikey Jerkson… You know, I never did figure

out where that one came from. Only the older Fangs seemed to use it.

The Fangs—who really, really hate that name—finished up feeding on Fred and took their time in turning him loose. He did his usual ritual of pissing and moaning, cursing their families and hoping all the demons in the universe chose to pay them a visit, but he put more feeling than usual into it today.

"Someone woke up on the wrong side of the kennel this morning." The Fangs never, never lost a chance to get in a dog reference. The few Furs I'd run into before this cruise all seemed really self-conscious about their animal sides, and Fred was no exception. Maybe it was because when they morphed out, they were pretty much ravening, mindless beasts on steroids. Poor Fred. All those moons meant he was wolfed out most of the time if he went outside or got near an unshuttered viewport. It wasn't that he had any choice in the matter; it was just automatic, as much of a physical necessity as the Fangs' need for blood, or a person's need to breathe.

When he did go all wild-eyed and hairy, it was best not to be anywhere nearby. Imagine a 5-foot-4 accountant-looking guy turning into an eight-foot-tall unholy terror that basically wants to rip apart and eat anything that looks like it might be made of meat. That's what Fred becomes whenever he gets hit with the light of any moons, if they're full. You would think that the moon phase wouldn't matter on a spaceship; hell, conversely, you'd think that *being* in a spaceship wouldn't matter if the moon was full. What do I know? Maybe the Norms figured out how to put anti-moon-phase shielding on the hull that didn't work on the open viewports. I'm just the janitor, and I wasn't exactly a rocket scientist when I was alive. Besides, in a 'verse where vampires, werewolves, and zombies exist as a matter of fact, some things just are and it doesn't matter that they don't make sense.

Fred was going on with his cussing for longer than usual too, his tirade becoming less profane and more inventive as time went on. "I'll tear you in half and throw you out of the airlock when we're parked next to a yellow star." That was new. Death threats are not anything that this lot hasn't already made before, but when you start working in the specific weaknesses, it strikes a chord. Fred's idea would probably work, too.

Class G yellow stars and those close to them in stellar classification are deadly to Fangs; the light crisps them nicely, and if they are out in it long enough, it reduces them to ash. There actually *was* a coating on the viewports that prevented yellow sunlight from hurting the Fangs—probably some kind of UV coating. That vulnerability was what had kept the Norms on top against Fangs. Norms were top-notch at finding and exploiting weaknesses.

Antonio sneered. Antonio *loved* his full name. Antonio della Contani, supposedly some sort of Venetian royalty, right? I'm laying bets on him actually being plain old Tony Conti from Brooklyn who was Turned in the '50s, based on his taste in music and the fact that he acts like a punk thug in nice clothes. "Promises, promises. Puppy didn't get his walkies." As usual, they were at each other's throats, verbally if not actually. Not that it mattered if they did tear pieces out of each other, they'd just regenerate. The same wasn't true for the likes of me. I would end up in a not so neat pile, with my parts wriggling around until my brain got tired, unless my bits got shoved into a recycling unit or someone was kind enough to stitch me up. And this wasn't exactly a kind bunch, if you get my drift. Besides, zombies are a dime a dozen; we're nothing more than part of the inventory.

Yeah, that's the other thing about being a zombie. Being undead is totally rad unless you're one of us. Vampires are strong and fast and persuasive. Werewolves are giant hairy woodchippers on legs. Zombies are janitors. Smelly janitors. Disposable janitors. Whenever one of us breaks, they just shove the bits into the recycler and grab another one out of the hold. I used to have a name, forever ago. I don't remember those days all that well. Now I just go by Skinny Jim, when there's someone that bothers to speak to me. Which, let me tell you, isn't all that often. Zombies are not exactly what you would call stellar conversationalists, so why would they?

That's another thing. Not a lot of zombies can talk. Most of us really are mindless; burnt out or burnt up by whatever made us the way we are. We can do simple tasks, sure, especially if shown what to do a few dozen times. But there's not a lot of intellectual stimulation amongst zombies, if you don't count munching on the occasional rehydrated brain. You don't find us sitting around discussing Kierkegaard.

So, I'm special in that regard; I've got some of my mind left, but no opportunity to show it. And no incentive, to tell the truth. The Norms—well there were no Norms out here in any great numbers so that was moot—still, what the Norms would do, I didn't like to think about. And the other Undead don't like the manual laborers to be too bright, and I'm not sure what *they'd* do if they found out I was different. They'd probably do what the Norms would do, and sad as my existence is, it beats the alternative.

✿

"Fuckin' elitist bastiches," Fred muttered under his breath. Fangs. Thought they were the kings of the universe. Ask any of them, and they'd tell you. Not a one of them was ever some wino that got rolled for Type O-Pos in an alley, or would at least admit to it. Oh no. All of them had longer pedigrees than the winner of the Kennel Club trophy. And they *all* had the goofiest names you've ever heard of. Always something faux-fancy or exotic sounding. You never met a Bob the Vampire. Fred hated them, this ship and—well not the job, exactly, but after the first few new planets it had gotten…routine. But this was a paying gig. Not the greatest gig in the universe, *except* for the pay, but it'd do for now. Now, of course, being quite a stretch— he'd signed on for 300 years for this tour, give or take a decade. They were about halfway through their supply of Reboots, with the other consumables—spare parts for the hardware, mostly—at about the same level.

Why would a bunch of monsters from ancient fairy tales and B-movies be out roaming the stars, anyways?

Why else—the ones that had the power and the money made the rules.

It was because the Norms were the real kings of the universe, or at least, of Earth. They had the lock on the stakes, the silver bullets, the Sun-guns. Oh, poor Norms, who just didn't have the weaknesses of the Undead. The light of yellow suns didn't make them fall into a coma at low levels of exposure or burn up at high levels. They weren't terminally allergic to silver or garlic. And they could run faster than any zombie *and* they had flamethrowers. Only thing they didn't have were long life-spans, long enough to do serious space exploration. Fangs, Wolves, and

Reboots did, though, and there wasn't much out here that could kill a Fang or a Wolf if it didn't already know the weaknesses.

The pay for a long cruise was excellent, and the Undead didn't have to worry about dodging religious fanatics, or wolfing out and maybe hurting someone, or worse, or going comatose and vulnerable once the yellow sun came up. So, for the ones out of the broom closet, space exploration was the mainstream place to be. There were more volunteers than there were ships.

So, things got along pretty smoothly, for the most part, back home, at least for the supernaturals that wanted to just get along with Norm society. Personally, Fred thought that a lot of them were sell-outs. You could still find a measure of freedom on some of the colony worlds, and a lot of the Paras that didn't get exploration gigs had shipped out for those, or so he'd heard. But back on Earth? Stuck kowtowing to the whims of the Norms, never daring to even stick a toe over the line, always afraid of setting a "bad example" for the rest of your kind? To hell with that noise. The Fangs and Furs (the ones that weren't Underground and actually had some moxie) all cued up for their shots at a ship as first choice, colony as second. Fangs for crew, a Wolf or two for crew and the fresh blood for the Fangs, and the zombies—the Reboots—for menial labor. Neither Fang nor Fur needed to worry about the Reboots chowing down on their brains. The Reboots ignored them both so far as feeding went. The Norms on Earth got rid of their problems, everything was one humming happy assembly line, and that didn't matter for crap out here. Because once you got out here you found out what the real pecking order was, and you were looking at 300 years locked up in the same tin can as the creatures that considered you "Lunch That Talks." And they'd really rather you didn't talk, but just grovel and do what you were told.

It was Fred's job to make sure that the Reboots were sent to the right places and made to do the right jobs. He was a supervisor, for the most part, only taking care of the most sensitive jobs personally. At least he wasn't *just* the Fang cafeteria; he'd been an engineer before he got bitten, and he still was an engineer now. Today, he had a sensitive job to take care of. The ship's main drive was being finicky, so

Fred had to eat some rads and fix it. On any vessel that held Norms, and there were a few, mostly Earth-system stuff, there were dozens of safeguards with redundancies and contingencies and so on. Not so for a ship like this. Supernaturals didn't get hurt the same way that Norms did, so it was more acceptable to cut corners, and thus costs. Ah, the joys of space exploration.

He'd take some Reboots along to hold lights and pass him tools. A few extra sets of hands never hurt, even if the hands were prone to falling off at the worst possible times. Antonio still hadn't let him live down the time a Reboot's finger had snapped off and shorted the grav generator.

Fred pointed at the three nearest ones. "Command phrase: come with me. You, you, and you."

They didn't bother naming the Reboots; they all were dressed in cheap red coveralls—which he thought was a nice touch—and all responded to "you" so long as they noticed someone was talking to them. One of the ghoulies looked somewhat startled—or at least as startled as a decayed corpse can look—when Fred spoke to him, but Fred shrugged it off and started marching them all to the lift that would take him to the reactor. It was probably nothing more than a nerve twitch. You never knew with the Reboots. Once he thought he'd caught the one that looked like a desiccated surfer dude trying to skateboard. He chalked it up to the Fangs trying to fuck with him.

Were all the crews this dysfunctional? How could they be? How would anything get done if they were? Then again…paranoia set in. Because it was true that it wasn't paranoia if "they" actually were out to get you, and there was no doubt that the minute the Norms thought the Paras just *might* get the upper hand, out would come all the stockpiled weapons, the stake- and Sun-guns, the garlic spray, the silver-coated *everything*, and lots and lots of flamethrowers. The Norms just preferred things to not be chaotic and messy and dangerous. So…*Maybe that was the plan; send our Kinds out in the stars to kill each other. And meanwhile, find some planets the Norms could use; y'know, as a "nice if it happens" bonus. That would just figure. Have the bad luck to get Turned, and as a Were no less, only to get shipped off to the stars to deal with Larry, Curly, and Shithead for however long it took until one of you snapped and you all killed each other. The way these lowest-bidder ships are built, the Norms could probably afford that, and it wouldn't be nearly as messy as a Norm versus Para war.* He shook his head. Thinking in circles like this was sure to drive him mad.

Or maybe this all was just paranoia, and the other crews all got along just fine, and the Universe had decided to stick Fred with the most petty, vain, and antagonistic bunch of bloodsuckers ever created. Given how his luck usually went...yeah, that would be about par for the course. It made more sense than some enormous Norm plot. Right?

Not that it mattered to him at this point anyway. Because whether it was part of a huge plot against the Paras, or whether it was just bad luck, he was stuck here with the Divas of the Damned for the foreseeable future. He muttered more curses as he made his way to the engineering section, thinking of all of the different ways he'd like to kill his shipmates. Well, re-kill. Actually, all things considered, he wouldn't feel unhappy if he got to re-kill all of them three or four times before finishing them off for good. *A wolf can dream...*

Man, Fred had it bad. Me, it didn't matter, the Fangs couldn't get a kick out of verbally tormenting me, and when they were in a bad mood, I could just make sure I wasn't the one within reach of their claws. It might get different later, when the numbers of us Reboots started getting a lot lower, but for now, I was just one more tree in the forest. Thing is, the Fangs could get all the reaction their hard little flint-like hearts desired out of Fred. The poor sap was a great big hairy ball of reaction, and the longer the trip went on, the shorter his fuse got. Reboots didn't have any brains except the ones we were munching on—har har—so we didn't notice and didn't react. Fred though, he was the only Fur on the ship, and the only one who acted with resentment when they were looking for someone to verbally abuse that wasn't one of them. The Fangs *loved* to make people squirm. I don't get it. I never had much to do with any of the Paras before I got herded up with the rest, shoved into a red jumpsuit and stuck in the hold, so...were all Fangs like this?

I don't know. But this lot really took the "fun" out of "dysfunctional." When Fred wasn't around, they fought with each other. When he was around, they ganged up on him. It was like they weren't happy unless they were spreading pain to something other than themselves. Maybe it was part of the pecking-order thing that Fangs always seemed to establish, and maybe they figured they each had to be the Alpha, Fearless Leader Supremo, at least over someone, or maybe that sort of thing came with being Turned. Or maybe we just got stuck with the biggest assholes the Fangs ever produced and the powers that be lumped all of them together to keep all the grief in one place.

We arrived at the section where the malfunction was. Fred started pointing at each of us Reboots, positioning us where he needed us, and then went about the task of fixing what was wrong. I was just supposed to flip a switch whenever he told me to. Looked like something dealing with the ship's coolant systems. A lot of heat got generated by the drives, and it needed some way to safely bleed off into space. I played along, allowing Fred to do his part and treat me like the others. It was boring, but it was better than...well, what? Rehydrating brains, I guess. Waiting to get broken beyond repair, like the others, like just another replaceable component on this ship? Or standing around and thinking? There's nothing much around here that makes for comfortable thinking.

Then things got even more "entertaining." Grigoire decided to make his entrance when we were about halfway through and the ship was running on the APU—which meant no one got to do anything that wasn't absolutely necessary. Grigoire took a special pleasure in torturing Fred; he really, really hated werewolves, more than the average Fang. Before Paras were outed to the entire world, Fangs and Furs were already at each other's throats in some kind of eternal holy war, or something. When us zombies started causing enough trouble for the Norms, both sides came to a truce to try and "save the herd," as it were. Didn't seem to do much to quell the resentment and hatred that immortal beings can harbor in the long run though; a grudge seemed to age like fine wine with some of them.

Grigoire was the vessel's astrophysicist, which meant on a scale of one to ten on "Uptight Asshole-ness," he scored a whopping seventy-three. He was probably the same when he was a Norm, if the near-ancient vids we have onboard of "Big Bang Theory" are to be believed.

"Hey, Fuzzy Wuzzy. How's it going with the re-pairs? Try not to get any dog hair in the components. It's a pain to get out, you know?" He slapped on his best smile, which looked fake and painful stretched across perfect and blemish-free dead skin. "Oh wait, that's right, *you're* going to be the one to clean them out!" He laughed at his own humor. "Never mind then, carry on."

"Grigoire, not now. Think of it like this: if I don't do my job correctly, then the ship falls apart. If the ship falls apart, you'll be getting really cozy with a couple of red dwarfs. And I'm not talking the Snow White kind either, sucker." Fred was pissed. Poor bastard. In another unlife, I would've really had my withered heart go out to him. Here, he was just another prisoner that might end up busting me to pieces. "I don't come tell you dirty jokes while you're piddling with your equations, so how about you go brood about the unfairness of un-life, pine over the women you aren't getting to bite, or write Goth po-etry or something while I do my job?"

"That's really funny, flea-bag. Make sure to comb some insect-killer into that hair."

I'm not sure why, because it's no worse than any of the other shit they call him, but there was some-thing about that name that always got to Fred. He put up with a lot of crap from the Fangs; but what other choice did he have? But whenever they called him that, he got mean. Fred put down his tools with a loud clang and turned to face Grigoire, an ugly smirk on his face.

"At least I still have all my hair. Must suck—har-dy har—that you got bitten so late in life you were stuck with a comb-over. Tony said you were looking lighter around the North, by the way. You been pick-ing at yourself again? You should know better than that. You haven't got anything to spare up there." Fred twirled a finger around the very top of his cra-nium, grinning evilly the entire time. And that was all that Grigoire needed. It's an interesting thing, to see one of the Fangs really vamp out. It's not too unlike the Weres, but a little more subtle. Grigoire's eyes filled with murder and a cold fury that always unsettled me. Something happened that seemed to make the shadows deeper around him; calling on the infernal whatever-the-hell that animated Fangs, I suppose. He bared his terrible canines and leapt for Fred, claws extended. Fred partially transformed; his features became more bestial, with his hair growing longer and his muscles rippling and growing under-neath his skin. He can do that half-transformation at will; he just can't completely wolf out. He still has full control over himself in the half-state, which was good because if the wrong stuff was busted in this room, the ship had a fairly decent chance of explod-ing. Ah, lowest-bidder contracts…

There was about sixty seconds of ultra-violence and way-too-fast ruckus, which was fortunately confined to a relatively robust part of the engine room; then Antonio appeared in the door, yelling at the top of his lungs. *Knock it off, morons!*

They froze. Antonio is the captain. Top of the Fang food chain. I *think* there's something in their instincts that makes the other Fangs obey him. Maybe he's been Undead the longest, or he was born or Turned with a certain whatever that just made the others obey. Didn't matter, they jumped when he said to. A good thing, too, since otherwise this would have been a hulk floating in space about three months into the mission, inhabited only by us de-cayed types until the brains ran out. Not so much because they knew how to kill each other without helpful tools like wooden stakes and silver, but be-cause they'd probably have blown something up and gone through a bulkhead, with the end result being the lot of them sucked out into deep space to form a fighting ball until they all froze solid, or Fred ran out of air. The Fangs didn't need air, but they wore suits to protect themselves from the cold—and to be able to talk to the ship and each other. At near zero Kelvin even a Fang will freeze solid and be unable to move. Fred, however, needed air, though he would last longer than a Norm would.

"You!" Antonio said to Fred, pointing. "Back to work. I want a hot shower and a movie. And you—" he pointed to Grigoire. "Act like a civilized noble, and not a thug. You can always be demoted if I choose. As far down the chain as I care to put you."

Antonio always tried to play at being sophisticated and a part of "undead royalty." I always thought it was a heaping pile of bullshit, personally. "So behave as if you deserve your position, or you'll be second-in-command to Fido." Tony got a wicked look on his face. "And I'll let him tell *you* when you can eat."

Grigoire hated being talked down to by Tony, even though it was his place in the chain of command, but that was just a whole new level of insult. I don't think it was my imagination, what there was left of such a thing, but matters were escalating around here. He shrieked a terrible and piercing wail, and then went to work on us Reboots. I've been around when either the Fangs go woolly, or Fred has his moon phases going on. But never in such close quarters. He ripped through us, pulling zombies apart with his hands, tearing at us with teeth. It was horrible to watch, but I couldn't move. He was working his way towards me, and I didn't dare run. To run would be to show that I knew what was coming—and that would show I could still think. I was dead either way. Well, dead again. Perma-dead. If I could have closed my eyes, I would have, but my eyelids are sort of glued in the open position.

"*Grigoire!*" Tony used a worse voice than before. It was the sort of voice that you used with a dog that just took a dump on the carpet in front of you. The tone…I can't describe it. If I'd had blood, it would have been frozen. More Fang powers. Even Fred went statue-still. Grigoire stopped with one clawed hand raised to rend me from stem to sternum.

Tony was really pissed now. "Not in front of the help, fool of a child," he hissed. "Back to your quarters! Now!" Grigoire fumed, shooting another savage look to Fred before he finally retreated. I tracked my eyes the barest few centimeters to look at Fred, then to Tony, trying to keep my face uninterested in the happenings around me. Kind of hard to be any more deadpan when you're already dead.

Fred cocked his head to the side. "That zombie looked at me funny."

Tony sighed heavily, squeezing the bridge of his nose with his fingers as if to stave off a migraine. I think that's just another affectation on his part; I don't think the Fangs have such human concerns as headaches. "That's because you're funny looking, Fred. Go take a flea bath or lick your ass or some-

thing. Just get the drives fixed first." If I could still evacuate my bowels, that would've been the moment for me to. That had been…way too close. And dusty wheels had started to turn in my head.

✧

"Pete, what other choice do we have? We're coming apart at the seams, here, literally." I pointed at Pete's left shoulder; he had been wedged between a mainframe core and its housing while trying to install some new wiring, and one of our less-than-awake Reboot brothers decided to push anyways. I was sewing him back up. "Nobody ever tries to fix us, because we're disposable!"

"Dude, what's the point? We go back home, and we're just more deadheads. You know what they do to us, especially if they think we can talk and think and feel. Well, feel kinda, at least." Every conscious Reboot remembered what happened to Xavier, the short-unlived "Lord of Zombies." It hadn't been pretty even by Reboot standards, which you had to admit were somewhere in the sub-sub-basement. "Get out of the gutter, so that those of us in the sewer can get some sun", that sorta thing. Xavier had been the reason why the Fangs and the Furs came out of the broom closet to help the Norms in the first place. Zombies on their own can be dealt with pretty easily, if a Norm has a lick of common sense. But, when you have one that can think and command all of his rotting brethren? One that can plan, make strategy, and has an almost endless army that doesn't care what parts get blown off while constantly replenishing itself? It was almost the end of the Earth. I wasn't there to see it; I was turned years and years after. Doesn't stop me from still getting shivers thinking about it.

I wasn't going to give up on *my* plan, however, because I didn't see how we had anything to lose. If we did nothing, we were consumables anyway, and eventually they'd be down to just me and Pete. "Do you want to get flushed out of an airlock? Our brothers and sisters can't tell the difference; they'd just float along, hungry as ever and not knowing the difference. But we're awake, man. If we're not insane now, think about what an eternity floating in nothing would do to you. Or if you got ripped apart—

there you are, conscious and watching your bits get shoved into the recycler."

"Dude, listen." Pete had been a professional surfer, or so he claimed, before he had become a Reboot. He retained the sometimes annoying habit of reverting back to his former speech patterns when he was perturbed. "I get what you're saying, man, really I do. But look at us. We're just a couple of stiffs, man. They're Fangs and a Fur. What do we got against all five of them, dude? Seriously."

Then it hit me. The last piece of the puzzle fell into place. Not only did we need to ensure we weren't in line for the next temper tantrum, we needed an ally. And it wasn't going to be a Fang. "Fred."

"Fred, what?" Sometimes Pete can be so dense. I mean, dense even for a Reboot. It clicked for him a few seconds later, and realization shone through his milky-white eyes. "Dude. You're fucking insane already. You know that?" But that wasn't disbelief I heard in his voice. It was cautious admiration.

"Yeah? Who else gets a shorter, shittier stick than us? Fred. Who's got as many brains as Grigoire, and gets treated like the third-world hired help? Fred. Who would give anything to see every Fang on this ship turned into corpsicles? Fred."

Pete rubbed his stomach woefully. "Man, you know better than to say brains around me. I still got the urges, dude."

I smacked him lightly. "Focus, butthead. Fred hates them worse than we do. And—" I paused for effect. "Fred can pilot this boat."

"Yeah but...oh, dude. If we come outta the closet..." he shook his head—carefully, to avoid dislodging anything. "Even if he's okay with it...that can't be taken back, like, there's no do-over, and he has that any time he needs to pull something out for the Fangs."

I laced my rotten fingers behind the patchy scalp at the back of my head. "Pete, sometimes...you've just got to look at the bigger picture."

☼

Whenever it was scutwork that had to be done outside, it was Fred that did it. Usually. He was actually getting out of most of it in this star system, with six *visible* moons at any one time dirtside for the planet they were orbiting, so there was a lot of "full

moon" time—during which he was pretty useless. Inside the ship, he could stay human as long as he didn't get mad and decide to go half-wolf. Outside? All bets were off.

Though, just before the "drive incident," Grigoire had locked him out to get back at him for some other petty damn thing, leaving him out for half a day. He'd pounded on the airlock door for an hour, screaming at them.

"Come on guys, will you let me in already? I've had like five minutes of me-time since you—HROOOOOOOOOO!"

"Someone turn Fred loose again?"

Yeah. Real funny. Wolfing out wasn't any fun for Fred, "he" got lost in the animal and he damn well didn't like it. After it ended, it was mostly a blur of images for him. Back on Earth? Lots of blood and terrible memories. Here, in deep space with nothing but Undead that he hated worse than the Dark Prince? Promises of dreams to come, and as a sort of compensation he could plant the Fang-faces over the vague images of whatever it was he'd ripped into. Still, he didn't like being out of control like that. Well, now they could tote their own barges and lift their own bales. He got to stay in the ship.

Which of course meant...he had to stay in the ship. Inside the same walls, breathing the same canned air, watching the Reboots. Reading. Watching the Reboots. Rewatching the vid library. Watching the Reboots. It was getting so he was even considering cracking into the opera collection that only Tony ever watched. The best thing about being able to get outside was the air on the planets that had them—even when he was human, his sense of smell was better than a Norm's. So even with the CO_2 and stink-scrubbers, there was always this faint stench in the back of his nose from the Reboots. The Fangs wouldn't notice, of course; he didn't think they actually had a sense of smell anymore; most of them didn't need to breathe, outside of speech. As far as he could tell, all they could smell was blood; and the only one with the fresh stuff was Fred. But Fred's sense of smell extended outside the bounds of known science; he could compartmentalize a million different scents, and discriminate among them. Almost all of them were disgusting on this cruise.

That made the times of being able to get out on a planet all the more important.

So he was stuck in here, which only made him think more, about a lot of uncomfortable things. There were only so many new deaths that he could imagine for his shipmates, so even that grew boring eventually. Ugly notions kept intruding. He knew the Reboots were expendable, but what if they all were? What if the Home Service actually expected them to kill each other out here? That might explain the fantastic rate of pay; if they weren't expected to make it back, it wouldn't matter how much the pay-rate was because no one would ever collect.

He shook his head, hoping to banish the ominous implications of his line of thought. There was work to be done, and it seemed like more than usual. The ship was always malfunctioning these days, but now that he was feeling irritable all the time, even the ship seemed to be trying to torment him. Such an idea, of course, was at odds with his logical brain; it was just the nature of such a sophisticated piece of machinery, just like it was in his nature to go berserk with a full moon and for the Fangs to be assholes. More so, really—the ship might be sophisticated in design, but she was still built by the lowest bidder. Still…things had been happening that just were not in the list of "malfunctions."

For instance, the lighting. It was never, never, never to have a UV component except in his personal quarters, or for the onboard hydroponics garden; a garden that was for his sole benefit. He had to eat, after all, and though Wolf might live by frozen steak alone, Man did not, and this thing supplied all the needs—veggies, algae, and this fish called tilapia that bred like rabbits and sucked up seasoning so at least it didn't taste the same all the time. Some of the bulbs had gone missing not long ago. He suspected at the time that one of his crewmates was going to be playing a particularly painful prank on him. So, naturally, as soon as one of the Fangs got a sunburn from a replaced bulb, he was the first one blamed.

Not a malfunction, and not an "accident." More like an "on purpose." But the Fangs all claimed innocence, and he knew that *he* hadn't done it—not that he could prove otherwise. It was almost as if there was a third party around here. Which, of course, was impossible. He'd heard of haunted ships before, but this one had been vetted back in dry-dock as spirit free; one of the few things that the Home Service seemed to have done correctly on this flight. Could a ghost have somehow hitched a ride? But how? Ghosts were chained to places or things, and they hadn't taken on anything new. Not even a spare part, much to his chagrin. And he'd booted all the gremlins out on their shakedown run as he was supposed to do; that'd been three days of nonstop fun, crawling through wiring ducts, Jeffries tubes, and hydraulics.

Hell, maybe he was sleepwalking and he really *had* done it.

Just one more charming item to add to his list of aggravations.

"He's dead, Jim." We were in the engineering section again. Whenever the Fangs or Fred didn't need us, those of us Reboots left outside of the holding pen were free to roam around, weighed down with tool belts. Kind of like free-floating tool chests with limited maintenance ability; if something minor was wrong, just point at one, give it the command, and have it do a job. If we got busted wandering around it wasn't as if it mattered.

One of our brethren had just that happen to him. I stared down at what was left of him. It wasn't even remotely pretty, and even as distant as my own emotions now were, I felt sick. "Must've been one of those damned Fangs; Fred doesn't really knock us around, unless he's wolfed out and can't tell the difference."

He was in pieces, some of which were still squirmy and half-attached. I looked down at him and felt a dim desperation. Pete stared down at the bits too. He made a grunt that sounded uneasy, but before he could voice any objections, I cut him off, so to speak. "Pete, we *can't* stop now. Do you remember what happened when you died the first time? Before you came back?"

Pete shook his head. "Naw, man. I do remember I had caught a killer wave the day I died, and had found some good herb, too, but that's about it."

What I half-remembered woke the one emotion I could really feel well—Fear. "Well, I remember. I didn't see any pearly gates, or fiery brimstone, or a light at the end of the tunnel. I sure as Hell didn't get reincarnated, unless someone stole my spot in line. I just remember darkness before waking up again." I played with a frayed tatter of the broken Reboot's red jumpsuit. It had been…well, empty, a void, a nothingness that is hard for me to describe now, and I doubt I could have described when I was alive. All I know is it was negation. The absence of life, the absence of *me*. It's what I imagined regular Reboots were like, all the time. Blank, empty on the inside, no purpose. "That scares the crap outta me, Pete. I didn't do much when I was alive, and I don't want to waste this second chance, such as it is."

Sighing out of habit rather than because I actually had breath, I took out a screwdriver from my coveralls, and plunged it through the eye of the ruined Reboot. Destroying what's left of the brain does destroy us permanently. It's about the only thing that does, other than incineration. Getting ripped to shreds will leave us helpless, but still "conscious" as long as the brain is mostly intact. Killing the shredded Reboot was a small kindness, all things considered.

✿

Good old Barny decided to get revenge on Fred *and* his fellow Fangs.

Someone reported a landing strut sensor misread. Fred went out to check it, during the twenty or so minutes when there were no moons up. And…tried to get back in, only to discover the airlock door mysteriously sealed, and he spent another forty-eight hours wolfed out and locked out. Barny wasn't too good at figuring consequences, however, because he'd locked Fred out under the moons with only a day's worth of stored blood left. Bad timing. Antonio was not happy. Come to think of it, he never was. This had pushed him from "glowering and miserable" to "glowering and furious."

The Fangs had been forced to go hungry for almost twenty-four hours, and once they got an exhausted (but well fed!) Fred back on the ship, Tony had ordered them up into orbit to keep it from happening again. Fred was not a happy puppy, and that was not the only reason. Today sucked, and in more ways than one. It seemed that the ship was being extremely touchy; there were a number of subsys-

tem failures that, while not serious, were time-consuming. Not only did he have to deal with the aggravation of having his crewmates bitch and moan to him about all of it and "Why wasn't this fixed already;" it was also a feeding day. He was due to report to the medical bay in fifteen minutes; and at the last minute, Tony evidently decided that this was enough time for Fred to check out a potential atmosphere leak in the observation deck, so that everyone didn't suddenly decompress. Not that decompression would bother the Fangs or even the Reboots, but *he* would die, and that would leave the Fangs without food. At this point, Fred thought that dying quick and easy like that would be better than continuing on this trip. He wouldn't have to listen to them anymore, and his own last thoughts would be of how nice it was that they would die slowly and painfully of starvation, or much more slowly and not so painfully of starvation while sleeping. Bad things happened to Fangs that don't feed and stay awake too long, and it wasn't much better for the ones that went into hibernation when food got scarce.

Grumbling loudly and cursing his lot in life, he stepped into the anteroom for the observation deck. Something that caught his attention was that the doors leading from the other sections were all locked, for some reason. He mentally shrugged; probably just another bullshit prank by one of the Fangs. Grigoire again, more than likely. Tony had come damn near to demoting Grigoire to "Fred's helper," and he'd only been talked down from it by the rest of the Fangs pointing out it would be a bad precedent.

Fred finally reached the observation deck—and immediately sensed that something was off. Next to one of the doors was a Reboot, and it was looking directly at him. Somewhere in the back of his mind, he recognized it as the one he'd caught on a skateboard.

And it talked.

"Sorry, bro. This'll only last a couple of minutes."

The zombie flicked a switch, and closed the door between the two of them. Before Fred could even register what had happened, the outer shutters for the observation canopy slid open, letting the cold light of three full moons in through the viewport.

"Goddamnit, Tony. Fred was supposed to be here five minutes ago. I'm hungry!" Hephaestus, the ship's navigator, was the whiniest of the Fangs. Whining was irritating to everyone, and only aggravated all the worst traits of the inborn jerk in each of the rest of the Fangs.

Not that any of them were going to win Miss Congeniality. Even *Fangs* considered all other Fangs jerks.

Tony scowled, and made a quick revision in the feeding order. "You'll get your share, Hephaestus, just like the rest of us. Today, you're going last, though, and if you make another single peep about it I swear to all the dark and sharp things of the Underworld that you'll be floating home."

Hephaestus looked down, cowed by his superior. Grigoire and Barnabas shared a nasty grin. Any suffering was good suffering, as far as they were concerned, and for Barnabas, this meant he got to move up one in the queue.

The intercom started up with a pop and a crackle. Tony rolled his eyes. Another malfunction. They'd stopped using the intercom on his orders because they were all playing "dueling DJ" on the damn thing for the first six years of the trip. Grigoire was the first to look up and cock his head to the side. "I know this song…"

I see the bad moon arising.
I see trouble on the way…"

Tony had particularly keen hearing, and he was the first one to hear the main doors for the medical bay open, even past the music. He turned away from Heph towards the door. "About time, Fred. The damn intercom is on the fritz again. Besides, this vampire likes his room service prompt—" Tony didn't even have to take the milliseconds to sweep his eyes to the door to know what was wrong. He heard it, and smelled it. Fred was a monster, and bigger than ever; the more moonlight he took in, the more powerful he became when he wolfed out. All Weres were that way; luckily, Earth only had one moon to shed its light on all the dark creatures she possessed. Fred had become a nightmare of eight feet of hair, claws and jaws, and had murder in his dark eyes.

They were running, but not nearly fast enough.

☼

Fangs and Weres were both blessed with many dark gifts. Strength enough to topple buildings, supernatural senses, and in the Fangs' case remarkable powers of persuasion. Provided, of course, the individual Fang trying to do the persuading wasn't a complete douchebag. There are some things not even supernatural manipulation can overcome.

Like being a douchebag. Or an enraged and moonlight-drunk Werewolf in full form.

They were also inhumanly fast. Of the two species, though, the Weres were faster, and Tony cursed this racial difference now more than ever. Fred had been on top of the group before anyone could even bare his fangs. They had been in the medical bay for blood, and blood they received; it was splattered messily on every surface. Some of it was Fred's, but most of it was his vampiric compatriots'.

Fred regenerated at an incredible rate; they could have, as well, if they were supplied with fresh blood, but the only fresh blood was in Fred's veins and…he wasn't exactly cooperating.

So they had run; Fred's Change could only last so long, if he didn't come in contact with moonlight.

For some reason, though, every single viewport shutter was wide open. Due to the way the ship was positioned above the planet they were supposed to be surveying and evaluating, they had visible moons on almost every side; three completely full ones above them, in relation to the ship's rotation. Fred kept getting stronger, and they kept running. There was no silver on the entire ship; the Mission Planners from the Home Service reasoned that Fangs or Weres killing each other would be suicide. Without food, the Fangs would wither and sleep and maybe die before they could get back to Earth. So no silver.

As for the Fangs, the planners counted on "safety in numbers," or so the brochure said. A single Were couldn't hope to overpower the rest of the crew by his (or her, though female Weres were much rarer) self. That *should* have kept the Fangs in control. Obviously, the planners hadn't counted on a situation like this one—multiple moons, all the viewports wide open, ship in orbit, and no way to get the ports shut without getting torn into tiny pieces. Well, someone *might* have been able to get the ports shut in one section, if he volunteered to be the one that would end up shredded. Right. *That* was never going to happen. An altruistic, self-sacrificing vampire? Get real. One of the reasons they made it through getting Turned in the first place, rather than ending up another messy victim on a slab, was the fierce determination to *live* no matter what it cost. Which was, when you thought about it, more or less the definition of being self-centered.

So they ran, desperately.

✿

"He's right behind us, we've got to move!" Grigoire's voice was a shrill scream; he had lost his left arm in one of the running battles, and it was only now starting to regenerate. Barnabas looked worse, almost as bad as a fresh Reboot; cuts and grievous wounds covered his entire body. He was holding his guts in with both arms and hobbling pitifully on a leg that had been twisted completely around in its socket. They all felt so weak. They were past due for their blood ration from Fred; it didn't help that he was spilling their claret, expending their life force with each swipe of his claws or flashing of his horrid jaws. They also were looking to each other with hunger; they could drain one of their own, replenish their strength…but Fred was chomping at their heels and they didn't even have time for that.

"I know, goddamnit, but we can't stop to open any of the doors, or he'll catch up with us!" Beneath the panic and terror clouding his mind—two sensations that Tony had not experienced in millennia—an analytical part of him wondered why most of the doors they came to were locked. It was almost as if they were being herded somewhere, driven ever forward by the beast at their backs.

"What're we going to do, Tony? Oh fuck!—" Hephaestus went flying ahead of the group, tossed bodily by Fred. He slammed into a bulkhead with a sickening and wet crunch; his ribs were protruding from his back from the force of the blow. Recognition clicked for Tony; they were at the airlock! Without thinking, he shoved the other two Fangs into it, then kicked Hephaestus inside, while hitting the activation relay so hard that the housing around it bent and creaked. In a split second, the inner airlock doors closed with a snap-hiss. Fred barreled into the door, his fury fueling strike after strike against it. His claws raked against the metal to fruitlessly send

showers of sparks into the air, and he howled impotently at having his prey so close but out of reach at the same time. Even if he'd had the mind to use controls, they weren't where he could get at them. Shipside door airlock controls were all on the inside of the airlocks for a reason. Nobody could get shoved inside unconscious and spaced that way, or at least, not easily. You *could* override from the main control room, but that would take some significant planning, and Fred was not exactly thinking in this state.

Tony put his back against the bulkhead. He was in better shape than the others, but only marginally.

They were safe. Tony automatically began to plan. They could put on suits to keep from getting cold-damaged and protect them from sunlight. Grigoire could get to either the control room or the aux control from outside and override the viewports. Without moonlight, Fred would change back to human form back eventually no matter where in the ship he was. Or, they could just wait him out, hoping he'd stay in this section.

They all began to chuckle, which broke down into fullout uproarious laughter. They didn't really breathe, but it was a stress reaction that their dead bodies still remembered. It was a ghastly sight, in truth: four broken bodies, dead in most ways that counted, laughing and spilling more blood all over the deck. Tony had to wipe blood-tears from his eyes, he was laughing so hard. Fred continued to rage outside of the door, pounding against it relentlessly with his impossibly powerful fists.

Their laughter died as one when one of the space suits that was stored in a wall alcove stood up straight. The blast visor flipped up to reveal a Reboot inside of it, illuminated by the harsh helmet lights.

✿

The grav kicked off, right on schedule, as I raised the blast-shield on the suit. I looked at them through the visor, and all they could do was look at me in stunned silence as they rose slightly from the floor. I knew that this made no sense to them, that this was so out of character for a Reboot even their lightning reflexes would not be able to save them, especially without footing. So, baring my busted teeth through my patchwork lips in the most evil Bond-villain grin I could manage, I said, "Adios, suckers." In two smooth motions, I flipped them "the bird," and then snapped up the safety for the outer airlock doors. In the old movies, they used to show people getting sucked into space in a rush of atmosphere, trying to scrabble and hang on to anything they could. It doesn't really work like that, though, not when no one is ready for it, anyway. One second, the Fangs were there. The next, I felt a slight jolt against my restraint harness, and they were gone into the blackness, like darts out of a blowgun. There was nothing in the airlock but me and my suit; it was like Tony and the rest of his bastard brethren never even existed.

Then I waited; being a Reboot, I'm pretty good at that. When the banging from the other side of the door subsided, I waited some more. Couldn't hurt to be too careful, and besides, we had a plan. Stick to the plan. In movies, it was when you didn't stick to the plan that things went off the rails. So, I just floated there, whistling some old commercial jingles to myself. Funny how that stuff sticks in your mind. I don't drink anything, but there I was, rattling the words to a cola commercial around in my head, or what was left of it. Halfway through it, the outer doors closed and the chamber repressurized, and the grav came back on again. I unhooked myself from the restraint harness, looking to the door. There was a flash of hazard lights, and the heavy blast doors opened. On the other side, as planned, was Pete.

"Dude…is that you?"

"No, it's Hannibal Lecter. I've come for you, Clarice." I trotted forward, enjoying the feeling of the artificial gravity again; weightlessness isn't my thing, even though my stomach doesn't really get queasy anymore. "Where's Fred?"

"Probably sleeping it off somewhere, man. When he trips bad like that, he usually gets a killer headache afterwards. Dude, are you sure that we can trust him?"

"Pete, we've gotten this far. Time to take it the last mile." Besides, he was the only one who knew how to fly this boat. While we could probably sit up here for a while, eventually orbit would decay and then… a very fancy cremation. It was now, or never.

✿

Fred did wake up with a headache. If he had been cognizant enough through the immense pain to think about it, he would have declared that this was the worst headache in the history of man, living or unliving. Once the pain went from mind-blanking to merely Olympic, he started to remember—or notice—a few things.

Like the fact that his clothing was in pieces, which meant he'd almost certainly Changed. And that his last real memory, before the usual flash of blood and screaming and then nothing but red, red rage, was of three full moons staring down at him, as if they were laughing at what would come next. And…and a Reboot opening the ports.

While *talking*?

No, that part had to be a hallucination. His mind did that sometimes, right at the Change, as if it was trying to protect him from what was coming.

Looking around, he took stock of his situation. He was in a storeroom for tools. Sometimes when he wolfed out, the others would corral him into a room and lock him in until his Change wore off. Then he noticed that the door was torn inwards, and that there was blood all over it.

"What the hell is going on?" His voice was thick and scratched. Even though he regenerated constantly, roaring and howling a lot took its toll on his human-again vocal cords. "Grigoire? Antonio? Anyone?" His eyes caught movement in the hallway beyond the door; a person-shaped smudge of shadow against shadows. Probably one of the Fangs here to chew him out for busting the door.

"Hey, which one of you assholes made a Reboot open the shutters in the observation deck? There were three goddamned full moons out there!" The figure stepped through the ruined door; it was dressed in a space suit, obscuring the identity.

"Oh, that was me. Sorry about that, friend." Friend? He'd been called plenty while on this flight, with some of it so off-color that the Dark Prince, hell-red bastard that he was, would've blushed upon hearing it. But he'd never been called friend.

"Seriously, who is that in there?" That voice wasn't familiar either. Had they—no, surely they hadn't been intercepted by another ship! Okay, there'd been rumors of FTL in the works but nothing but rumors…

The figure seemed to look down at itself.

"Oh, the suit." The suited figure took off its helmet; beneath was the Reboot that had looked at Fred funny-like a few days ago. It grinned. A Reboot grinning…

"I'm the local Sheriff," it drawled. "Heard there was some trouble. Looked like you could use a hand, pard."

He felt exactly the way he'd felt when he'd been taze-stunned at the end of his first Change by the Norm cops. "All the demons of hell, it talks!"

Could a Reboot look sheepish? This one shrugged, anyway. "Uh, yeah. About that. Name's Skinny Jim. Pleased to meet you, Fred."

Fred was so flabbergasted by this turn of events, that he found himself deep in a conversation before the "stunned" wore off. Oh, he had heard about the "intelligent" Reboots, but he'd always thought they were an urban legend. The entire "zombie uprising" had occurred decades before Fred was even born, after all, and the general consensus among people of his generation had been that the "King of the Zombies" had been nothing more than a figment of the fevered imaginations of the authorities. Either that, or a manufactured "threat" to give them the power to do pretty much what they wanted to do with the Paras.

Joke was on him, it seemed.

Joke was—even more so—on the Fangs, who were drifting in a decaying orbit right now, and who would, if not rescued, eventually come to a fiery end, conscious and starving most of the way. *Serves the bastards right, all said and done. Just wish I could see it.*

They spent a good long while talking. The Reboot explained his plight, and what he had done about it. Fred wanted to be angry, wanted to be filled with righteous fury for being used. He knew that he should destroy the Reboot, and flush the rest out of the pen and into space, then report back to the Home Service immediately.

But he couldn't bring himself to do any of these things. It didn't take him long to decide that things had just become a lot more interesting on the UES Cenotaph, and he suspected…a lot more peaceful, too. No more getting drained to feed evil bastard Fangs. No more orders from Tony, needling from Grigoire, bitching from Hephaestus, or dueling with

Barnabas. Taking stock of everything, Fred was suddenly happier than he had been in over a century and a half.

"Well, how about that. You know, Jim, I'd shake your hand, but—" He shrugged uneasily, looking at the deck.

Skinny Jim didn't have much in the way of an expressive face, what with the sunken eyes, retracted lips displaying broken teeth, and shriveled-taut skin, but somehow he conveyed resignation. "Yeah, I know, I'm a zombie."

"Hey, it could come off!"

They both shared a laugh, although the Reboot's was kind of wheezy. It was the first real laugh that Fred had had for many, many years. One not tainted by *schadenfreude*, or at the expense of someone else. It felt good, and it felt clean. Fred also noticed that it was as if a weight was off of his shoulders, and that was also good, welcome.

A smile broke out over his face. He didn't immediately notice when another Reboot trudged up behind Jim.

"Oh, Fred, I want you to meet Pete. Fred, Pete. Pete, Fred."

The skateboarding one! Fred goggled. He felt his eyes bulging when it opened its mouth. "Yo, dude. 'Sup?"

"Ye gods, two of them! I mean…two of…you…" It wasn't every day that a werewolf met a talking zombie, much less two of them. The shock wore off quickly, though; after the rollercoaster of emotions, combined with his still monstrously bad headache, he didn't have the energy to stay stunned and stupid for too long. "So, why didn't you guys talk earlier? Why didn't you flush me out of the airlock with the rest of those scum-suckers?"

Jim stepped forward. "You remember Xavier. Right? The 'Zombie Emperor'? After that, any of us that seemed to possess any greater cognitive ability than your average jar of mayo were exterminated. Being anything but another mindless deader didn't do much for anyone's survival chances."

"Yeah, but that still doesn't answer why you didn't flush me out of the ship, also. If I weren't cool with this, I could take the ship back to Earth. Or just rekill you myself and save the Home Service the trouble." Fred placed his hands on the hips of his tattered jumpsuit, trying to present a strong front, even though he wasn't truly feeling it.

"Honestly, that was the weakest part of the plan. But, you suffered just as much as we had under the Fangs, if not more; they actively hated you, while we were just scenery and mildly useful furniture. So, I—I mean, we—took a chance. It was worth it to see Tony's face when all the atmo got sucked out into the aether and them with it."

A fiendish smile crept across Fred's face. "Damn, I wish I could've seen that, actually."

"Good news is, I recorded it via the ship's security system. Wanna see it?"

"Bet your ass I do." He paused, thinking for a moment. "Well, what do we do now? We can't really go back to Earth, which isn't that big of a loss. Place is a hole, or at least it was when I left."

Skinny Jim nodded. "Me and Pete thought about that. We figured that finding a decent planet with lots of yellow sun would be a good start, one that can bake us nice and leathery. High UV to sterilize the bacteria. Kill the rot, and a little oil solves most of our problems. For you, well, pick one with no moons and plenty of stuff for you to munch on, or only one moon and stuff the Were can eat, and when you go human again you've got the ship's garden. As for everything else—" he pulled out a deck of playing cards from his pocket, "have you ever played poker?"

✧

It took us a while, but we found pretty much what we were looking for. Yellow phase star, no moons and not a lot of exploitable resources. Someplace that wouldn't off-hand look too attractive to the Home Service. We called it "Planet Hawaii," since it was mostly islands and mostly tropical. And contrary to what you are probably thinking, "island paradise" planets are not on the top of the list for places to go. Home Service wants *commercially viable* resources, and the number of people that can afford to take off-world trips to tropical islands that vary only from the same kind you find on Earth by the exotic flora and fauna are...well, you're not going to be able to find enough to support a single trip, much less a resort. Never mind that none of them would ever live long enough to get here, even with hyper-sleep tubes. You still age, even when you sleep.

So this was our little pocket paradise. Screw the non-contamination directive, our seeds would grow here, so besides the hydroponic garden, we figured we'd have the Reboots out there doing the slave-labor for a little plantation for Fred, and what with the place being mostly ocean and all, the water wasn't salt, so we just needed a nice big lagoon we could cut off from the rest of the oceanic biosphere. We'd find an island that had one, sterilize it, and seed it with algae. Once that got started we could transplant more tilapia, and bingo. Fred would be set forever. We did all that, and settled down, happy as beach-bums can be.

As for us, all we needed was that nice hot sun and oil. Fish and some of the peanuts that the greenhouse had in it provided oil. We Reboots really didn't *need* to eat brains to keep going, so we saved the freeze-dried stuff for me and Pete for kicks, and let the others do without. They wouldn't touch Fred—more of the Para influence than anything—so although they moaned a lot, it was no big deal.

In six months, we were self-sustaining. Then it got better, because even the moaning stopped, and I found the Reboots scrounging some sort of fungus that they seemed happy to munch on. At least, I think it was a fungus. It was spongy, neon-orange, and when I tasted it, it was actually better than the freeze-dried crap we subsisted on. I figured I would wait and see what happened to them in the long term before I moved the stuff onto *my* dinner plate, but it looked like a viable option for the others now.

I kind of hoped whatever the orange stuff was wasn't sentient, but hey. Survival of the fittest and we were only harvesting one island, so screw it. If it wanted to survive here, it could evolve a mouth and talk to us, or grow some legs and run for it.

Naturally, Pete didn't hold any of my reservations, and started chowing down as soon as he tasted it. Whatever. While I dimly liked him for our mutual plight of undead sentience, if he wanted to risk himself, I wasn't going to stop him, and I could watch *him* for signs of lapsing into the usual Reboot coma due to his new diet.

Fred and I could always change over to chess from poker if that happened.

So, Pete and I baked to a nice, healthy, flexible brown in the tropical sun. Fred got a tan. Pete taught us both to surf, such surfing as there was on a planet with no moons, and we all settled down to a pretty nice and quiet life, even if I did smell like Planters Best from the peanut oil. Fred said it was a much-appreciated change from perma-rot. Me, I never had noticed.

☼

"Ante up, sucker," I said, pushing my chips across the table. I had a good hand. A really good hand. Which meant that when Fred lost, he'd have to do my bidding, muwahaha. I was trying to decide what that would be. I was powerfully inclined to an external speaker system so we could play some music out here. I was pretty sure he could rig it, and reasonably sure we could weatherproof it. We didn't have crazy tides due to lacking a moon, but we did have some powerful weather systems and seriously impressive storms.

Fred scratched the back of his head. "I feel like I'm forgetting something." It was our third year on planet, and things had been humming along fairly smoothly for a while. The other Reboots were all doing their thing, we had the luxuries we wanted, and there wasn't anyone to bother us in this corner of the galaxy. The orange sponge hadn't evolved a mouth, and Pete hadn't turned into a wandering corpse, so I'd added the tasty stuff to my menu. We hadn't bothered to check on the subspace radio for news for over two years, since it was all more of the same. So-and-so tin-pot dictator was toppled, new government rises, such-and-such planet was annexed for whoever corporation, Home Service celebrates the whatever. We in the ships might have been taking the long and slow route, but communication was still at real-time speeds. It mattered little to us; we were separate, insular and sufficient unto ourselves. The *only* thing we got from the rest of the civilized galaxy was that we'd set up the computer to continue the automatic downloads of entertainment stuff, which flooded in faster than we could watch or listen to it. Home Service did that much for the ships, probably because otherwise the crews would kill each other from boredom; providing they'd been less like ours had been, that is. Life was good.

I should have realized it was too good. But, when you're on top, after having been in the gutter for so long…

So here we were, at our usual game. We had a comfortable table and lounges pulled out of the ship, set up under what passed for trees—more like giant ferns, but they kept the sun off. Since there wasn't a breeze at the moment, a couple of the Reboots were working one of those overhead pulley-fans they used to have in India in the bungalows the English overlords lived in. Fred had a storage-closet-brewed beer next to him. Trust humans, once you get past basic food and shelter the next thing we think about is booze. About a hundred yards away, little waves lapped on the black sand—this was a volcanic beach. Behind us was the ship, nestled up against a cliff. I had to laugh when I thought about our landing.

"Y'know…I'm not sure that that was much of a landing."

"What?"

"Well, you did shear off a quarter ton of rock off of that cliff…"

"Y'know what they say? Any landing you can walk away from, is a good landing. So, stuff it, Wrinkles."

We could still lift the ship if we had to. Like, oh, if one of the really *big* hurricanes decided to bear down on us. The fish and the veggies could survive one—better we got the hell out of Dodge if one of those things put a target on our island. So…screw it. Fred had been right. It had been a good enough landing.

I grinned, staring at him. I could grin, now. The last time Fred lost to me, he made me—well, I guess you'd call them tooth veneers—to give me something that looked human-ish again, and the oil had given me nice, flexible lips, even if they were a bit thin. "You're stalling. Even Pete has folded already."

"No, it's not that." A perplexed look crossed Fred's face. "It feels like there's something I should have remembered. Something important. I just can't place my finger on it." I could tell that whatever it was that Fred was thinking about, it was bugging him immensely. I decided to take his mind off of it.

"No use, *compadre*. I'm not letting you out of this hand. I've got plans for my winnings, and you can't get off that easy." I gave him my best "gotcha" look.

He was an aggressive player, normally. That *should* have gotten him back in the game, but it didn't.

I put my cards face-down on the table. "OK, if it bothers you that much. Did you leave your lunch on the stove?"

He shook his head. "No, it's not that. It feels… important."

"Is there an experiment you started and forgot to check on?"

Fred scoffed. "I haven't done an important experiment after the time I tried to stick three Reboots together for that—"

"I know, I remember!" If I slept, it would have given me nightmares. "Was there a news alert? Have you checked for one lately?"

He shook his head again, looking down at his cards. "No, I've scanned for our names, the ship's name, the Fangs' names, everything. Got it on automatic for the ship's computer, set up in a way so we don't get traced. Nothing on any of us, so far as I can tell. It's not that."

"Forget to check the weather?" That had happened once. It hadn't been drastic, but three of the Reboots had gotten washed out to sea, never to be seen again. No clue what happened to them. We hadn't exactly been vigilant about checking for aquatic monsters. We'd pretty much figured that if something couldn't crawl up on land to get us, we were good.

Suddenly, we all heard the whine of a extra-planetary booster engine powering up, quickly building to a frantic roar. All of us turned to look at the ship; even the Reboots craned their leathery necks in that direction.

"The *hell?*" I said. A single streak of fiery exhaust burst away from the top of the ship, with the bright point of light at the end of it blinking out of sight quickly, leaving only the thick plume of smoke pointing like a finger, upwards.

A big, fat, middle finger to our entwined destinies.

"Oh," said Fred, guilt plastered over his face. "Shit."

"What?" I asked, sharply. Then even more sharply, "*What?*"

"That's what I forgot." He laid his cards on the table, face up; nothing at all but stray cards. "Ship's emergency beacon. Launches automatically if the ship's captain doesn't check in after a predetermined amount of time. It's so the Home Service can re-cover the ship and any assets that are left. Tony was the only one supposed to know about it." Fred looked up to meet my gaze. "I discovered it while I was bored and poking around some of the auxiliary systems one night. I kept meaning to deactivate it, but I never got around to it." He looked down at his hand. "So…y'all got your bags packed?"

Oh hell. But…no point in making a deal about it. If there is one thing I am at this point, it's pragmatic. So Fred screwed up. Right now screaming about it wasn't going to change anything; the Fangs had tried that often enough, and look where they were now. "Any more of those things on board?"

"Just the one that I remember finding."

"Should we change islands, or whole planets?"

"With the Home Service involved? If we could scoot out of this galaxy, it'd be just barely far enough."

Bugger. Oh well. We could dump some Reboots to leave room for food for Fred, harvest what we had, and be off here in a reasonable amount of time. The Dark Gods in charge of our fate only knew how far we would have to go to get out of reach. Or if we even could.

Right. "Let's check the news. See how close they are to here." That would let us know how long we had to get a good head start. Twenty years would be nice. I could scream at Fred all I liked once we were on the run.

Then again, given the guilt on Fred's face, maybe I should just let him stew on his own. Without him, we'd have probably been drifting forever, and our plan never would have worked. Still, it was a colossal, colossal fuckup. *Deal with what you can, while you can.*

We ran for the ship, and started the computer scanning through the news. I checked the "colonized planets" list, Pete for the "messages from near-space" and Fred for stuff that needed a little more hands-on than what we were doing.

Fred made a strange noise. I looked over at him. Under his tan, he was pale. "Uh…looks like things have changed while we've been going with drive on full for the past century and change. We've got new neighbors. And they didn't get there by the long haul like us."

Oh, I did not like the way that sounded. My brain might not have been the best in the world, but….

"Please tell me that doesn't mean what I think it means."

"We've got not a whole lot of room to run, and we're a lot slower than the competition." He grimaced. "That's the long and short of it, as it were."

Oh…*hell*. The Dark Gods Above *and* Below were laughing at us. That rocket's contrail had been a middle finger after all. "No. FTL? Portal tech?" I begged him to say no with my beady little eyes. Fred merely shrugged. A lot changes in one hundred and some odd years. And we hadn't been looking for it until now. And that was *my* fuckup. Fred was the techy, I was the one that had told the computer what to watch for in the feeds. But…dammit, when we left, *everyone* said FTL was impossible, and the most anyone could manage would be near-light!

So everyone was wrong. OK, fine. Now we could both wallow in guilt. Wallow later, move now. Definitely abandon some of the Reboots. Run a couple of wires into the lagoon, stun the fish, flash-freeze. We'd been taking care of the hydroponics garden in the ship instead of letting it go to pot, so Fred was set.

"Dude. I'll get the Reboots harvesting brain-balls," Pete said, and headed out of the ship. I looked at Fred.

"Ship's mine," he said. "If you guys can handle everything else."

It was hard to think this fast. I hadn't needed to in a long time. "Can we decide where we're going once we're up?" I asked. That would take one thing off the list.

"Yes," he said instantly. "If you guys can get everything loaded back in, and whatever consumables—"

It had just occurred to me that there was something else we could leave behind…all the crap we'd needed for the Fangs. Best thing to do would be to sink it, so no one knew we'd lost them. The more we could confuse the issue, the better.

The blood-store room could hold a lot of brain-balls…

"Have I got determination on what to dump?" I asked. Fred just nodded. He was already busy with what I assumed was pre-flight, pre-readiness stuff.

"As long as it isn't me," he added, jumping to another set of controls.

Right. Stun the fish and harvest. Harvest what we could from the garden and the rest of the island.

Strip out the Fang crap. Sink it in the ocean. Would it be possible to simulate a wreck? Probably not, dammit.

I realized I was wasting time. I could think and plan while I did the first stages.

That, and curse all the Dark Gods.

✡

Seamus Murtaugh Ian ap Llowynn, who answered to "Ian Lonagan" so far as the Home Service were concerned, sauntered back to his office in an exceedingly contented frame of mind. A delightful three-hour lunch in the presence of the equally delightful Sharice from Planetary Resources Accounting, coupled with the high probability that he would be completely idle this afternoon, made this Púca one happy puppy. Oh sure, *technically* he wasn't supposed to be fraternizing with other employees except under very specific and Home Service-sponsored circumstances, but she was Planetary Resources and *he* was Extra-Planetary Exploration Incidents (aka, "oh fuck, we got a beacon") and it wasn't *really* fraternizing when they weren't even working in the same mega-block, much less building, much less department, now, was it?

Ian was on his three thousandth game of Spider Solitaire for the day when the e-mail came. This job was virtually perfect for him; lost in the bureaucracy of Home Service, there was very little work he was actually expected to do.

Besides, he worked hard enough chasing after tasty tidbits like Sharice.

Home Service just didn't appreciate that sort of thing; heaven knew he'd petitioned to open a new position that would let him get paid directly for just that. How else was she supposed to stay content in her dead-end, soul-sucking Accounting job, unless someone like him made her life exciting? Parahumans were always a hundred times more attractive than Norms, a thousand times better at evading actual commitments—Home Service would be annoyed if Sharice actually *got married* and had a real life and real responsibilities, as opposed to the illusory life and very real thrills Ian was giving her. Home Service would have been even more annoyed if someone like a Fang had moved in on her, and possibly even Turned her. Whereas, with a Púca, she was safe from Turning into anything, and Ian had several hundred years' worth of experience at ditching someone if she somehow did begin to want more out of him than she was ever going to get.

Annoyed at the distraction from his diversion, Ian closed the game and opened his e-mail. "Well, *this* is depressingly different."

It was an automatic notification from a broadcast repeater satellite on the edge of the Solar System's frontier. It was dated as having been sent three months ago, which was strange until he read further into the e-mail; usually any beacons that came in were within minutes of "Special Circumstances." Those circumstances usually being that another crew had gone batshit insane and torn itself to pieces, or that a ship had pancaked into a rogue asteroid or some other such cosmic mishap. Lowest bidder, after all, and it was difficult to find *competent* Fangs or Fur engineers. Paras still made up most of the crews, even with third-generation FTL. They were still the toughest things around, and with what was Out There, you wanted a crew that was hard to kill.

"That explains it." The e-mail listed that the beacon was one hundred and forty eight years old, launched four months prior. The older generation ships were very bare-bones affairs, and the tech capabilities were almost literally light years behind what was available now. He hadn't seen a beacon from one of these babies in…well, more than a year. He checked the ship list; this one hadn't been heard from in three years. Plenty of reasons for that, really, so no one had checked on it.

What was interesting was the partial log recovered from the beacon. The ship had *landed*. And had stayed that way, while still receiving Galaxy Net feeder streams.

"Keeping an ear to the ground for the cavalry, huh?"

No moon. Lots of sun. Looked as if the onboard Fur had done the impossible, overcome the Fang crew, and hijacked the ship.

I seriously don't have the time or patience for a wolf hunt. Who'll wine and dine Sharice in the meantime? He'd have to check out a scouter from Home Service—oh, the paperwork!—put in an appropriations request for ship, cash, and supplies, head out to that backwater, look for the ship…

And unless the Fur in question was a terrible pilot and the ship had been so damaged in landing it couldn't take off again, it was unlikely that the ship would still *be* there. Which meant *another* round of paperwork, getting authorization to search the galactic neighborhood…

"A fracking snipe-hunt," he said aloud with disgust. It could be months. Years! And at the end of it he'd have to try to wrangle a pissed off Werewolf. A pissed off *old* Werewolf, which compounded the problem. The older a Fur got, the tougher he got. And meaner. And this one had dispatched a full Fang crew, which argued that he was very tough and very mean indeed.

It was the same for many Parahumans, granted. Still, far more aggravation than Ian wanted to deal with. And no prospects for romancing tasty females, human *or* Para. What to do? How to avoid this? He'd been hired to deal with dead ships, not rogue ones. This was *not* his skillset!

Inspiration struck Ian like a ton of bricks. Why not just do what he always did when responsibility came a-knockin'?

He opened up the Rolodex—an antique novelty gift from one of his exes—and started flipping through it. *Someone reliable, but replaceable. No one from in-house. Inexpensive is a plus…there!* Ian punched up the ident number into the vid-phone, which picked up on the first ring.

"HB Investigations." The face was male, and rather forgettable, the sort of face that could get lost in any crowd. It was also not the face of a receptionist, which meant the Boggart in question was not in a financial position to hire anyone. Good. Lean and hungry; he'd probably jump at the chance to get a case from Home Service.

Ian licked his lips, smiling. "Mr. Boggart, I represent Home Service, Extraplanetary Incidents Division. It seems that I have a job for you."

(to be continued in issue #16)

THE BEST OF THE NEW AND THE OLD
✶New and Old Stories by Masters of Science Fiction and Fantasy✶
✶New Stories by Emerging New Talents✶
✶PLUS Columns, Book Reviews and Interviews✶
✶Serializations of Great Novels & Stories✶

DON'T MISS OUT ON ANY ISSUE
SUBSCRIBE
www.GalaxysEdge.com/sub.htm

Or send a check for $37.74 for a one-year (six-issue) subscription
(save 10% off the cover price) with this form to :

Subscriptions: Galaxy's Edge
Arc Manor Publishers
P.O. Box 10339
Rockville, MD 20849

Currently, subscription to the paper edition is only available within the United States.

Your Name_____

Full Address_____

_____

_____

Ph. No._____ Email_____